STEFANIE LOZINSKI

Maelstrom

Storm & Spire Book 3

Cover by Etheric Designs.

Map created in Wonderdraft, using assets by Evitcani & Nexoness.

Ave Christus Rex. ☦

First edition

This book was professionally typeset on Reedsy. Find out more at reedsy.com

To Mom

*Thank you for always teaching me
that I can do hard things.*

"The true soldier fights not because he hates what is in front of him, but because he loves what is behind him."

G.K. Chesterton

The glorious realm of
KAVERYTH
and the Four Kingdoms

GALEHARBOR

ARIDMOOR

SILVERFELL

BONESHIRE

UMRYM

NOX

Windehvar

Gravenheim

Karmere Lake

Redvale

High Kep

Varear

Dread Ruins

Rill

Edgairn

Wyrmere River

Riverspeak

Strongbollow

Old Hill

Briarcliff

Claymud

Whitespur

Azaranth

The West Strait

The Black Bends

Helmm

Prologue

ORIA

There were no ribbons, no candles, no flowers.

The trees that lined the halls of Stronghollow palace were decorated only with what remained of their own leaves, curled and desiccated in the late summer heat. No gardeners could be spared for something as frivolous as bringing water to indoor trees, not anymore.

As Oria walked down the long passage, she could hear crunching beneath her boots, a lonely sound amid the silence.

Sometimes the mobs outside would continue to pelt the palace walls with stones long after sundown, shouting at the few who remained sequestered inside, but tonight the citizens of Silverfell were quiet. This fact surprised her. The summer Feast of Offering was near, and the suffering people had been forced to give up their treasures, even without an Envoy to properly offer them to the Dracodei. Rage lingered in the city like a fog, even she could feel it. If it did not erupt now, it would soon.

It always did.

One Guardian. Only one Guardian came to our aid, and even she was too late.

Oria shook her head as she reached the door. What had happened was terrible, but it hadn't been surprising. After all that the Septemvirate had done, she should have realized that there could be no other outcome. The justice of men was corrupt, but the vengeance of elves was another thing entirely.

It is too late for bitterness.

She forced a smile onto her face as she entered the large dining room, balancing the tray that she carried in the crook of her arm. The soup was hot, and the smell filled her nostrils as she approached the table. The bread was fresh, and the cheese looked wonderful, though there was less of it than she would have liked to be able to offer. Even the residents of the palace had not escaped the poverty of these dark days entirely.

And yet the dragons have. The dwarves have. As we grow weak, they rip treasures from our hands. She felt her knuckles tighten against the edge of the simple metal tray, taking a few slow breaths in an attempt to get herself together.

"Are we safe?" she asked, placing the tray down at the head of the table and glancing around the room. She could see nothing of concern, only the wood-paneled walls interspersed with the few remaining paintings that had not yet been sold, but her sense of paranoia lingered just the same.

Elder Bram sat in silence, his hands folded as he bowed his head in a brief prayer.

"As safe as usual," he replied, raising his head to give her a quick smile. "Please sit for a little while. This soup looks wonderful, it would be a pity not to be able to share it."

He reached for the small silver cup that held a paper-wrapped piece of butter, tipping it out onto the tray and moving to pour the soup into the now empty vessel.

"I already ate," she said, reaching to touch his hand, still hovering over the soup bowl. "Please, enjoy all of it. It does smell lovely."

"You ate a bit of dry meat and a hunk of stale bread," he

accused, a wrinkled finger pointing in her direction.

"Yes. And I am not hungry," she said firmly, giving him another smile, genuine this time. She was happy to forgo luxury. Poverty had been her fate for as long as she could remember, and she was accustomed to it. She did not wish for her grandfather to suffer, especially when for her to suffer in his stead demanded no real sacrifice at all. For as long as it was possible, she would make sure that he lived well. He deserved that much.

They sat in silence for several minutes as Elder Bram ate. Oria placed a hand on her own stomach, underneath the table where her grandfather could not see it. She could hear a slight rumbling, but felt no real discomfort. The dry meat and stale bread were boring, but they were enough to satiate her. After all, she was only a child, and now, with the palace in a state of such decay, her work as a servant was not as physically demanding as it once had been.

Wes Cervos was gone, his rooms locked up and left to dust and gloom. The few children who had been about the palace were gone now, whisked away to safer villages deep in the forest, taking their laughter with them. Silverfell soldiers, craftsmen, cooks, gardeners, servants, so many had already gone. And now that the elves had come, the silence was heavier than ever.

Finally, Elder Bram spoke.

"Do you think it was worth it, my love?"

"What?"

"All of it," he said, making a sweeping gesture with his hand across the empty dining room. "Everything that I've done, everything that I've kept hidden. Everything that you have helped me to do."

"Yes," Oria said fiercely, without a moment's hesitation, leaning toward him and placing her hand atop his once more. "I do. The dragon chose the very worst time to tell the Envoy about the High One, but you never could have predicted it. No one could have."

He nodded, and Oria felt a warmth filling her chest. Even though she was still young, her opinion meant something to him. And that meant something to her.

"Well then, my love, despite everything that has gone wrong, the time has come to act."

"There won't be a better moment," she agreed, reaching for the remains of her grandfather's dinner and tidying them up. "You're head of the Septemvirate, just as we'd hoped. What's left of it, anyway."

She felt a pang of sadness at the thought. Whatever the Elders had done, what had happened was unthinkable. Even those deserving of death were owed their dignity. The elves had offered none.

"I still fear that it is entirely too late," Elder Bram said, coughing into the edge of his sleeve. "Wes Cervos has never been given a reason to trust me. I fail to see why he would be willing to listen now, but there is no other option but to try."

"We made our choices, and there is no way to take them back. We couldn't have expected that Wes would break out of prison like he did."

"I thought we could protect him," he said. "I tell myself that I did everything I could to keep him safe, but I suppose I'll never stop second guessing how I might have done more."

"You're human, grandfather. Only the High One can truly make plans. Ours are always vulnerable to change."

"How humbling it is to know that you have wisdom to see

what I cannot," he said, giving her a smile that made the edges of his aging eyes crinkle. "But how I hate the lies."

"I hate them just as much," Oria agreed. "Mother does, too."

"Every day I look at this place, and guilt grabs me straight around the gut. How can I live in luxury as my only child and grandchild suffer poverty?"

"Because it's the only way. Because it is for the greater good."

Oria looked at her grandfather for several seconds, wishing that there was anything that she could say to lessen his guilt, but she knew from experience that there was not. Instead, she got up from her chair and took hold of the dinner tray.

"Wes does not trust you, but he does trust me. There is still hope that he might listen, given time."

Several seconds of silence passed between them as her eyes met his. *The High One is with me, I will not fail, not in the end. Not when it counts.*

1

Chapter One

WES

Wes Cervos leaned forward on Celesyria's back, gripping the leather straps around her neck as the dragon dove. He tried to look down at the approaching ground below, but within moments he had pressed his eyes shut, letting his forehead rest against her orange scales.

"I trust you, you know," he said with his mind, trying to take in enough of the thin air into his lungs.

"And I try my best to deserve it," Celesyria replied, the flap of her wings sending air whipping past his face as she leveled out. Wes forced himself to open his eyes.

The mountains that surrounded Auranth were vast, their crumbling brown peaks stretching out high into the gray clouds. They were flying along the western edge of the range now, the steep mountainsides far closer to Celesyria's right wingtip than Wes would have preferred. To their left lay the West Strait, the waters flat and dark beneath the gloom that rested overhead.

"We're close, right?" Celesyria asked, banking to the left to

avoid a large rock formation that jutted out from the nearest slope. Wes breathed in and out slowly, focusing his gaze on the horizon rather than the treacherous terrain below.

For several seconds, he thought that he could see only mountains ahead, the ugly expanse of brown scree and lonely stone seeming to go on forever. The whole world seemed to bounce as Celesyria flapped her wings, gaining momentum as they flew over a large field of wayward boulders. But as she glided back down, he saw what he had been looking for.

"Trees!" he shouted aloud, feeling a smile spread across his face despite the sick feeling in his stomach. "At the foot of that narrow peak."

"I guess I'll find a good place to hide once we reach our old camping site," Celesyria said. Wes could hear a hint of resentment in her tone, and he couldn't blame her. Far too often, she was forced to hide away like a criminal as her friends carried out their plans. This time, though, he was confident that things would be different.

"Only for a little while," he replied, gripping the leather straps white-knuckled as she glided down, impossibly close to the tops of the pines. *"I'll speak to Bargren."*

Clearing the stand of trees, Celesyria tilted her wings and allowed the trapped air to slow their descent. Wes hoped that the landing would not worsen the pain of her damaged ankle, but he was thankful that the injury forced her to be more careful. A few seconds later, her clawed feet touched the ground without incident, and Wes wasted no time in climbing off of her back.

"How's the wound?" he asked, bending to examine it.

"Better than I'd hoped it would be by now."

The thick manacle obscured his view, but it seemed that the

2

swelling had gone down. She had received the injury just over a week ago, held prisoner during a disturbing meeting of elves, dragons, and dwarves. Her friend Gramnok Beastbane had set off a bomb in hopes of freeing her, but she'd been injured in the process.

He straightened, giving her a pat along the side of her broad chest. She would be back to normal within a few days. And, better yet, there was a chance that someone in Auranth would finally be able to remove her restraints. But first, he would have to ask Bargren if he was willing to openly harbor a dragon who happened to be a wanted fugitive.

"*You should hunt,*" he said, turning to look at the tight stand of pines that they had flown over. It wasn't quite a forest in his estimation—having grown up in the heart of Silverfell, few other areas in the Four Kingdoms could compare—but he was hopeful it held a deer or two. "*I want to set out while there's still enough light.*"

"*Don't you think that Kessara and Alder should be here by now?*" Celesyria asked.

"*We don't know how far they had to travel,*" Wes reminded her, glancing in the direction of the West Strait, which was hidden behind the trees. "*Nor do we know which route they might take.*"

"*I miss them. I will worry until they're within my sight.*"

"*They'll be here. Perhaps they're already with Bargren,*" he said, not quite believing it. Though he didn't want to admit it and add to Celesyria's anxiety, he feared for them as well.

Despite his own best attempts to keep everyone together, Alder had not agreed with his strategy. They had been separated for several weeks, and news did not always travel fast, especially not now, when so much of Kaveryth was on the brink of war. "*I will return for you as soon as I can. Perhaps even*

3

tonight."

"Just be careful," the dragon said, leaping back up into the air and disappearing behind the trees that surrounded him.

The walk toward the southern gate of Auranth was a difficult one. The path weaved along the base of the mountain ridge, twisting and curving around trees, boulders, and bodies of water. Wes was nearly out of dried meat, and would have been sick of eating it even if he still had plenty to spare.

He listened to the sounds of the sparse forest as he walked, pulling off the hood of his cloak and enjoying the slight breeze rippling through his dark brown curls.

The birds chirping from within the depths of the pine branches sounded positively cheerful, and before long, Wes was beginning to enjoy himself despite the gloom.

As they'd flown over Umrym, they'd seen dozens of bandits and other suspicious individuals hiding amongst the stones, but here, it was quiet.

It feels like the way Stronghollow used to be. Safe. Happy.

The thought caused his whistled tune to falter for a moment.

He brushed past some pine branches, feeling the stickiness of their sap against his cloak as he came up over a small rise. How could Auranth ever be home without oak trees, or maples, or the song of mourning doves?

Another half hour passed, and he reached out to Celesyria with his mind again, warning her that they would probably not be near enough to speak again until he returned.

As the great stone wall at the southern edge of the city rose before him, he rested his hand on the pommel of his sword.

He was no longer alone.

Behind the open gate up ahead, he saw two men peering through the bars at him, their fingers clasped around the

4

spears that rested at their sides.

"Halt!" one of them shouted, raising his spear and striding toward him. "Drop your sword and get on your knees."

Wes obeyed, his fingers shaking as he undid the leather strap of his scabbard and let the enclosed blade fall. His heart hammered in his ears as he dropped to the ground, his knees smarting against the hard-packed dirt. Both of the guards were on him now, one of them grabbing his sword and the other reaching for his pack.

"Not a Blackmask, at the least," one of them said loudly, rifling through Wes' belongings. There wasn't much to find, and, satisfied, he slung the leather strap over his shoulder and stood, beckoning for Wes to join him.

"I'm not going to bind him," said the other, nearly shouting as Wes got to his feet. "He'll come easy enough."

Both of the men closed in at his sides, looking him up and down.

"Really? You were just going to march up to the gate? That was your plan?"

It took Wes several seconds to realize that the soldier to his left was speaking to him, his voice scarcely loud enough to be heard even in the quiet of the forest.

"What else was I to do?" Wes replied, stopping himself from mentioning the possibility of flying a dragon over the wall just in time.

"I'll just bring him to the hold," the other soldier said from his right, ignoring his protests as he reached over and drew the hood of his cloak back over Wes' head. "We'll ask Lady Garbella's men to talk to him in the morning."

Wes looked between them in bafflement. "What is–"

He felt droplets of spittle hit his ear as the quiet soldier began whispering again.

"Are you trying to get the attention of every soldier in the city?"

Wes said nothing, trying to look around as they approached the gate. Past the edge of his hood, he could see five archers standing atop the wall to their right, and he imagined there were more to his left. He'd never been alone after all. Perhaps they had even hidden guards among the trees, where they could watch the approach to the city. He could only hope that none of the men patrolled as far as Celesyria's camp.

He started to whisper to the soldier at his left, but the man held up a hand and gestured that he go through the gate. Wes decided to follow along, pulling the hood of his cloak lower so as to hide his face—and his scarred cheek—in shadow. Whatever was happening, it seemed that these men were trying to help, and besides, there was no way he would be able to break free of them even if he wanted to.

Several minutes passed in silence as they walked into the city proper, Wes keeping his head as low as possible. He watched as the men nodded to their brothers in arms, looking very much at ease, just ordinary guards bringing a strange newcomer in to be questioned.

Although Auranth was part of Silverfell in terms of adminis-tration, for decades the city had operated largely on its own, with its own small armed force. A nagging idea that had already begun to form in his mind only grew more detailed as he caught glimpses of the city as it existed today, even more isolated and self-sufficient than it had been the last time he'd been here.

While the rest of Kaveryth was fracturing, the people of Auranth seemed to be coming together, shoring up their resources for greater resilience.

It could be perfect...

Before he could think about it anymore, however, they had reached their destination, not far from the entrance to the city walls.

Ahead of him was a great door, leading the way into a massive stone building. As soon as they crossed the threshold, he felt the air turning thick with heat. Sweat began to drip from his curls onto his neck, and he knotted his hands in the fabric of his cloak to avoid flinging back his hood.

As uncomfortable as he was, there was plenty to distract him.

Huge stone shelves stretched ahead, as far as Wes could see, their racks and cabinets filled with thousands of swords, axes, and pikes. A few paces to his left was another row, this one holding bows, arrows, shields, and spears. Several more rows lay to the right, no doubt filled with more weapons. He could see stands of armor on the far side of the room, enough to shield a thousand men, all shining steel and neatly hammered edges.

"Welcome to the armory. You can take these," one of the soldiers said, handing Wes his own pack and sword. "The boss wouldn't want you getting too jealous."

The boss. Is it possible?

Wes smiled, relief rushing through him as he glanced down at his curved short sword and battered leather pack.

"A little late to avoid envy, I think."

"Come this way," the man said, pointing down the main row of swords and toward an archway at the other end of the room. Wes followed, happy to feel the weight of his sword on his belt again even if it was not quite so magnificent as the weapons that surrounded him.

When they crossed the threshold beneath the arch, the heat grew so intense that Wes wished he could remove his cloak entirely, and perhaps his other clothes, as well.

They were standing in a huge smithy, filled with no less than a dozen active forges. Each one had a man working at it, seemingly unbothered by the suffocating heat as they hammered, poured, and shaped the molten steel.

"Bargren's over here," a man called out, looking up from the shield that lay on his work bench. "He's hammering. Talk loud."

They moved deeper into the space, the sound of metal on metal making Wes' teeth ache. He watched in amazement as they worked with astonishing speed, leaving piles of new weapons, shields, and armors at their stations, ready to be cleaned. He knew that Auranth was renowned across Kaveryth for its weaponmaking, but he hadn't realized just how large the operation really was.

To think that the entirety of the Four Kingdoms relies on this little town, hiding in the mountains.

It seemed to him now to be an absurd reality, and yet, there was that idea again, swirling in his mind like the smoke that clouded his vision.

"Bargren!" one of the soldiers shouted at the top of his lungs, startling Wes even over the sound of hammer-blows. "Bargren!"

The man sitting at the nearest forge threw his hammer to the side, sending a spray of sparks flying in all directions.

"By the Dracodei, what is it! I nearly bashed my thumb–" Bargren roared, the words dying in his throat as he turned to see who exactly had caused the interruption.

Wes pulled back the hood of his cloak.

The big smith, head of the Armory Guild, got up at once, and for one terrifying moment Wes thought that he would hug him, soot and sparks and all. Instead, the man restrained himself by giving Wes a heavy clap on the shoulder, sending a small poof of black dust into his face.

"Wes Cervos! I was beginning to wonder if I would ever see you at my door again."

"We found him at the gate, sir. He tried to walk straight in," one of the soldiers said, shaking his head. "He wasn't even trying to hide."

"The reward will be large, gentlemen. I'll be sure to offer extra payment as recompense for the foolishness of our guest," bargren said, straightening up. "Now, the Envoy and I have much to discuss."

The soldiers nodded, heading toward the front of the armory.

Wes was growing hot and longed to chase after them out into the cool autumn air, whether they thought him foolish or not. Instead, he waited as Bargren gave a few parting instructions to the other smiths.

To his relief, there was a back door close by, and within a few moments they were outside, blinking away the surprisingly bright glow of the overcast sky.

"What was that all about?" Wes asked after taking several moments just to breathe. He felt rather terrible after standing in the smoke and heat, and his head had begun to pound. Bargren seemed unphased, though Wes supposed that he must have been very used to the conditions by now.

Bargren said nothing, instead wiping the soot from his hands onto his leather apron and reaching to grasp a piece of paper that had been stuck against the outside wall.

Wes extended a hand to take it, a sinking feeling burrowing into his belly.

Etched onto the paper in spindly black lines was a rather accurate drawing of his face, followed by a few lines of text.

Envoy Wes Cervos, wanted on charges of blasphemy, treason, and other crimes. Reward in coin for capture and delivery to the Protectorate. No reward will be given if fugitive is delivered deceased. Warrant given by order of King Kylan Ursa, Sovereign of Aridmoor and Steward of Silverfell.

"Well," Wes said after a long pause. "That's a pleasant welcome." Bargren gave him a pinched smile.

"I bribed the guards, as I'm sure you ascertained. I'm not about to turn you in. Come," he said, beginning to hurry along beside the wall. "I have something to show you. Let's not draw any more attention."

He ducked his head into a doorway and gave instructions to one of the men inside. Though he shouted over the sound of hammer blows, Wes could not hear a word.

"You'll need a smith's uniform," he explained, gesturing to his own clothes. "If we're lucky, you may even be able to pass off that ruined moonscar of yours as an ordinary burn."

Wes touched his cheek, feeling the rough skin beneath his fingertips. The memories of that night flooded into his mind.

The fire. The forest. Celesyria.

If there's any hope at all for my plan to work, I have to tell him the whole truth.

"Er, Bargren," he started, trying to keep up with the big man's surprisingly quick pace. "I have a confession to make.

10

I did not come alone."

2

Chapter Two

CELESYRIA

"Alright, it's time."

Celesyria could hear a voice, though for a second she was confused about who it belonged to, and whether she had heard it through her ears or inside her head. The dream she had been having still lingered, and she felt off balance, like she couldn't quite make out what was real and what she could leave behind in the bottomless memory of sleep.

The dream was always the same.

She could see the masked bandits swarming Windshear like insects. She could hear the screams of pain and death, smell the metallic stink of fresh blood. The little Vilzanian boy was there too, his brown face peering out at her from a window as she flew toward the bandit that chased him.

As always, she woke up just before she swiped the ladder out from under the boy's pursuer, sending him to his death.

Could I have made another choice? Could I have saved that boy without resorting to murder?

She blinked her eyes several times, as though she could wash away the images that haunted her. Even though the bandit's death was not part of the dream, she could still hear the crunch of his bones breaking as his body hit the ground.

Wes' voice was there again, inside her head, breaking through the horrible thoughts. She looked around, noticing that the grim sky overhead had given way to darkness. Some of the clouds had shifted, and between them, she could see a small blanket of stars. She had been sleeping for at least a few hours.

"Is everything okay?" he asked aloud, his face near hers, eyes filled with concern.

"Yes, fine. Just a dream," she said in his mind, nearly hitting him with her front claws as she stretched out against the ground. Part of her wanted to confess to him, to tell him not only the details of the dream, but to share the feelings of guilt that had plagued her ever since that day.

She knew that the High One did not condemn killing if justice required it, but still, she could not doubt that the act had wounded her deeply in a way that only He could heal.

"Are you sure?" Wes asked.

"Yes," she said firmly. There was nothing that her friend could say. For all she knew, she would soon be forced to kill again. She would just have to learn to cope with it.

Wes nodded, seemingly satisfied. *"I have good and bad news."*

"Give me the bad first."

"The people of Auranth know what I have done, and they've already given up their treasures to the Septemvirate for the summer Feast of Offering."

"Wonderful."

"It gets worse. There are wanted posters with my face on them

all over town."

"By order of King Ursa, I assume."

Wes nodded.

"The good news is that Bargren is still willing to help us," Wes said, a smile tugging at the corner of his lips. *"Both of us. He thinks that the King is a bully and a tyrant, and seems rather pleased to be given an opportunity to disrupt his growing power over Silverfell."*

Celesyria gaped at him. She scarcely heard the rest of what he'd said. All this time, she'd felt like more of a liability than an ally to her friends, always hiding out, away from the action. Could things really be different now, just as Wes hoped?

"You told him I'm here?"

"I did. And then he showed me the perfect place for the both of us. And for Alder and Kessara when they arrive.

He paused for a moment, as though considering he might say more before thinking better of it.

"Big enough for a dragon?"

"Big enough for ten dragons. Perhaps more."

She wanted to ask more about it, eager to know what sort of place would serve as such a perfect refuge, but then she thought of their friends.

"How will Alder and Kessara find us if the whole city is on the lookout for you?" she asked. *"If they know what you've done, they probably have an inkling about our ex-Protectorate soldier at the very least, if not the princess."*

"Bargren bribed guards at the gate to apprehend me before city officials could do so. I'm hoping he will do the same for them as well," Wes said, looking back toward the lights of Auranth in the distance. *"In the meantime, I told him we would take a detour toward the mountain range and approach our new hideout from*

the east."

As Wes climbed onto her back, Celesyria looked to the stars, finding a familiar constellation as she took flight. As she climbed higher into the night, relieved to be off her sore ankle, she thought of the High One. He had protected her and Wes thus far, against terrible odds. She had to trust that He was looking out for Alder and Kessara as well.

KESSARA

"Let me get this straight," Princess Kessara said, clutching the leather reins with white-knuckled fingers. "You're okay riding these beasts, but find it too uncomfortable to ride a deer?"

"I also like riding dragons," Alder quipped from his own saddle, glancing over at her with a playful grin. "In case you haven't figured it out yet, I quite enjoy my life as a walking contradiction."

"If you say so," she said, rolling her eyes.

Before he had a chance to respond, Kessara noticed that the entire company of horses ahead of them were being pulled to a halt by their riders. Scrambling to do the same before she caused a collision, she yanked a bit too hard on the horse's mouth, causing the large black animal beneath her to give a small buck in protest.

She pitched forward, her stomach bumping into the horn of the saddle before she settled down hard on her bottom.

"Are you alright?" Alder asked, drawing his own gray horse up next to hers and grabbing the side of her horse's bridle.

He patted at the animal's neck, whispering soothing sounds at him until he stood still.

"I'm fine. It isn't the first time I've been bucked," she said,

15

trying her best to hold her head high rather than staring at the ground. It would have been a long fall to the grass below. "Though I suppose it would be rather worse to be bucked off of an Aridmoor plains horse."

Alder grinned at her, letting go of the horse's bridle as the group began to move forward again. "Best warhorses in all of Kaveryth. They just need a firm hand."

"I've been riding since I was six. I know how to handle a horse," Kessara said, narrowing her eyes at him.

"I suppose we'll see tonight, when we gallop," he whispered, leaning toward her in his saddle, his face dangerously close to her own. He smelled rather sweaty, but she found that the scent was not unappealing.

To her great annoyance, his mare did not so much as flinch as he shifted his weight. How she had ended up with the plucky young gelding and him with the gentle older female, she had no idea.

"Shh," she whispered, daring to take one hand off of her reins to wave him away. He winked at her as he settled back onto his own horse.

They had been trying to stay away from one another, but here on the road, far from anyone who knew them, it was difficult. She sighed, relaxing her grip as the riders ahead slowed once more.

Up ahead, she saw nothing but open space, the usually bright green grass dulled from months of summer sunshine.

Being near Alder felt about as safe as running through the dry prairie and striking flint to steel.

"Down here," a voice from up ahead was calling. The whole company of riders—a bit more than twenty men and another ten women, if she had to guess—directed their horses to the

16

left, forming a neat line along what looked like a game trail. She glanced at Alder, trying not to meet his eyes, and they both waited until all but a few of the slowest riders remained behind them before joining the line.

The sun was nearing the horizon, and despite the season, Kessara was beginning to feel the chill of the approaching night. The plains of Aridmoor were often windy, and when a cold front blew in from the faraway sea, there were few forests or mountains to stifle it.

All she wanted at that moment was to curl up beneath a blanket and rest her tired muscles, and she was thankful when the riders up ahead began to slow. They came to a stop near a low hill and riders began climbing down from their horses' backs, heading for a watering hole nearby. Kessara did likewise, with Alder following close behind. Their horses got to work immediately, finding the patch of grass that was most to their liking and beginning to graze.

As soon as she could reach the edge of the small pool without drawing undue attention to herself, she filled their waterskins, taking out a dainty bottle from her pack and adding a few drops of its contents to the drinking water.

To her pleasant surprise, Alder made none of his usual objections about "superstition and nonsense" as he accepted his portion of the cool but rather grassy-tasting water. After taking a few sips, he rose, gesturing off toward the far side of the hill.

"I'll go get your tent set up."

She opened her mouth to argue, but he cut her off.

"Don't worry. You'll be nearer to the water. I'll be the one who has to fight off the wolves at the edge of camp." He looked almost delighted at the prospect.

17

She would have scolded him for joking about such terrible things, but before she could, another woman came to fill her own waterskin nearby. The stranger flashed Kessara a quick smile, and Kessara felt a blush rising to her face. These people would think that she and Alder were sleeping together, in their tent that was big enough for two.

That's the plan, after all.

Kessara had taken Alder's shabby army-issue shelter for herself, figuring that if anyone was going to try and rob them or if anyone found out who they were, they'd be more likely to attack the nicer tent.

She fiddled with the simple silver ring on her left hand, twirling it around as she smiled at the other woman. All around them, people were setting up their own tents and unpacking saddlebags. Another man was scraping the grass nearby, creating a round section of dirt where they might safely light a fire.

So far, their entire plan to sneak into Auranth had gone better than she'd expected.

After they'd watched Alder's mother and sisters ride off from Raela's hut, they had gotten straight to work. Kessara had been the one to find the most useful treasure. Raela's lime-burner's uniform was perfect for their purposes, especially the white linen cap covered with a leather helmet. Kessara used it to hide her blonde hair, which would have surely given away their charade among the redheaded people of Aridmoor. Alder already looked halfway the part in his farmers' tunic. Once he had borrowed a spare leather apron and let Kessara cut his red curls short with kitchen shears, the disguise was complete.

The two of them had walked into Claghan village with no

18

one giving them so much as a second glance. To Alder's great excitement, they had immediately found two retired warhorses for sale and purchased them just in time to join up with a merchants' caravan headed west. There, too, no one had shown any sign of suspicion.

The large group of riders had been waved through several Red Army checkpoints along the main roads without issue, until finally they had reached the river near Vaevar. They had headed down a smaller road, one that Alder had frequented when he was a member of the Protectorate, and since then, they had met with no more checkpoints.

Kessara sat by the little pond for a while, watching the pink and gold gleam of the setting sun drift over the camp.

High One, You have watched over us thus far. Help us to make it the rest of the way.

3

Chapter Three

WES

Everything was completely silent.

Even the birds seemed to have ceased their songs for a moment, hiding away amidst broken stones and lonely trees. Wes climbed off of Celesyria's back, turning in a slow circle, trying to take everything in. The dragon simply stood still, her clawed feet planted firmly amid the untidy grass.

The walls of the old armory were marred with rust stains and pocked where pieces of stone had broken, but they were sturdy and tall. The ceiling was almost whole, vaulted in stone like the walls, but there was a section on the south side that was big enough for a dragon to fly into.

Currently, rain was pouring through it at a rapid pace, but at least it didn't seem to be causing any flooding in the rest of the room.

"If you plan to stay into the autumn and winter, we can fix the hole," Bargren cut in finally, breaking the almost reverent silence from his spot near the door. "I can get men on it within a couple of days."

"I'm not sure we should," Wes said, glancing up at the slice of gray sky overhead. "This place is big enough for dragons, and it seems easier to let them in that way than to build a door for them."

Bargren gave him a strange look, and Celesyria's voice entered his mind.

"What other dragons are you planning on inviting?"

He forced a smile onto his face, chiding himself. His plans were coming together, but he wanted to tread carefully. There was still much to sort out, and he wanted Alder and Kessara's input as well.

"I'll explain later," he replied to Celesyria, hoping she wouldn't press the issue.

"That's true enough," Bargren said, still eyeing him but saying nothing more.

"The floor seems to have seen the worst damage," Wes said, glancing around. The stones had been torn up in several areas, leaving dirt and grass exposed. In several places, trees had grown, sustained by the sunshine that entered through the battered ceiling above on clearer days. "But I like the trees, and a cold floor isn't such a bad thing, when it's surrounded by solid walls."

For a moment, Wes was swept away by his memories.

Growing up in Stronghollow palace, there had always been trees growing indoors. The forests of Silverfell were precious to him, and he'd loved the way that the forest was not shut out, but rather invited into the home of the House of Cervos.

"Thank you for allowing me to come, Bargren," Celesyria said aloud, bowing her huge head until her chin touched the grass. "You have offered me an extraordinary kindness."

"You are welcome here," he said firmly, glancing back at the door. "I will have meat brought to you as soon as I am able."

"I'm sorry if our presence brings you distress," Wes said, noting the man's nervous posture. Celesyria was right. Bargren was taking a huge risk by allowing them to stay here. He may have been the head of the Armory Guild, but there were even more powerful men in Auranth who could cause him trouble if they wished.

"I can't deny that I'm afraid, Wes," bargren said simply, giving them a brief smile. "I would be a very stupid man if I wasn't. But as I said to you before, I do not trust King Ursa to be my Steward. I remain loyal to King Gadan Cervos, even if only his memory lives. Aside from being a worthy king, your father was one of the greatest people I have ever had the privilege of knowing. I will not face my death knowing that I could have helped his last surviving child but did not do so out of cowardice."

For a moment no one spoke. Wes watched as a breeze rushed in through the ceiling, making the leaves and grasses dance between the stone tiles that made up the floor. The calm of the place reminded Wes more of a temple than a smithy. It was difficult to believe that this place had once been filled with thick heat, molten metal, and men with burn wounds.

"Well," Wes said at last, returning Bargren's smile. "Thank you. For everything."

"Don't worry, son. I have other reasons as well to hope for the success of you and your friends in freeing this land from the worship of the Dracodei."

"You believe in the High One?" Celesyria asked, sounding surprised. Wes shared her sentiment. The first time that

Bargren had aided them, he had not known the extent of their plans. Auranth was remote, and before King Ursa's Red Army had begun recruiting all over Kaveryth, news traveled much more slowly. Now, they could not hide, and Bargren seemed to know a great deal more about their affairs than Wes had realized.

"I don't know if I believe in Him or not," Bargren answered, his words slow and careful. "What I do know is that the Septemvirate continues to extract our treasures, supposedly in devotion to the Dracodei, and yet the skies remain empty even in our hour of greatest need. I have lost faith in the current order."

"I can understand that," Wes said mildly.

Bargren nodded. "It may not be as noble as your own faith, but that is the truth of it, for the time being at least. In any case, I'm also concerned about my sons. A conscription campaign for King Ursa's Red Army is well underway in Aridmoor and Silverfell proper, and I'm sure that the more remote cities will be called upon eventually. I was beginning to give up hope that you would return before my four boys were called away."

"Well, we are here, and we will do all that we can to prevent it," Celesyria said, her voice booming across the open space. Bargren nodded, gesturing toward the entrance of the room.

"Indeed. As I've said, you will be safe here. For a time, this building was overrun with prostitutes and drunks, but the city administrators finally cracked down. Better yet, my boys grew up friends with the lads who have been given guard of the place. They will divulge nothing about your presence here."

"You've done so much for us," Wes said, giving a bow of his head. "But I confess I have one more favor to ask."

Well, several more, but that's a problem for tomorrow.

"Of course, my dear Envoy."

"Can you keep up your bribe with the city guards a little while longer? I need them to keep an eye out for a pretty blonde woman with blue eyes, and a tall Aridmoorian with red hair and freckles."

"That describes half of the men here," Bargren objected, gesturing to his own red hair. Wes knew this, of course, but he had no better ideas.

"Bargren is very handsome for an older man," Celesyria noted in his mind. *"Though perhaps not quite as handsome as Alder."*

"So ask them to apprehend the blonde woman and her companion, whoever he may be," Wes said, resisting the urge to stick his tongue out at Celesyria. "My friends should have money to pay you back once they arrive. Alas, I cannot pay in advance."

"I will see it is taken care of," Bargren said, bowing to Wes and turning toward the door. "I'll call for refreshments. You both need to rest."

"Thank you. And Bargren?" the burly man stopped, waiting. "The man's name is Alder Cadogen, if it helps, though I am not sure he will divulge it."

The smith stopped short before the door, turning on his heel.

"*The* Alder Cadogen? The boy soldier who single-handedly turned the tide in the Battle of Halgrad?"

"Er, I guess so," Wes said, glancing over at Celesyria. He could almost see the gears turning in her head, and he knew that she must be thinking over the hundreds of books she had read and about whether or not such a battle had been mentioned within their pages.

"Military history is of interest to me, and his name has come up more than once. Quite remarkable for someone barely into his twenties."

"Indeed," Wes said with a pinched smile, unsure of what else he could say, having never heard this tale from Alder.

With a final nod, Bargren left the two of them alone in the vast room.

"*Any clue what he's talking about?*" he asked Celesyria.

"*No idea.*"

"*Fascinating. Alder did something for the history books and didn't even brag to us about it.*"

Not long after Bargren had left, two teenage boys who looked very much like him returned, bringing huge plates of food for Wes and promising Celesyria that she would get a whole live deer to herself just as soon as their two other brothers returned from hunting.

Thanking their hosts, they ate in companionable silence, Wes sharing bits of meat with Celesyria, though he supposed it would not do her hunger much good.

"*Wes?*" Celesyria asked after a while, her nose buried in a large wash tub that she had been given as a water dish.

He paused before acknowledging her, a smile rising to his lips. She knew him far too well for him to hide anything for long.

"*I know what you are going to ask,*" he said. "*And yes, there are things I am not telling you. Plans for this place, for it to be more than just a place to hide.*"

"*But you won't tell me.*"

"*I will. Just as soon as Alder and Kessara arrive.*"

ALDER

Alder sat in his tent, looking out through the open door flap as the moon rose high over the camp. He could see no clouds, and though the stars were not quite so magnificent as they would be in the wintertime, they were still pretty to look at. He thought of Kessara, sleeping in her tent nearby, and a familiar twinge of anxiety shot through him.

Celesyria would tell me that true love should not be anxious, and she would be right.

The thought brought little comfort. He had no other word for how he felt about her, no other way to describe the fierceness blooming in his heart when he looked into her eyes. But he knew it was impossible, a word that would remain unvoiced, a fire with nothing to consume.

A flame that must be quelled.

He realized that he was fidgeting, pressing his dirty finger-nails into the side of a wooden tent pole again and again. There had been a time when he found it easy to wait in silence, with only his thoughts to keep him company. The discipline of life in Aridmoor's army was only deepened when he joined the King's Protectorate. But those days were gone, his old life swept away like dust. He served the High One now, and that required even greater personal discipline than he'd had before.

So why is it that I falter so easily?

He got up from the floor of the tent and began to gather up his scattered belongings. He knew exactly why he faltered. He knew exactly why he struggled to be still, let alone to pray.

Princess Kessara Manta was a shadow over his life, beautiful and dangerous, and his thoughts were constantly drawn to matters of her protection and happiness.

Alder slipped out into the warm summer night, leaving his packed bag at the edge of his tent. He would be back for it.

Kessara's little tent stood dark and silent, and he continued past it until he reached the edge of the pond. Another man stood there, dressed in a style Alder recognized as originating from the northern mountains of Vilzan that lay between Galeharbor and Silverfell.

"I'll take a watch," Alder offered, sidling up beside the merchant and clapping him on the shoulder. "The moon and stars are beckoning me, anyway."

"I never quite get my fill of them, but my eyelids are growing heavy," the man conceded, skipping a stone that he had been holding across the still water. "It's been quiet. Not so much as a wolf's howl, and certainly no bears or anything else exciting."

Alder smiled. *The curse of all watchman. Hoping to see nothing, and hoping to see something.*

"That's certainly good to hear," he replied, glancing around the entirety of the camp, wanting to be sure that the man was correct that they were entirely alone. After all, they were about to find themselves without a watchman.

The man yawned, and within a few minutes he had retreated to his tent, leaving Alder to turn to his silence and waiting once again.

The minutes moved slowly. He managed to pray to the High One a little, mostly because it gave him an excuse to talk to the night sky without feeling insane.

Finally, it was time.

He picked up a large rock from somewhere near his feet and threw it into the water, enjoying the satisfying splash as it struck the surface. He listened for any sign of movement from the surrounding tents, but there was nothing to hear besides the occasional chirping of a restless moorbird.

He kept quiet as he approached Kessara's tent and entered

through the door flap. She was sleeping soundly on her bedroll, her mouth hanging open with a bit of drool dribbling down onto her chin. He reached over and shook her gently by the shoulder, hoping that she was not the sort to leap up in bed. If anyone else in the camp woke up, they would be furious to find that Alder had left his post vacant, making a second chance to slip away much more difficult.

Kessara did not so much as flinch.

Alder just looked at her for a moment, drool and all, his gaze falling upon the silver ring on her left hand. It was plain and cheap, and if he looked closely he could see that it was bent ever so slightly out of shape, but that didn't matter. Even the illusion of a wedding ring on her hand was enough to make him feel sick.

"You will wear a beautiful ring when you marry Wes," he whispered to her sleeping form. His voice shook with each word. "You will be Queen of Silverfell. The House of Cervos will rise from the ashes. And you will be safe and happy, better off without me."

He finished then, letting the fierce words die off in the dark. He took a few breaths, trying to push aside the foolish dreams and desires that would only bring him—and worse, her—pain.

Discipline. That's all it takes.

He shook her again, harder this time, and she jolted awake. He brought a finger to his lips, and wordlessly she helped him to gather her own belongings.

They emerged into the night, and it seemed to Alder that in the short time since he'd entered her tent, the moon had grown even larger and more bright.

"Wow," the Princess whispered, staring out over the pond. Her hair was mussed from sleep, and it fell over her back like

28

spun gold. She reached out as though she could clasp the moon in her delicate, tanned fingers.

Discipline.

"We're not on a sightseeing tour," Alder hissed as he strode up beside her, gesturing toward the far side of camp. "We need to get to the horses."

He saw her brow furrow in annoyance, but she said nothing as she hefted her leather satchel onto her back and followed him.

A few minutes later, they were on horseback, trotting away across the plains. They had forded the river easily on their huge mounts, and now the edge of Silverfell's forest was near enough that they would easily reach it before dawn. They were not safe on the roads that crossed Aridmoor. Even if they managed to avoid Red Army soldiers, there were roving bandits and wandering elves to contend with. At least in the forest, they would have the advantage of stealth.

'What's that?" Kessara asked after a few moments of quiet, gesturing at the ground.

"What?" he said, nudging his horse over to where hers now stood. In a little hollow there was loose dirt, and in it, he could see a distinct shape.

"It looks like a stag print," Kessara said, squinting. "A recent one."

He ignored the adorable way that her brow furrowed and dismounted, landing carefully so as not to disturb her find.

"It is," he said, crouching down and pointing at the front end of the impression. "A stag with a rider. It was wearing shoes."

Satisfied, he returned to his horse, hauling himself up onto the saddle with some effort. Kessara was looking around, her gaze swiveling over the empty prairie.

"The town of Vaevar lies just a little to the northwest," he said, giving Kessara what he hoped was a reassuring smile. "They're not on the route that the Red Army would likely take, and in any case, there's nothing to bring them there anyway. Just the Academy."

As he was sure Kessara knew, the scholars and students there were exempt from offering treasure to the Dracodei, so it was unlikely that these prints belonged to any Septemvirate lackeys, either.

What she didn't know was that anyone just passing through would almost certainly have made their way around further south, to avoid fording the river.

He sighed. He didn't like keeping things from her, but there was no reason for him to give her additional reasons to worry. They would be long gone before anyone else could make it back from Vaevar, but still, he had no interest in waiting around for trouble.

"Are you still nervous to canter?" Alder asked, looking back over his shoulder to make sure that no potential threats had snuck up on them. He saw only rippling grass. Whoever had come through here was long gone.

Kessara rose in her stirrups, leaning forward slightly over the huge horse's neck and turning to grin at him.

"Race you to the forest," she yelled, urging the eager gelding into a gallop. Before Alder could react, she was well ahead of him, her hair gleaming in the moonlight as she raced toward the distant trees. He could almost hear her laughter over the thundering of hooves.

Discipline.

4

Chapter Four

KESSARA

Despite the closeness of the trees, their huge horses still managed to make quick work of their travel. Kessara quickly grew accustomed to their dizzying height, and her smaller stature enabled her to win meadow races with Alder more often than not. Though she grew more comfortable on her horse with each hour spent in the saddle, his temperament left much to be desired.

Still, she could see why the horses were often used as messengers, especially when stags could not be procured. Their speed was second only to that of dragons, and they were capable of going long distances without needing to stop and rest.

The summer heat had grown cloying as they rode through the thick forests, and the biting insects had not improved her gelding's attitude. They had all been relieved–horses included, Kessara was sure–to reach the outskirts of Briarcroft, where the trees had become sparse and the flies were less numerous.

Alder had gone into town for food and other provisions,

keeping his face well-hidden in the shadows of his cloak, and though she had been anxious the whole time he was gone, he had returned to their camp unharmed. There had been no trouble, but he had seen Silverfell and Red Army men passing by on stagback, their mounts laden with treasure in preparation for the upcoming feast.

Just as soon as they reached the foothills of the mountain range that bordered Auranth, the rain began. They dismounted and gathered up as much of the food as they could under their cloaks as the clouds unleashed their fury, but by the time that they remounted, the hard-pack of dirt and fallen leaves had already transformed into a slick mire.

As they pressed forward, Kessara could feel the cold rain dribbling past her hood and through to the back of her neck.

Can't wait for wet bread tonight.

She chided herself for the thought. They were both safe, they were nearing Auranth, and at least they would have something to eat, however unpleasant it tasted. She had been raised to be patient and calm when things didn't go her way, and she was determined not to lose her composure now.

"Careful, there's a—" Alder started. Before he could finish his sentence, she felt her horse's right front hoof push downward into a deep divot of mud. She lost her balance, only barely managing to stay on by grasping the animal's mane as she tumbled forward. Mercifully, the animal did not attempt to buck.

Biting her tongue against a string of curses, she settled back into her saddle as the horse backed up, shaking mud from his front leg.

"You need to be careful," Alder ordered. "The path is going to get even more uneven as we ascend. Sit deep, and keep your hands on the reins from here out."

"I'm fine, by the way, thanks for asking," she snapped. She did as he said, however, and felt somewhat satisfied to see that he was tightening his own reins as well.

Without another word, Alder moved a couple of horse lengths up ahead, presumably to find the most tolerable path forward. The rain continued to pour until Kessara's cloak was soaked and heavy. She was certain that none of the food could possibly still be dry. Despite her resolve not to complain, she felt she was ready to snap at any moment.

It's probably good that he's barely speaking to me. I might tear his head clean off if I get any more annoyed.

After they rode in silence for what felt to be at least another hour, however, she began to feel her bitterness slipping away. Truth was, she was more hurt than angry. Alder was all she had right now, and his hot and cold behavior was exhausting.

Was he really upset with her, or was it merely a sign of his hurt? She knew for herself that it was easier to be angry than to admit to feelings that she was not allowed to feel. Perhaps he was the same.

O High One, soften his heart. And mine.

As they reached a small clearing where the mud was not so thick, she nudged her heels into her gelding's sides and pressed him into a trot until she came up beside Alder's mare. They were riding at a decent incline now, and she was sure the horses were growing tired. Perhaps she could convince him to make camp soon.

"Hey," she said, forcing a smile. "How far is the pass from here?"

"Not far. We'll make it before sunset."

She wanted to retort that they could hardly discern the

location of the sun through the rain and trees, but restrained herself. Drawing a slow breath, she tried again.

"The horses are tired."

"You're tired, you mean," he said, continuing to face forward.

She took another breath, suppressing the urge to shove him from his saddle.

He had removed his cloak and cap, and the rain was slick against his closely shaved head. He looked fierce, like he was about to ride into battle.

Not everything has to be a war. I'm on your side.

There was so much that she could not say.

"Yes," she said finally. "I am. So are you. Which is what I'm telling myself to explain why you have been either distant or outright rude to me all afternoon."

"I'm sorry," he said flatly.

"No you're not."

"Now you're being rude."

She balled her hands into fists, bending the leather reins against her palm. They had reached the thick trees again, but there was still just enough room to ride side by side.

"Alder," she started, trying to infuse a gentleness into her voice that she was very far from feeling. "You're all I have right now. I just want you to be my friend."

She could feel her voice quavering. She swallowed, blinking away the sudden tears that were stinging at her eyes.

For several seconds, he didn't speak. He turned to face her, his eyes hard.

"Maybe I don't want to be your friend, Kessara. Maybe I can't be."

She felt like she'd been slapped. Swallowing tears, she

kicked her horse into a trot, unconcerned with the increasingly steep grade, scattered stone, and pits of mud that littered the trail. Within moments she had pulled up ahead of him, her hands loose on the reins as she let the spirited animal pick his way up the slope.

"Be careful!" Alder shouted from somewhere behind her. She ignored him, focusing on staying balanced in the saddle. A few seconds later Alder had brought his horse up beside hers again, the two animals so close that Kessara could have reached over to touch Alder's mare's flank.

"Fine. If you won't treat me decently—"

Before she could finish her sentence, she heard Alder's horse give a loud snort. Kessara watched as the mare's foot slipped on the edge of a large rock, sending her tilting to the left. Before Alder could so much as unleash his usual flurry of soldier's curses, he was on the ground, the huge animal narrowly missing him as she landed on her side. Her own horse dashed up over the offending rock, throwing his head up and giving his own snort of protest.

Once they were on relatively flat ground, Kessara told her horse to woah, and to her relief, he listened without his usual fuss and stood still as she dismounted. By the time she reached Alder, the mare was already on her feet, standing forlornly beneath a large, dripping tree. She seemed to be bearing weight on all of her hooves.

Thank you, High One.

She grabbed for the mare's reins, eyeing her own gelding who was calmly nibbling at a patch of sodden wildflowers, and bent to examine Alder.

"Are you okay?" she asked, realizing that her heart was racing. He was laying rather still, half of his body covered with sopping mud. To her relief, he got up at once, sitting and scraping the muck from his cloak with a nearby stick.

"Fine," he said, his eyes flashing with annoyance. "More importantly, the letter is safe."

He drew a small envelope out from the depths of his cloak. Raela's dying words. Proof of Holga's true lineage. Proof that the House of Noctua had not fallen as all had assumed.

"Thank the High One," she said softly, getting to her feet.

"Now," Alder said, the slightest hint of a smile on his lips. "Can you please refrain from running away?"

"Can you refrain from acting like a savage?" she countered, though she could not keep her face entirely serious. He was so impossibly handsome, even covered with mud. His green eyes met hers, just for a moment, and the pain she saw there took her breath away.

Even if he would cooperate, could she bear to be his friend?

Perhaps he was right. Perhaps tenderness was too painful for them both.

She looked away, down at her feet, and the moment passed.

Neither of them spoke as they strode toward her horse. He offered her a leg up, and she balked at the thought of putting her dirty boot into his hands before realizing that he was already so covered in mud it would make no difference.

"I'm sorry," Alder said as she settled into the saddle. "I mean it."

She couldn't bring herself to meet his eyes, instead focusing on convincing her horse to leave the enticing flowers behind. "You're already forgiven."

As they reached the entrance to the narrow mountain pass that led to Auranth, the rain had finally ceased, but the heavy cover of clouds continued to shroud the moon. The trail was treacherous, and more than once they'd had to get off of their horses and lead them over particularly dangerous terrain.

She had wanted to stop and camp before now, but she could see why Alder had decided against it. Everywhere she looked, the ground was sopping wet, and their food and supplies were no better off. Their choice was either to spend a miserable night in the mud, or to spend a miserable night on the pass, at least making progress.

By the time they emerged into the foothills on the western side of the range, they could see a hint of sunlight washing over the sky behind them. The clouds were clearing, and the air felt fresh and new.

"I love the smell of rain," Kessara said as they rode through the silent, sparse forest. She craned her neck every few seconds, waiting for Auranth to appear in the distance. Her stomach growled so loudly that she was sure Alder would hear it.

"It is a nice morning," Alder conceded, giving his mare a pat on the neck and murmuring something to her about a fresh blanket and a nice bed of warm straw.

Before she could say anything else, she saw a glimmer of light poking out from between two trees. A few steps forward, and there was another. And another.

She glanced over at Alder as his face broke into a smile.

"Welcome to Auranth. Home of the finest smiths in the Four Kingdoms, and perhaps all Kaveryth."

A few minutes later the sun had risen over the mountains behind them, and she could see the city in its entirety, resting below them along the West Strait.

Like her own home city of Windshear, it was made of stone, but the architectural style was entirely different. While

Galeharborian design tended to be delicate and whimsical, the buildings in Auranth seemed built mainly for utility, likely by sourcing nearby brown and dull gray stone from the mountains.

It looks like a city for men.

She felt a shiver ripple down her spine, followed by a flash of anger. She had never been intimidated by men before. As Princess of Galeharbor, she was used to interacting with everyone from noblemen to sailors.

But that was before she was assaulted by a group of men in High Keep.

She pressed her eyes closed, as though she could stop the images of that night from replaying in her mind. Her knife plunging into the eye socket of one of her attackers. The hard stone floor pressing into her back. The blows to her head.

But I woke up, and Alder was there. And he was there because the High One was taking care of me.

"Everything okay, Princess?" Alder asked, giving her a funny look from over on his horse. They had both continued to ride forward, but she realized that she had allowed her gelding to wander off of the trail and toward yet more of his favorite wildflowers.

"Fine," she said quickly, pressing her heel into her horse's side and guiding him back closer to Alder's mare. "Just nervous to meet bargren."

"Don't be. He likes Wes and I just fine, and you're way more pleasant to be around than we are."

However minor the compliment may have been, she was so starved for his affection that she found herself blushing. Alder grinned and held her gaze, and she was sure he enjoyed her discomfort.

"Oh, nevermind," she said, flustered, caught between annoyance and longing. The truth was, she would have given anything to hear him call her beautiful. Or to feel his hand brush against her own. "Let's hurry. I'm starving."

The ground was too muddy and uneven to gallop on, but she wished that she could.

As long as she was running, she could just about forget the love that she was being forced to leave behind.

CELESYRIA

As night fell over Auranth, three hunters, two of them looking very much like younger versions of Bargren, came to the old armory bearing their prize.

Celesyria took the deer into the huge room, thanking the men profusely until they had gone, and now she was enjoying a late evening meal of the best venison she'd ever had.

"I still don't understand how you can eat like that," Wes commented from his place several feet away, his nose crinkling in disgust. "We could cook it, you know. Though it might take a little while."

"Aren't you humans always going on about the superiority of rare steak?" Celesyria asked, giving him a grin which she was sure was somewhat gruesome.

"Rare. Not raw," Wes protested, rolling his eyes.

Celesyria chuckled deep in her chest.

She hadn't eaten so well or felt so safe in a very long time. It was nice simply to rest, and being with her dearest friend made her feel even better.

"I spoke to Bargren about your manacles," Wes said, pausing for a moment to flash her a pained look.

"He can't take them off?"

Celesyria lifted an ankle, feeling the unwanted weight of the iron that had been weighing her down since her imprisonment back in the spring.

"No, he can," Wes assured her. "He's the head of the Armory Guild and a master smith. Of course he can."

"But..."

"You can't fit into the working forge where he has the proper equipment. He did assure me that he's working on a more mobile solution."

"Fair enough," she said, letting out a slow breath and trying not to let her frustration show. She'd been wearing the heavy bonds for so long already, and she longed to be free of them as soon as possible. But she couldn't blame Bargren for not being able to accomplish the impossible.

They sat in silence for a moment as Celesyria finished up the last of the deer meat, a nagging sting of guilt rather ruining the rest of her meal.

"Wes?" she said finally, glad to be able to speak aloud here without worry. Though mindspeaking was comfortable for her, for humans it was much more exhausting than normal speech, and she knew that her friend could use a break.

"Everything okay?" he asked.

She let out a sigh. "I'm fine. I'm just worried. And then I feel guilty for worrying about myself and my silly concerns when I have so many more important things to worry over."

"I don't think the High One wants us to worry at all."

"I suppose not," she said, feeling even guiltier than she had before, though she was sure Wes had meant the statement to be comforting. "But I do. I worry about all of the people that got hurt back in Whitespire, not least of all my mother."

"I really do think that she's fine. She had a lot of warning time, and besides, she was near the surface."

"What about my father?" she asked, surprised at the edge she heard in her own voice. "Is he fine too? Alone in Nox, while I sit here eating like a queen, complaining about a bit of metal on my legs?"

Wes only stared at her for a moment, and she immediately regretted the harshness of her words. None of this was his fault. None of it was hers, either. She could find some blame for Gramnok—after all, he'd been the one willing to detonate a bomb in order to free her from the council room, putting hundreds of innocent dragons and dwarves at risk—but he was dead. In the end, he died to save a portion of the Codex Veritatis.

In any case, she was sure he had his reasons for what he had been willing to do, reasons even she did not fully understand.

"I never said I didn't worry," Wes said. "I'm afraid, too."

"I need to find him," Celesyria said, surprised by her own feeling of conviction. He had probably been tortured by now. Perhaps even killed. She couldn't sit here any longer while he was in danger. "I can't just wait around for Alder and Kessara. We don't even know if..."

She drew her eyes away from Wes' gaze, looking down at the haphazard stones that lay across the ground.

I have to believe they're going to make it back here unharmed, even if I can't be here to greet them when they do. They have to be alright.

"Just a little longer," Wes said, ignoring the implication of her half-finished words. "Please. Just until the summer Feast of Offering has passed. It will be busy in Umrym, anyway, with the Septemvirate lackeys swarming the mountains with their extorted treasure."

She had to admit that he had a point, but she suspected there was more to his worries than mere logistical concerns.

"Are you afraid of what will happen when the day of the Feast arrives?"

Wes didn't answer for a moment, instead casting a glance up at the hole in the ceiling. The rain that had plagued them all day had ceased, leaving only occasional clouds to block the bright moonlight filtering into the space.

After a few moments, he continued. "It's as I said. I have faith in the High One. I know that I should not be afraid, that I should trust Him to take care of me rather than falling to worry. But I'm human. It's hard."

Celesyria took a couple of steps forward and pressed his arm gently with the tip of her snout.

"Anyway, to make a long answer short, yes, I am afraid. None of this is supposed to happen. The only time that the Feast is disrupted is when an Envoy dies and his replacement is too young or too injured to take his place even with the aid of others. For an eligible, healthy Envoy to cease the sacrifices is unthinkable, Celesyria. It's never been done. As far as I can tell, it's never been thought of."

"And you're not thrilled to be the first."

"To put it mildly. I don't even know what I'm up against. It's hard to know if even what little I've been told of the Dracodei is true. What if they retaliate? What if harm comes to those that the Septemvirate is using to deliver the treasures of the people?"

Celesyria did not have any good answers for him. Before Gramnok and Wes had freed her, she'd been imprisoned and brought to a strange council room filled with dragons, elves, and dwarves. One of the elves, Falloren, had let her in on a secret, assuming that she would soon be executed. Of course, her execution had not come to pass.

"Well, we know that in the early days, the elves and the dragons were allies," Celesyria reminded Wes, wishing that she'd been able to get more information out of Falloren before the explosion interrupted him. "That's enough for me to know that we can't trust the official mythology of the Dracodei, be they gods or mortals."

"The impoverished people of the Four Kingdoms have already had their treasures stolen from them by a bunch of corrupt bureaucrats," Wes said with a bitter smile. "Though I suppose I must have merited some punishment of my own."

Celesyria's guilt returned in full force.

"If you hadn't met me, your life would have been so much easier," she said, trying not to let her voice waver. "You'd still be living in a palace. You would have been admired as Envoy. Everything would have been different."

Wes' eyes met hers.

"If it were not for you, I would not know the High One. You have given me the greatest gift in all the world, and I won't have you apologizing for it."

Before she could decide whether to apologize anyway or to thank him, they heard a pounding at the door. They strode over the stone floor as bargren entered, followed by two people wearing sodden black cloaks.

"My loyal guards came to wake me, told me they'd captured a blonde woman and her companion just outside of Auranth. It seems your friends have indeed arrived," Bargren said, grinning as Alder and Kessara drew back their hoods. Celesyria felt tears springing to her eyes as Alder rushed over to stroke the scales on her flank and Kessara flung her arms around Wes.

43

Faith.

Whatever else I lose, whatever else I doubt, the High One has never failed us.

5

Chapter Five

ALDER

Alder and Wes sat near the embers of the makeshift fire pit in the middle of the old forge, watching through the hole in the ceiling as the moon signaled midnight. The dragon snored.

"Maybe we should have made her sleep outside, after all," Alder said, picking up a small piece of scorched kindling and chucking it across the room at her. She didn't even flinch as it ricocheted off of her tail. If anything, her snoring grew even louder.

Wes laughed, shaking his head at his friend. "She can't help it."

Alder grinned back at him. Wes had offered to take the first watch, but Alder had been unable to fall asleep and figured they may as well take time to catch up while the others rested. He glanced over at the corner of the room where Kessara was sleeping behind a curtain that Bargren had hung for her. It had been just the two of them for so long, it was strange to be back with his other friends.

They had spent the past couple of hours catching each other

up on the adventures they'd had, but finally the women had decided that the conversation would have to continue in the daylight hours.

He and Wes had set up bedrolls in the opposite corner to Kessara, bringing them closer to Celesyria, a decision he now regretted. Wes had pointed out a couple of small rooms that were sectioned off in the other corner, saying that they might serve as sleeping quarters if they could get them cleaned out. Alder wondered why Wes was so eager to stay, but when he had asked, Wes had told him that there was a lot that he wanted to discuss a little later, when everyone had gotten the chance to settle in.

"So," Wes said after a while, adjusting his feet so his boots rested closer to the smoldering fire. "Are you planning to apologize for locking me out of the palace back in Windshear?"

Alder had been anticipating that question, though so much had happened since it was still difficult for him to know whether or not he regretted it after all.

"No way," he said, giving Wes a playful punch on the arm. "By the sounds of it, I was doing you a favor, sending you off on a wild adventure."

He expected Wes to smile and possibly hit him right back, but he didn't. "I know why you did what you did. But..."

His words trailed off. Alder shifted his own body a few inches closer to the warmth, waiting.

"There was a lot that happened in Umrym. Celesyria and I both saw things that I doubt we'll be able to forget. And I guess a part of me wishes that you'd stood in my place. You would have handled it better than I did."

Wes looked at his feet, his cheeks red in the dim glow of the dying firelight. "I'm a coward, I know," he added.

No. You're blessed. You didn't have to join the army at fourteen. You didn't have to see so many terrible things that you began to numb yourself to evil.

"I understand, and I don't condemn you," he said instead. "But you can't run from these things. The world is growing darker with every passing day. If there are no men like us willing to stand and to fight, we have already lost."

They sat in silence for a moment.

Alder breathed deeply, enjoying the smell of smoke in his nostrils. He had good memories of his time as a soldier, too. Memories of laughing with his brothers near a roaring fire, swigging ale and telling stories. But even those memories were tainted, especially after what had happened to Kessara.

I stopped it. I protected her, and she's alright now. Nothing happened.

He rubbed at his eyes, a wave of tiredness washing over him with sudden intensity. He was thankful for the distraction.

"There's something else that I need to tell you," he said, his voice loud in the silence of the open space. "Before I fall asleep sitting here. You can tell Celesyria, but no one else, promise?"

"Who would I tell?" Wes asked, giving him a half-smile.

Alder figured that he was mostly forgiven.

I wish I didn't need to be so harsh. But it's for your own good.

"Bargren, I guess. Anyway, it has to do with the girl that you rescued with her brother, back in the spring."

Wes' jaw nearly fell open.

"Holga?"

"Yes."

"Is she alright?"

"I don't know," Alder said, shaking his head. "But I'm going to find out. As soon as I can get away."

47

"You're leaving?" Wes asked, his voice so loud that for a moment Alder thought even Celesyria would stir.

"Shh!" he snapped, reaching into the front of his tunic and pulling out a thin envelope. "It's better if you read it for yourself."

Wes took the letter, his brow furrowing as he read the first few lines. "Who is Raela?"

"She helped to raise me and my sisters. She's like a mother to me," he said, looking over at Celesyria as she shifted onto her other side, her scales making a tremendous noise as they scraped over the floor. "Just read it."

For a long while, they sat in silence, Wes poring over the letter and Alder using a stick to poke at the last few gleaming cinders.

At long last, Wes looked up, letting the letter rest on his lap.

"The House of Noctua lives?"

"Yes."

"Are you sure that you can trust this letter?"

"I'm certain," Alder said firmly, taking the paper from him and gently returning it to its envelope.

"Then we need to tell her, and then we need to help her," Wes said. "She has no one else back home, only her little brother Gohr. She's not going to be able to restore a noble house on her own."

"No. But we need to take time to plan our next move. There's a lot at stake here."

"Agreed."

"In any case," Alder said, his words interrupted by a yawn that seemed to make his entire body shudder. "I do not trust myself to come up with any brilliant plans until I get some sleep."

Wes hesitated.

"Do we even need to keep a watch here?" he asked, gesturing vaguely at the heavy stone walls.

Alder found himself grinning, a feeling of peace washing over him that he hadn't felt in a long time. "No, I suppose we don't. The men who took hold of Kessara and I when we arrived seemed to keep a pretty close eye on the city. It's just become a habit for me to expect death at any time."

Within a few minutes, he was laying on his bedroll, looking over at the stars and listening to the comforting rhythm of Celesyria's snoring.

WES

The next day passed in a flurry of activity.

It was Wes' eighteenth birthday as well as the Feast of Offering, and his friends were ready to celebrate together after so much time apart. With the help of Bargren and his sons, they managed to make the old armory a little more comfortable, and his wife Mella had even baked a proper birthday cake.

He had woken up with a terrible headache, which had been happening often as of late, but despite his general malaise he found himself full of energy. The sky was clear, the air was warm, and he spent most of the morning and afternoon working with Celesyria and Alder to tidy up the huge room. He even helped Kessara to prepare for the party she insisted on throwing for him, though he still wasn't particularly thrilled to be at the center of attention.

"You're the Envoy of the Four Kingdoms," Kessara said

after hearing him complain for the tenth time. "You're used to attention."

"I hated it then, and I still hate it now," he said, prodding the scar on his cheek with his fingertips as he often did when his past life was mentioned.

"Nevermind. Help me hold this chair steady," she demanded, gesturing to a rickety wooden stool that she'd placed beneath one of the trees that grew up through the stone. "Actually, you shouldn't even be helping me with this. It should be a surprise."

He said nothing, focusing on steadying the tall, wobbly stool as she climbed it. It was only when she had climbed safely back to the floor that he realized what she had done.

The tree was covered with colorful ribbons, dancing in the air as the breeze caught them. For a moment, he could almost see himself back home at his palace in Stronghollow, walking amid dozens of brightly-decorated trees.

"It's beautiful, Kessara," he said, giving her a quick hug. "Despite everything that happened the last time I was there, I miss home."

"We will return there eventually," she said, giving him a smile that didn't quite reach her eyes. "I'll be queen, and I promise that I won't throw you into prison."

He chuckled without humor as Alder crossed the room toward them, carrying a large tray of sauce-covered chicken drumsticks. As he and Kessara bickered over whether or not everyone would be ready for dinner in a half hour, Wes couldn't help but to notice the glances that kept passing between his two friends. Had he not known them both so well, he would see only the fire behind their eyes. But he could see that there was a tenderness, too, that they were failing to hide.

"*Celesyria?*" he called out in his mind, excusing himself from Kessara and Alder's quarrel and looking for his waterskin. His head was pounding again, and though water never seemed to help, he hadn't yet worked up the courage to ask Bargren if there was a healer who could find him a better remedy. War drums were beginning to sound across Kaveryth, and he felt foolish for concerning anyone else with something as trivial as a headache.

"*I'll be back in a minute. Mella has me moving rubble in the old courtyard,*" she said, her girlish voice filling his mind. He watched as his friends continued to argue, Alder wearing an amused grin as the princess scolded him.

"*Have you noticed Kessara and Alder lately?*" he asked.

"*What do you mean?*"

He paused as he took a few long sips of water. Kessara had insisted on dosing it, and everything else that any of them drank, with the potion the herbwoman had given them back in Galeharbor. He found the practice silly, but he supposed it could not hurt.

"*The blushing. The constant arguing. And the annoying puppy-dog stares whenever they're in range of each other.*"

"*Wes, honestly,*" Celesyria said, her voice filled with laughter. "*One would have to be blind and deaf not to notice.*"

He felt rather miffed at that, but did not comment. He couldn't help but to think that those of the female sex—including dragons—seemed to have some kind of magic power when it came to sensing such things.

Wes watched as Kessara brushed past Alder and headed to the door, where one of Bargren's sons was waiting. Alder stared after her, his eyes trained on the back of her blonde head as she flitted around the room, fixing a few loose ribbons on the trees.

Will Alder still be loyal to me when Kessara and I marry?

The thought troubled him. Ever since they had met, Alder had displayed a steadfast faith in the High One that Wes often envied, and his loyalty extended to his friendship with Wes as well. But even without much in the way of personal experience, Wes knew that there was nothing like a beautiful woman to turn wise men into fools.

"Kessara, this looks incredible," Celesyria said as she flew in through the hole in the ceiling, landing gently on an intact section of the stone floor. "How long until we start the party?"

Wes looked around at the number of plates that had been set out along the long table, relieved to find that the guests would likely consist of himself, his friends, Bargren's family, and a few others who already knew they were in Auranth.

He wasn't sure that he would have been able to handle the sort of party that Kessara would have thrown back in Galeharbor. He'd never been much of a fan of royal galas, and certainly not ones that held him as the guest of honor.

"Soon, I hope," Alder answered, rolling his eyes. Kessara was kneeling at the fire pit, absorbed in starting a fresh fire for the evening's festivities.

"I'd finish faster if you helped me," she retorted, brushing sweat from her forehead with the back of her sooty hand.

"You haven't let me do anything!"

"I would if you listened to my instructions," she chided him, picking up several pieces of kindling and placing them in a tent-shape over the tinder. "Only a soldier would mistake a soup ladle for a soup spoon. Can you imagine?"

She looked up at Celesyria, who, being a dragon and therefore having little use for cutlery, gave her a bewildered expres-

52

sion. Wes, having been raised in a palace, knew exactly why such a thing was ridiculous, but it was more amusing to keep silent.

"Only a princess would insist on three different spoons for dessert," Alder retorted, grabbing them from the nearest place setting and holding them up for effect.

"That's not a dessert spoon, you brute," Kessara said, standing up from her spot near the half-built fire and striding over to snatch the silverware from his hands. "It's a cream ladle!"

"Maybe we don't have much to worry about after all," Wes said to Celesyria, watching with some amusement as Kessara rubbed ash onto the end of her hair by mistake.

"You can't be serious. I was just about to say that it seems they fancy each other even more than I thought," Celesyria said, striding closer and lowering her head between Alder and Kessara.

Wes rolled his eyes, deciding then and there that he would defer to Celesyria when it came to matters of the heart. All he knew was that she had to marry him, not Alder, whatever they all felt about it. There was no point in worrying about something that none of them would dare to try and change.

"If you two would call a truce, I believe our guests have arrived," Celesyria said, cutting Alder and Kessara off before a second debate could begin. The spoons that the Princess gripped in her palm were almost as black as her fingers.

"In the end, I must concede that the Princess is right," he said, placing his hand on the small of her back and leading her in the direction of the door. "She's always right, just like she thinks she is."

Wes stifled a laugh. He was certain Kessara would have

denied it, but she had no chance to say another word. Bargren, Mella, their four sons, and several of the men from the Armory Guild were coming through the door, and within moments they were all chatting and laughing together, though Kessara slipped away for a few moments to wash up.

Time passed in good cheer as Wes enjoyed his birthday with friends old and new, and his cheeks began to ache from smiling so much.

The food was copious and expertly prepared, but still it did not take long for the party to move from the table to the open space near the fire. Night had fallen, and only the fire gave light.

Mella and Bargren began to sing, their boys dancing along to the old songs of Silverfell and Aridmoor, and soon enough Alder was roped in. They called Kessara over shortly after, who grabbed Wes by the hand and half-dragged him away from the biscuit he'd been snacking on while he watched.

"You're not going to make Celesyria dance?" he said to no one in particular, laughing as Kessara attempted to give him a twirl. Usually, he found dancing incredibly embarrassing, but he was too happy to be bothered. It felt good to move his body, there beneath the stone and stars.

"She already told me that if I tried it, she'd light me on fire," Alder said in the middle of performing a complicated step in perfect time with all four of Bargren's sons. Wes made a face, unsure if Alder being able to dance along with everything else was annoying or amusing

"Correct," Celesyria said aloud from the other side of the fire, and Wes noticed that she was tapping her foot along to the music.

Bargren grabbed an empty bread basket off of the table and

turned it over, using the flat of his palm to strike it like a drum.

For several minutes, everyone was dancing and singing together. It was a dwarf song, a common tune sung to children, but they all knew it, and the bouncing melody was perfect for the evening's mood.

Just as Bargren banged out the last few beats on his makeshift drum, Celesyria lowered her head toward the flame and exhaled, sending a perfectly timed wave of sparks up into the air. For a second they all stood where they were, mesmerized as the sparks danced like fireflies.

Kessara rested her head on Wes' shoulder, her cheeks bright red as she tried to catch her breath. Without realizing what he was doing, he found his hand was pressed gently against the back of her head, his fingers entangled in her blonde hair. His instinct was to pull away, especially when he noticed Alder standing nearby, an unmistakably crestfallen look on his face, but he forced himself to be still.

The fire had calmed, and the sparks had winked out, but no one seemed in a hurry to move. Everyone was standing there, wiping sweat from their brows and tears of laughter from their eyes, and Wes realized that standing there with her wasn't really so bad.

Can I do this, High One? If I'm given more time, will I learn to love her as my duty demands? Will I ruin my friendship with Alder when we marry?

Before he could think about it any more, Kessara stood up straight, fixing her hair back into place and shaking out a few wrinkles from her simple blue dress.

"There is still cake, if you will excuse me for a moment," she said, her voice breathless as she pulled away.

The others offered to help her, and Wes allowed Mella to

lead him back to his seat at the head of the long table. Celesyria wandered over to keep him company as the others disappeared into the shadows near the front door.

"I wouldn't mind a cake," she said in his mind, poking at the tablecloth with a single claw. *"A big one. My birthday is in the spring, so you'll have time to plan how to fit it into the cookstove."*

"If we stay here, I see no reason why not," Wes said, his eyes meeting hers.

"I can't stay. You know that. I agreed to wait until Kessara and Alder arrived, no longer."

"But you could come back."

"So you wish for me to go to Nox alone?"

"No, that's not what I meant."

Celesyria looked at him as Kessara set a huge piece of cake in front of his chair. It was frosted neatly with chocolate cream, and little pieces of crushed nuts covered the edges.

"Thank you," he said as she beamed at him.

"Mella made it," she replied from over her shoulder as she continued down the table, setting out somewhat smaller slices at the other places. "Baking is a skill I haven't mastered yet."

He took a few bites of his cake, refusing to meet Celesyria's eyes.

"Stop speaking in riddles, Wesley," the dragon said. *"I'm tired of waiting. If you have a plan, the time to tell us about it is now."*

Wes cringed at her use of his full name. He supposed it meant that she was serious, and quite right. He could no longer keep his ideas to himself. It was time.

6

Chapter Six

KESSARA

Kessara shot a final glance down the table before digging into her own cake, pleased to see that her friends and guests all seemed to be enjoying themselves. The mood had remained merry, and she was thankful for the distraction. Ever since they'd arrived, she'd thrown herself into serving her friends in whatever way she could, trying not to think of Alder and the confusing feelings that plagued her whenever he got close.

Unfortunately, Alder was never content to leave her completely alone. He was always there, either picking a fight or looking at her with a longing that made her knees go weak. Then again, she picked plenty of fights herself, hoping to bring him closer and then kicking herself for it. Neither one of them was innocent, but it made her feel better when he made her angry.

Just as she finished the last couple of bites of dessert, Wes was standing at the head of the table, tapping on his ale mug with one of Mella's dainty silver butter knives. She rolled her eyes, but decided not to scold him. She had had enough arguments over utensils for one day.

"Speech!" one of Bargren's boys shouted—she still struggled to remember their names—and soon everyone else was cheering and banging their mugs against the table. She joined in, though she was careful to slam the vessel down lightly on the aged wooden surface.

"I've never been a fan of speeches," Wes said, looking off somewhere in the distance over their heads. "But I do want to thank Bargren, Mella, and their lovely family for their kindness. Kessara, thank you for making tonight so special."

Everyone cheered again, chugging back ale. Kessara wiped the foam from her lip and expected Wes to sit back down, but instead he tapped the knife again. Everyone went silent, and she caught Alder's gaze, his eyes filled with puzzlement. She shrugged.

"You have all shown yourselves to be trustworthy," Wes began, grabbing his mug and taking a long swig of ale before continuing. "We are thankful for your hospitality in allowing us to stay here, and most of all for your discretion. King Ursa wishes for me to be arrested, and you're taking a risk by hiding me along with my friends. I cannot thank you enough."

Everyone at the table clapped, though Kessara was relieved when it died down quickly. She wanted desperately to know what Wes was going to say. Though her father had agreed to let them delay their marriage a little while longer, a part of her was nervous that he might make an impromptu proposal.

He wouldn't, not here. Don't be foolish.

"Look around this room," Wes continued, and Kessara noticed that he was finally looking in the general direction of the people he was talking to. She smiled at him, hoping that

Celesyria was encouraging him from within his mind as he held the room's attention.

"It is a fortress in all but name. First of all, it's big. There's enough space here to hold a lot of people. The walls are heavy and strong. There's a large outdoor space that is still secure. And it's not too close to the city."

Kessara glanced over at Bargren, who was stroking his thick beard between his fingers, looking intently at Wes.

"It's defensible on all sides," Alder chimed in.

"Exactly," Wes replied, clearing his throat loudly before pressing on. "You all know by now that ever since I met Celesyria and she told me of the High One, my friends and I have been running. Now, as we rest here with good food and good company, I've had a chance to think about the reality of our situation."

Kessara caught Alder's eye again, and he smiled at her, giving a shrug of his own. Somehow, even that gesture made her breath catch in her throat.

Well, so long as the reality of my undeniable feelings for Alder is not up for discussion, we should be alright.

"We are a small group, and we are vulnerable to the greater powers vying for control of Kaveryth. When we are separated, we're even weaker. We have been going along so far without much of a plan, just hoping that we will all make it through, but I do not think that our blessings will continue if we carry on like this. The Red Army is growing larger every day. The elves have ventured deep into our continent. Bandits, slavers, and the rest are becoming emboldened without the sight of Guardians in the sky,"

Wes was speaking louder now, his cheeks flushed as he leaned over the table, meeting the eyes of those around it in turn. Kessara hoped that her smile was encouraging, though she had to admit that his words made her feel rather anxious. She had known long before now that their situation was precarious, but to hear it laid out so clearly was somehow much worse.

"With the High One on our side, even our weakness will be enough," Celesyria reminded him as Wes paused for breath, her voice seeming to startle a couple of the guests. "He does not require great armies or the stratagems of men in order to be victorious."

"You're right," Wes agreed. "He has helped us until now. Even so, does that preclude us from gathering a force of our own? A force that fights under the banner of the High One, determined to free the Four Kingdoms from this tyranny of lies and return worship to Him?"

For a moment, the room was entirely silent aside from the crackling of the renewed fire. Celesyria's face showed no emotion. Bargren and Mella both sat with their hands folded, sharing glances between each other. The others present looked excited by the speech, though she hoped that Wes had not made a mistake in allowing them to hear it. Though she supposed that they already knew quite enough to cause them trouble, anyway.

Finally, Alder spoke. "I would be honored to be a part of such an army."

"As would I," one of Bargren's sons added.

"Now let's just wait a moment," Bargren said, planting his palms against the table. His deep voice thundered throughout the room. "I assume by all this talk of a fortress that you want to set up your headquarters right here on the edge of Auranth."

"Yes," Wes said firmly. "I can think of nowhere better.

The people here are already suffering under the burden of the sacrifices, and now they must face the possibility of conscription into King Ursa's Red Army. It seems very possible to me that many of them would be willing to enlist with us instead."

Bargren grunted, and Wes continued to make his case. Kessara had to admit that the plan was not a bad one, but it was certainly not without risk. It would require a ton of work, not only from their small group of friends but from everyone who sat at their table tonight, and she feared that they were asking too much. Still, she sat and listened, impressed by the strength of Wes' ideas.

You underestimate yourself, Wes. You would have made a very good king.

"The treasures of Auranth have been taken to the great spire on this very day. Within a matter of weeks, many of the people here will be questioning why their hard-won treasure did not bring the promised protection from the dragon Guardians. If we can offer them a real chance at protection without the need to impoverish themselves, I believe they will respond."

"I have another concern," Celesyria said. "If we create our own force, we could find ourselves fighting a two-front war—the elves and bandits on one side, and the Red Army on the other."

Kessara watched as others nodded in agreement, including Mella. She wasn't sure what she thought about it. For a moment, she wished very much that her mother was here. Queen Manta would come up with an angle no one had considered yet, and she'd know exactly what to say on both sides of the issue.

Wes spoke. "That is a reasonable concern, but what is

the alternative? King Ursa probably does not care one way or another about the High One on a personal level, but he will not allow mass blasphemy to disrupt his hold on the Four Kingdoms. The population suffering under Feast of Offering-induced poverty may lead to increased petty crime and unrest, but at least it ensures that they are at the mercy of his leadership. In any case, he still has the elves to worry about, and he can't risk antagonizing the remaining Guardians by allowing their gods to be cast aside."

"And that's just it," Alder chimed in, standing up in his own place near bargren. "He has the elves to worry about. And the bandits, and the slavers, and all the rest, just as we do. I know the way that the King thinks. He has no reason to want to fight us, at least, not while we are small. It is easier for him simply to tolerate us and stay out of our way. If anything, he'd be glad to let us help to pick off some of his more powerful enemies. By the time he realizes that we are having a real impact on the worship of the Dracodei, we could be in command of hundreds or even thousands of men. And at that point, we have bargaining power, especially with many of his own army's weapons being made here in Auranth. It's very possible that we could avoid conflict with the Red Army altogether."

The whole table was silent again, everyone lost in their own thoughts.

Kessara cleared her throat. "Bargren, we are asking a lot of you, and of your family," she said, glancing over at Mella. "If you do not want to work with us, no one is going to hold it against you."

She was sure that Alder was glaring at her, and possibly Wes as well, but she ignored them. Everyone at this table had to understand the real risks of what they were proposing. In any case, if they chose to help despite the possibility of imprisonment or violence, it would go a long way toward proving their loyalty.

To her surprise, it was Alder who spoke next. "Kessara is right. But I do believe that an alliance is the best option for the safety of your family and your people. You and your men are the best weaponmakers in all of Kaveryth. If you are able to bring a large number of them on board, there will be absolutely nothing that the local government can do to stop us from building a force here. I'm sure I don't need to tell you that if the forges stopped burning, the damage to the economy would be catastrophic."

"I can assure you that it's not the overstuffed bureaucrats that I'm afraid of. I'm much more worried about the Septemvirate and the Steward," Bargren said, taking hold of Mella's hand and giving it a squeeze. Kessara glanced up and down the table, noticing that every pair of eyes was trained on the burly smith, hanging on his every word. "They can cause a lot of problems for us, even if our administrators leave us alone."

"But there is something else you fear even more," Celesyria cut in, hanging her head over the table and catching bargren's gaze. Everyone went silent as they waited for the dragon to continue.

"You fear that harm will come to your sons if King Ursa conscripts them into service," Celesyria said, her voice firm, almost a challenge. Kessara caught Wes' eye, but even he looked surprised by her words. The other men at the table looked between one another and began to speak in hushed voices, the incomprehensible gossip filling the air like the buzz of summer flies.

And then Kessara understood exactly what game Celesyria was playing. A part of her was annoyed that she hadn't thought of it. Her mother certainly would have.

As if on cue, Bargren stood, raising his forefinger until it rested mere inches from Celesyria's snout.

"Forgive me, dear dragon, but you misunderstand my apprehensions. I dread the death of my sons. I dread the sorrow of my wife. But what I *fear* is the loss of my kingdom to a usurper."

Celesyria said nothing, though Kessara could see that she had drawn herself back a little.

"King Ursa wishes to exploit the cowardice of our men to serve his own ends. Most of them no longer have children to defend, and they have lost regard for their womenfolk as well," Bargren continued loudly, his cheeks flushed with anger.

Kessara was impressed by Celesyria's stoic expression in the face of his tirade. Most of the men present, on the other hand, looked about ready to start cheering for a brawl to break out.

"When men lose their families, the enemy knows that they have already won. A man who has nothing to fight for quickly becomes a slave to the strongest horse. So no, Celesyria, I am not afraid for my sons to die, and I am even less afraid of my own death, so long as we are dying in defense of the legitimate ruling House of this great kingdom. We will not fight under the Steward's red banner of tyranny masked as unity."

Everyone sat silently for a moment, as if to be sure that bargren would not say more, and then applause broke out. Kessara joined in herself, glancing over at Wes and then at Alder who were doing the same, though she figured Alder was cheering with some reservations.

In order for the legitimate ruling House in Silverfell to reign again, Wes and I have to marry. There is no other way, and I suspect Bargren knows it very well.

Kessara caught Celesyria's eye, and the dragon gave her a wink. Wes stood and took his ale mug in his hand again, tapping the side with a fork this time.

"So you agree to help us?" he asked Bargren, his smile lighting up his eyes.

"The blood of King Gadan Cervos runs in your veins," he replied. "I already promised before he died that I would aid his son without question. It would be an honor not only to hide you from those who wish you harm, but to fight at your side for the freedom of the Four Kingdoms!"

The table erupted into clapping and cheering again, and Kessara joined in, feeling more hopeful than she had in a long while about the future of their continent. It was a long road that lay before them, and it would not be easy, but with the aid of the High One she was confident that Wes would be victorious. Whether or not bargren and his people would embrace the High One if given time remained to be seen, but she had to hope that even an imperfect army would be pleasing to Him.

Wes was right. There were no better options. The time for running and hiding was over, it was time to stand and fight.

CELESYRIA

Celesyria watched as her friends cleared up the mess from the party. The other guests had tried to stay and help, but Kessara had successfully shooed them out into the night, and now the old armory was quiet.

The dragon would have helped herself, but she had never

had very much luck being around small, breakable dishes.

"So," Alder said after the table was mostly cleared, brushing a bit of chocolate from his fingers. "We have a base."

"We have a *fortress*," Wes replied, grinning from ear to ear. "Great work, Celesyria. You closed the deal."

Celesyria gave a sharp-toothed smile, but inside she felt a strange melancholy. She couldn't deny that they were taking the best course of action that was open to them, but she was afraid, too. They had all seen violence, but she did not relish the thought of how much more she might see before this was all over.

If this ever ends at all. If the High One is ever worshiped throughout Kaveryth again.

She stretched out her folded wings, giving a yawn that sent a plume of smoke toward the ceiling. She couldn't think like that. She had to have hope, even when it seemed that everything was always falling apart.

"I'm glad that we will have more allies," she said finally. "But I need to remind you all again that my father is still imprisoned in Nox, and my mother is still missing."

She glanced about for Kessara, who was carrying a large tray of plates toward the back courtyard. After a moment had passed, the Princess returned to the table, sinking heavily into the nearest chair.

"They can hang on a little bit longer," Wes said, his voice pleading. "Please. Just stay until we're set up a bit more, and until we know we can trust the loyalty of Bargren and his men."

Celesyria gave a humorless chortle. Setting up here in Auranth would not be easy. They had to find not only soldiers, but an entire support infrastructure to sustain them. Weapons, food, armor, clothing, the list went on. She hoped that Wes was prepared for the reality of the path that they were choosing to take.

"I don't think we will ever be certain. You're seeking to turn craftsmen into warriors, and on a volunteer basis at that," she said.

"Assuming that they are willing to join with us at all," Kessara added.

"They will," Alder said.

"But what if they don't?" Kessara asked, the hint of a smile tugging at the corner of her lips. Celesyria would have rolled her eyes if she could. Another bit of flirting disguised as disagreement.

"They'll join, I promise. Don't underestimate the call to glory and doom. Men are drawn to it like flies to light."

7

Chapter Seven

WES

Wes sat in the back courtyard of the fortress, watching as the sun descended beneath the stone walls. He would have liked to sit near the front entrance, where he could see the red and orange light glimmering off of the distant West Strait, but he didn't feel like running into strangers at the moment.

Almost everyone had left the old forge for the day, leaving only his friends and Bargren's immediate family behind. They were all busy with their various projects, and had left Wes alone to think for the first time in what felt like several days.

Three weeks had passed since the summer Feast, and so far things seemed quiet in Auranth, but he couldn't be sure about the world that lay outside. The uncertainty made him anxious. His people could be suffering, and he would have no way of knowing.

Usually, Bargren relied on traveling merchants for news, but ever since their arrival the caravans had grown scarce. Wes found this troubling, especially considering that Kessara and Alder had been able to find a party bound for Auranth within mere hours of looking for one. It seemed the trade disruptions were getting even worse.

He got up from where he sat, brushing bits of dry grass off of his trousers, and glanced up at one of the huge old chimney towers. At Kessara's urging, some of Bargren's men had added a platform, a window, and a ladder, converting it into a rudimentary watchtower. He thought of venturing up into the stench of old smoke and darkness, dismissing the idea as quickly as it came.

I am unlikely to see bandits prowling around these lonely mountains, but that is no assurance that the rest of Kaveryth is safe.

Not for the first time, he thought about the necessity of finding allies not only within Auranth, but throughout the Four Kingdoms, as well. They needed to know what was going on if they were going to be effective as a force. Still, he was thankful for those that had joined their cause. When he'd first proposed the idea, he'd had to sell it to the others with much more confidence than he himself felt, but it was nice to see that things seemed to be working out nonetheless.

It seemed nearly a third of Auranth was supporting their burgeoning army, and most of those who did not—including much of the city bureaucracy and various Lesser House nobles that resided in the area—largely ignored them. Some of the children even made a game of bringing his wanted posters to him in return for treats from the kitchen Mella and Kessara had set up.

It takes a brave man to stand up for what is right, but even a coward can stand beside him. He smiled to himself. Now that he had become the quasi-legitimate leader of an armed force, Wes had come to learn that Alder was fond of such military proverbs and had one at the ready for most occasions. Most of the time, they elicited groans or eyerolls, but every so often a nugget of wisdom could be found.

The goal of their army was to exalt the High One across Kaveryth, and they all hoped to find more passionate supporters who would fight and die alongside them to do just that. But Wes was beginning to realize that a broader strategy was needed, and fortunately, they had already begun to enact it without his intent.

Within a matter of weeks, they were already beginning to draw the ordinary citizens who saw that the tides of power were shifting. So long as the Red Army remained at a distance, most people were content to turn their loyalties elsewhere, even those who worshiped the Dracodei seemed willing to stand with the army that opposed them.

Celesyria and Kessara saw this as a mark of weakness on the part of the civilians, but Alder insisted that if it was, it was only the weakness into which all men are born. Wes' opinion rested somewhere in the middle, though he hoped that by prayer and example they would be able to convert the people from fair-weather friends into true followers of the High One.

As the sun dipped lower and dusk began to fall, he watched as Kessara and Alder strode into the courtyard, carrying several folded canvas tents between them. For once, they did not seem to be fighting, and actually managed to get their burdens safely to the ground.

Wes got to his feet and went over to help. He and Alder went back into the fortress to grab another couple of tents, leaving Kessara outside to mark out where they would be setting them up. After a few trips, Wes was sweating all over, and it was becoming difficult to see as the last of the sunlight faded.

Celesyria flew in through the hole in the ceiling and proceeded to light the torches that had been set up along the walls, bathing the enclosed courtyard in a warm, pleasant light.

A few days prior, Mella and bargren had moved into the fortress permanently, and Mella had promptly declared that the place looked like a bandit's camp. Kessara had agreed, and the two women had brought much needed order to the fledgling army base, though they were still preparing for it to be able to house their soldiers.

"Where have you been?" Wes asked the dragon as they dropped the last batch of tents onto the grass. He and Alder fell to the ground along with them, resting on the canvas packs and catching their breath as Kessara placed rocks as markers along the huge expanse.

"Hunting," she replied aloud. "The mountains are quiet, but there are deer hiding in the foothills. I ate two."

Alder stared at her, incredulous, as she picked up several of the tents in her front claw with ease and carried them over to where Kessara's markings began. "You couldn't have hunted later? You could have gotten the tents out in five minutes!"

Celesyria picked up a nearby twig with surprising dexterity and threw it at him. "You two are getting fat sitting around here all day. You should thank me."

Wes gave her a look of mock offense, grabbing a rock of his own and chucking it in her direction. It bounced off her scaly shoulder without her noticing. "I kind of miss it. My life was a lot easier back then, fatness and all."

"That's true," Celesyria said, showing her pointy teeth. Wes was glad that he knew her well enough to ascertain when she was in fact smiling. "But Alder wouldn't survive the loss of his abdominal muscles. He'd lose his mind."

"What would he do if he couldn't admire himself in Kessara's mirror when she isn't looking?" Wes teased, poking Alder in the ribs. Alder shoved him to the ground in return, smiling as he pulled him into a headlock.

"I heard that," Kessara called from somewhere toward the far wall.

Wes and Alder fought playfully on the ground, with Celesyria acting as referee. To his surprise, Wes found himself more or less able to hold his own for a few minutes before Alder pinned him face-first into the grass, forcing him to surrender.

Alder let him up with a final slap on the back, gasping for breath. "Okay, the dragon's right. I am getting fat. Usually I pin you before you can even get a punch in."

Kessara wandered over, sitting down near Celesyria against the pile of tent bags. "Thanks for the help, guys."

"Come on, Princess," Alder said, placing a hand to his chest in mock-innocence. "Your rows are perfect. Ours would have been a mess."

"It's true," Wes added.

Celesyria leaned over and butted his shoulder with her snout. "You two should let Kessara sleep in tomorrow while you set up the tents. It's only fair."

"Great plan," Kessara said, smiling.

For a moment they just sat there in the torchlight beneath the stars. Wes looked over at each of his friends in turn, feeling a rush of gratitude. They were all here, together, and they were safe.

The fortress was coming together. Mella had even begun turning one of the separate rooms inside into a bedroom for him. She had assured Wes that it would be nothing next to his palace bedchambers in Stronghollow, but at least it would be a place of his own. After what felt like a very long time traipsing all over Kaveryth, it felt good to be building a home, even if he knew that he would soon be leaving it again.

He thought of what it would be like to go to Nox and search for Celesyria's father, and the thought sent a shiver through him despite the warm summer night.

Finally, Alder got up and stretched out his arms over his head. "I'm turning in. Bargren has me helping to fit new recruits for armor tomorrow, and before that, apparently, we're building tents."

"I'll be up to help," Wes said as Alder gave him a final punch on the shoulder and headed inside. Celesyria stretched out her wings and turned around a couple of times before curling up against the stone wall. "It's too beautiful of a night to sleep without the stars," she said, giving an enormous yawn.

Wes got up and stretched, preparing to follow Alder inside, but Kessara placed a gentle hand on his forearm. "Can we talk?"

He looked at her, searching her face for any sign of what she might wish to say. He felt a twinge of nerves in the pit of his stomach, but her eyes revealed nothing.

"Of course."

He followed her as she made for the watchtower and began climbing the ladder, surprisingly agile in her skirts. He did not enjoy heights, but managed to get himself onto the platform above without his knees shaking too much. "Is everything okay?" he asked, walking over to stand beside her at the small window. The moon and stars gave enough light for them to see the mountains, the trees and stone veiled in a soft blue glow.

"I wish I could see the West Strait from here," Kessara said, her delicate lips curving up in a small smile as she continued to gaze into the distance. "It's not the same as looking out at the North Sea at home, but it would at least be something."

He wanted to assure her that soon they would be able to move around Auranth without fear, and that Bargren would be happy to find her a high place where she could see for miles. Even now, it was unlikely any trouble would meet them, but they were exercising an abundance of caution.

But something about the expression on her face made him stay quiet as she turned to face him. "Even so, it is lovely here. This old armory will soon be a fortress fit for a future king. Even one who cannot rule."

He wanted to say something, but his tongue seemed to stick behind his teeth. She reached out a hand and pressed it into his own, and he did not pull away. Her skin was soft, and some deep part of him enjoyed the smallness of her hand in his. He was so used to comparing his physical strength to Alder, and yet, standing here with the Princess, he could see that he was not as weak as he thought.

As she pressed herself against him, he breathed slowly, trying to settle his nerves. Her entire body felt soft, somehow, even though she had always been quite thin. She rested her head against his chest, and without him realizing what he was doing, his arms were wrapped around her, pulling her in close.

"It can all be ours, Wes," she said, her voice a soft whisper against his tunic. "A future. A world where our people are safe."

He had hoped that when this moment came, he would feel attraction, butterflies swirling in his belly, something that a man was supposed to feel for his future wife.

As they stood there in the moonlight, his chest rising and

falling against Kessara's cheek, he felt nothing.

No, not nothing. I feel a fiercer love than I ever expected to have for the Princess of Galeharbor. But it's the wrong kind of love. It's all wrong.

He pulled away from her with a quick intake of breath, suddenly desperate for air.

"Wes, are you alright?" she asked, her eyes wide with concern. He nodded mutely as the feeling passed and he began to catch his breath. "You look like you're going to be sick."

"No, no," he stammered, looking at his feet for a moment before forcing himself to meet her eyes. "I'm sorry. I'm fine."

"No, I'm sorry," Kessara said. Wes was sure he could see a flush of red rising to her cheeks as she gazed back toward the stars. "I should have..."

Neither of them spoke for a long moment. Wes wanted to kick himself. He was relieved to be free of her embrace, but he did not want her to feel that she had done something wrong. None of this was her fault. He took a couple of steps closer to her, wishing that he could know what she was feeling deep inside.

This couldn't be easy for her, either. She had lost the man she loved, and now she was expected to marry his younger brother for political reasons instead of being with the man she was quite obviously attracted to. He could hardly blame her for trying to foster a deeper connection between them, desperately searching for some assurance that she was doing the right thing.

I have to be honest with her. I can't hold anything back.

If they were going to be together, to raise a family, to set their place firmly in history, they were going to have to work together.

"I'm terrified," he said, his words sounding very loud in the silence of the tower. "I'm terrified to marry you."

The princess said nothing, but she gave him a small smile, and it was enough. He pressed on.

"It is not easy to marry out of duty. I know that. But I also know how blessed I am. You're a wonderful person. Kind, smart, genuine and beautiful on top of it all. I'd be lucky to have you," he continued, placing a hand on her shoulder. He hoped that she believed him, because he meant every single word.

"But we aren't in love," Kessara prompted.

"No, but that's not the problem. Love can grow. Celesyria's parents were married by arrangement, and they fell in love later. The problem isn't a lack of love, it's..." he paused for a moment, wishing that he was better with words. "There are competing loves. I love you like a friend. Like a sister."

"It is super weird trying to be all romantic with you," she chimed in, smiling. "You hugged me like I was going to explode if you got too close. And your hands are clammy."

Wes smiled back, a bit of the weight on his chest beginning to lift.

"Yes, but that's not what I meant. I want you to be happy, Kessara. Even though I was young then, I saw how happy Roven made you. And now, I see how happy Alder makes you."

He paused for a moment, but she made no attempt to deny it.

"I can't bear the thought of watching you be unhappy for the rest of your life. I know that you would hide it. You would put on a brave face and you would do your duty, because as long as I've known you, you've always put the good of others above your own desires. I don't know if I can handle that kind of life," he said, the words coming out in a torrent. "It's not a selfless concern, I admit that. I don't want you to be unhappy, but I also don't want to be the husband that makes you unhappy. I don't know if I'm strong enough."

Kessara said nothing for several seconds, her face unreadable.

I would never be able to figure out exactly what she feels. She's too smart. I would always be one step behind, trying to console a woman who could never be consoled, trying to wipe tears that she would be too brave to shed.

High One, please, do not make me do this.

Finally, she broke the silence, turning to face the mountains again.

"Before we left Windshear, I convinced my father to give us more time," she said.

His breath caught in his chest. Even the temporary relief felt like cool water against a wound.

"King Ursa is urging him to order our men to join the Red Army. He's under a lot of pressure, but he knows that if I become the Queen of Silverfell, Ursa's Stewardship will end. Many of the soldiers will follow me rather than joining the Red Army. And that's not even including the forces we're already amassing here. Our army could be the biggest in Kaveryth, in the end."

"So how did you convince him to wait?" Wes asked. His hope deflated as he considered her words. It was hard to deny the huge benefits of having Kessara as queen. King Manta would not be willing to defer victory for long.

"I spoke his language. I appealed to politics," she said, turning to him and offering a small smile. "Sure, if I become queen, we will have control over a larger army. But if the

77

people of Silverfell still believe in the Dracodei as firmly as they currently do, it's going to cause as many problems as it solves. The Septemvirate will continue to demand sacrifices, and I have no doubt that they will do all that they can to engender hatred for you. You will be a ceremonial king who is hated by his own people for ceasing the sacrifices. The persecution you will face if you marry me will only increase."

"Fair point," he said.

Perhaps waiting was not only what he desired, but the right choice for their people after all.

Could it really be so?

"Even if the Septemvirate doesn't stoop to direct treason against me—and I wouldn't put it past them, even now that Elder Dorold is dead—they will still hold most of the power in the Kingdom. For five years now, the people have grown used to their indirect rule. The shifting loyalties of peasants and mercenaries is one thing. But the loyalty of the lesser House nobles and the rest of the upper class will not be so easy to gain. Even the Steward knows this, which is why he continues to back the Septemvirate for the time being."

"So what do we do? Hope that at some future date, they will accept you as queen?"

"We do just what we have been doing. Ideally, we bring a significant number of the people to the High One so that they will not be blinded by the demands of the Dracodei and the Septemvirate."

"But how will we do that?" Wes asked. "The portion of the Codex Veritatis that Celesyria and I recovered from Whitespire is something, but I'm not sure it's enough to convince those who are set in their worship of the Dracodei. And I fear that the rest of it is lost forever, buried beneath the wreckage of the city."

"We have to find a way to make them see."

"I agree, but it's not so simple. These people have been lied to about everything for generations. Even we do not know the whole truth, which makes it difficult to offer it to others."

Wes thought of Celesyria's visit to the secret council beneath Whitespire. One of the elves had told her that his race had once been allied with the dragons. He could only guess at what other facets of history they were ignorant of.

"It certainly doesn't help that Celesyria's dwarf friend blew up the whole city just as she was about to get some answers," Kessara said, exhaling a long sigh.

"We have to keep praying to the High One for guidance. It's the best we can do. But I have a feeling that your father is not going to wait for us much longer once he learns that the Codex fragments in Whitespire have been destroyed."

"You're probably right," she said. "I'm sorry. I tried, but my father's stubbornness is legendary."

"Will the fact that you and Alder have discovered the existence of a lost queen sway him?"

Kessara gave him a weak smile. "If anything, I fear it will sway him in the wrong direction. Even if Holga is alive and well, and prepared to take up the crown, Boneshire is divided and unstable. He won't count on them as an allied kingdom, even if they inherited the best monarch in Kaveryth."

He had nothing to say to counter that point. King Manta may have been stubborn, but he also happened to be right.

They stood in silence for several seconds, watching the moon. Wes knew that he should head down to the main floor to sleep, but he felt no tiredness. Worries about the future swirled in his mind, and each time he tried to think of a prayer to push them back, he found himself distracted by new fears.

He looked over at Kessara's pretty face. As usual, it revealed little of what she was thinking, though if he had to guess, he figured that she was probably feeling the same way that he was.

A moment later, he saw her expression change. Her brows knit together, wrinkling her forehead.

"Do you see that?" she whispered.

He leaned out the window, squinting in the dim light, and then he saw it.

On a small trail that wound through the mountains was a cloaked rider on stagback. And he was coming straight toward the old forge.

8

Chapter Eight

ALDER

Alder lay in the dark, staring up at the stone ceiling. Every few moments, he could hear a faint hint of Kessara's lilting voice, followed by Wes' deeper one, but he couldn't make out any words. He had seen them climb the tower together, and though he knew he should try and sleep, he couldn't help but to try and listen.

His imagination wandered. He thought of them holding hands, embracing one another, perhaps even kissing. He found himself clenching his fists beneath his blanket.

She was never yours. She always belonged to him. Ever since Prince Roven died, there was never going to be any other way.

His own words felt hollow. The fact that none of this was Wes' fault did little to quell his rage. For so many years, he used his fists to solve his problems. In the Aridmoor army and even in the Protectorate, it was often the only tool that he had. It was not so easy for him to learn to surrender.

You also learned discipline in the army. You learned to put aside the desires of your flesh, the boredom of your mind, whatever it took to carry out your mission. You will do the same thing now.

The thoughts surprised him. They were his, but somehow they were more than his. He smiled a little, even though there was no one to see it. The High One was with him even now, and he would get through this.

No matter how badly it hurt.

He closed his eyes, praying silently and pushing aside thoughts of Kessara. None of it mattered. Only the High One mattered, only the High One could bring him peace...

"Alder!"

A voice shattered his thoughts, and he found himself awake sitting up on his cot and blinking away the sleep from his eyes. He wasn't sure how long he had dozed, but his mouth tasted foul. Swallowing the thick saliva in his throat, he got to his feet.

"Someone's coming. A single rider, on stagback. He's on a path that I doubt the Auranth guards patrol."

It was Wes, standing beside him, his face a mask of anxiety.

"Is Kessara alright?" he asked, getting to his feet and grabbing his belt and sword from the floor. He got his boots on within seconds, and strapped the weapon around his waist before Wes could answer him.

"She's fine. I told her to wait in the tower until we see who has come."

Alder nodded. "Good. How far away is he?"

They heard stern voices from outside the front door, on the side of the building that faced the rest of the city. The old forge had already been assigned guards before they arrived, to discourage the return of squatting and prostitution, and Bargren had been able to convince them to stay on as volunteers.

Alder made for the heavy wooden doors and Wes followed. As he lifted the large bar that held them shut, he heard Celesyria's heavy steps behind him.

"I'm going to stay back here in the shadows. Let me know if you need me," her voice sounded in his head, and he assumed she would tell Wes the same. He thanked her aloud, surprised that she was staying away from the action willingly. Perhaps the new freedom that she enjoyed here in Auranth was enough for her, or perhaps she merely realized that the sight of a dragon often complicated things.

He and Wes dragged the door open just as the guards ushered the cloaked figure forward.

"Who is he?" Wes asked the two men, closing the distance between him and the prisoner. Alder stayed a step back, his hand on his sword. The rider looked very small, but he knew that dwarves could be very skilled fighters despite their size.

"He would not answer, my lord," one of the men said, adjusting his grip on his prisoner's thin arm. "Asked to speak to Wes Cervos."

"Well, here I am," Wes said, crossing his arms. "Speak."

The prisoner threw back his hood. It was not a man, nor was it a dwarf. Staring back at them was a little girl.

KESSARA

"You can sleep here for tonight," Kessara told the girl, handing her a couple of blankets and gesturing to a bedroll on the floor. "We'll find you a proper cot tomorrow."

"I'm not sure I will be able to stay another night," she said, accepting the bundle from Kessara's hands. "But thank you. I promise, I will explain everything."

Kessara waited as the child got into bed before turning to

leave the little storage room. "If you need anything, I'll be sleeping one room over. Please do not hesitate to come and wake me."

The child nodded, and Kessara could see the exhaustion written on her drawn face, half-hidden beneath a curtain of flaxen hair. She seemed to be somewhere between nine and eleven, though she was so thin it was hard to be sure. Kessara hoped for her sake that she was a little older than she looked.

"Get some rest, Oria," she said, closing the battered door behind her and heading back into her own makeshift bedroom.

Wes had assured them all that she could be trusted, but Kessara was not so sure. As soon as the child had introduced herself, she recognized the name. She had been a servant in Wes' palace back in Stronghollow, and had helped Wes and Celesyria before they were both imprisoned by King Ursa and the Septemvirate. In the end, however, Oria had been threatened, and she had told the Septemvirate that Kessara was hiding out in the city.

But the child had told Wes that she came bearing news, and news of life outside of Auranth was something that they could not pass up. The isolation of the northern mountains had kept them safe from various spies and listeners, but until they could gather loyal eyes of their own, they were left at an extreme tactical disadvantage.

As she climbed onto her cot and tucked the simple blanket around herself, she thought of home. Her parents would still be worrying about her. Her people were likely facing bandit attacks or worse.

I couldn't stay. I would have been no use to anyone standing around the palace. And if I'd followed Wes to Whitespire, I might have been killed. At least Alder was able to protect me. No, none of it matters. My people are fine, they must be fine. My presence would have made no difference, whatever has happened since.

Arguments with herself swirled in her mind. She had followed Alder for purely selfish reasons, and that was the truth, no matter how she tried to justify it to herself. She pressed her eyes closed. She hoped that sleep would be enough to wash away the lingering haze of guilt.

CELESYRIA

As dawn broke, Celesyria was already awake, fidgeting in her corner of the forge. Though she understood why Wes had insisted that they all get some sleep, most of all Oria herself, she wished that they had just convened a meeting in the middle of the night. She feared that the child had come bearing dark tidings, and trying to go back to sleep had been impossible.

"Celesyria, can you bring some wood over from the court-yard?" Mella asked as her skirts swished past, gone before the dragon could reply.

Glad to be able to do something other than staring at the ceiling, she made quick work of delivering and setting up the firewood before poking around the fortress in search of her friends. She had not seen Wes or Alder leave their rooms yet, but Kessara was in the kitchen and had gotten to work on preparing a massive pot of pancake batter. Mella returned from a brief excursion toward the city bearing several trays of bacon.

Celesyria's stomach rumbled loudly, and one of Bargren's sons called over from out in the courtyard that he had procured three roast pigs for her. She found herself standing about uselessly once again as the others finished getting the table prepared, thinking to herself that the mood in the room was quite strange.

As if reading her mind, Alder emerged into the main room and proclaimed that it looked like they were preparing for a noble's dinner rather than what was almost certain to be a gloomy meeting with a peasant.

"A noble's brunch, you mean, dear," Mella said, nearly shoving him down into a seat near one end of the table. "If we are to hear unpleasant things, we should hear them with full bellies."

"Oria looked sickly," Kessara added, taking a seat beside him. "Whether she turns out to be a friend or an enemy, I cannot bear to see a child go hungry."

Alder rolled his eyes. "You have not seen the sorts of things children will do in times of war."

"She's just a peasant!"

"Wes, hurry up," Celesyria said in her mind. *"Please, if you value my sanity whatsoever."*

Five minutes and nearly as many arguments later, Wes joined them at the table, leading Oria gently to her seat at the end. Bargren and the rest of his sons had arrived, each giving Mella a kiss on the cheek as they took the remaining seats.

"This looks wonderful," Oria said, her voice small as she gazed at the pancakes, bacon, and fruit that the women had prepared. "I do not deserve such hospitality, but I appreciate your kindness."

Wes reached out for her hand on one side and Bargren's on the other. Kessara looked surprised for a moment before she took Oria and Alder's hands in hers. Celesyria lowered her head and closed her eyes as her friend gave a quick blessing over the food.

Oria did not seem fazed by the action, though Celesyria wondered if she was a believer herself. Not so long ago, most of the people of Kaveryth didn't even know the High One's name. Things had changed so much that she struggled to keep up.

She found herself pleasantly distracted as she turned to her own roast pigs, eating them whole several feet away so as not to disgust their guest. The others dug into their food with equal enthusiasm, and before long, the sun was drawing up over the hole in the roof and plates were being pushed aside.

"So," Alder said finally, placing his elbows on the table and leaning toward Oria. "How did you know that Wes was here? You knew not only that he was here in Auranth, but in an old abandoned forge, as well. Should I be seeking out a spy in our midst?"

Celesyria glanced over at Kessara, who was giving Alder a murderous glance but said nothing.

"It's a meeting, not an interrogation," Wes said before Oria could answer.

Alder said nothing, but leaned back in his chair, crossing his arms across his thick chest.

"*Let Wes handle this,*" Celesyria told him in her mind, lowering so that she could prod the back of his head with her snout. "*He knows the child already, and if you frighten her, she might hold something back.*"

The fact that Alder was not yet capable of projecting words with his mind was just as well. She hoped he would listen.

"It's alright," Oria said, an amused smile stretching her gaunt cheeks. "I have lived my entire life as a servant. I've heard much worse, from employers much less pleasant to look at."

Celesyria grinned, fearing that she might knock the remaining dishes from the table if she laughed. Alder looked pleased at the compliment, and Wes rolled his eyes. Even Kessara was smiling.

"In any case, I found you here easily, just as many of your enemies could," Oria said, leaning over the table, her expression suddenly sober. "This new situation in Auranth has not passed without notice. King Ursa certainly knows that the nobles and bureaucrats of this city are neglecting to capture a wanted fugitive. Of course, his Red Army and his remaining Protectorate men have other priorities at the moment."

It was all Celesyria could do not to ask the child how she possibly knew this information, but figured that she would tell the full tale if given time. She glanced around at her friends, who seemed just as taken aback as she was at the sudden transformation of the emaciated little servant. She looked as though she had aged ten years in an instant, her chin held high, her words careful and articulate.

Oria continued. "Elves have been pouring into Umrym, building up settlements that they had already begun and starting new ones. The Red Army is trying to hold control of the region, but many of the dwarves have sided with the elves."

"And the dragons are allowing this?" Bargren asked, sounding incredulous. "I thought that the dragons were compelled to fight the elves. That's the entire promise that the sacrifices of the Envoy rests upon!"

"Only the Guardians are bound by oath to fight back in defense of Kaveryth," Oria said, gesturing to Celesyria.

"She's correct," the dragon said. "In the past, civilian dragons would often fight alongside the Guardians, but no oath demanded that they do so."

"In any case, the oath is only binding when violence has been committed," Oria added. "And the settlements in Umrym have remained peaceful as of now. And if you recall, when a Witness and the Envoy's deermaster was killed during the spring Feast, it was dwarves who did the dirty work."

Celesyria couldn't help but to feel ashamed as Bargren and Mella looked at one another, astonished at all that they had not known. At minimum, the majority of dragons and dwarves in Umrym were turning a blind eye to great evil. It was hard for her to believe that there were many who truly did not know. Then again, it would be a mistake to underestimate the power of the elves' manipulation, especially considering what she knew of their clandestine council.

"In any case," Oria continued, "the elves have no doubt promised the dragons and dwarves of Umrym that they will be better off with the settlements than without them. With the Envoy ceasing the sacrifices, the treasures that they are being brought will lessen with each passing Feast. As I'm sure you all know, their numbers have dwindled in recent years, especially the dragons, and they now must face the possibility of bandit attacks like the rest of us."

"In other words, ancestral enemies have entered into a pathetic alliance based on greed," Alder spat.

Celesyria felt a pang in her heart. She hated what the dragons were becoming, and she found it difficult to argue with Alder's analysis, as much as it made her feel sick with shame. For too long, her race had grown accustomed to wealth and ease, and now their evil ways were catching up to them and putting the whole continent at risk in the process.

"Have there been any messages from the Dracodei?" Bargren asked. "Not that I'm sure I believe anyway, but it's good to know," he added quickly.

Oria shook her head. "Not a word. Not since Whitespire fell. It seems the citizens of Umrym are acting without any higher guidance."

Celesyria caught the young girl's eye for a moment, but Oria quickly looked away.

Could the black obelisk have something to do with it? Or the council?

"Anyway," Oria continued, clearing her throat. "The current talk is that Galeharbor's navy will be deployed to the West Strait, to stem the tides of elven boats coming into Kaveryth via the Black Beach. The King wishes to order his men to join the Red Army."

"No," Kessara said sharply. "My father has not agreed. Not yet."

"Apologies, my Princess. In any case, none of this is why I have come," Oria said, lifting her chin and looking out over everyone sitting at the table. Celesyria shifted her weight and glanced over at Wes, giving him a draconic imitation of an eyebrow raise. He shrugged.

"I've come to arrange a meeting between the Envoy and the new head of the Septemvirate."

Celesyria could hear Alder chuckling quietly to himself.

What makes her think Wes is going to trust them ever again after they threw him into prison like a common criminal?

"Who is their new leader?" Wes snapped.

Oria's steely expression faltered.

"Elder Bram."

9

Chapter Nine

WES

Wes stared at the servant girl, trying to calm himself before he raised his voice at her again. His head had been pounding since he woke up, but it was growing worse by the minute. He could feel a pressure behind his eyes, as though something deep within his skull was trying to force its way out.

"Elder Bram is head of the Septemvirate," he said, his voice just above a whisper. Everyone at the table leaned a little bit closer to him, waiting for what he would say, but he did not know himself.

Leave it to that traitor Dorold to ensure that the most wicked man possible would succeed him.

"Please," Oria said, her eyes pleading. "It's not as simple as you think."

"Elder Bram threw Wes in jail. He had his men drag me into Stronghollow palace like a prostitute caught on the streets. He was probably behind King Ursa taking over as Steward of Silverfell," Kessara said, her voice rising in volume. "I'd venture a guess that it's probably even worse than we think."

Wes watched as Alder reached a hand under the table. He had little doubt that he was reaching out for Kessara. She was right.

Elder Bram had hated him since he was a child, and after what had happened after the spring Feast, he hoped never to have to look at his pompous face again. Still, Oria had come a long way at great personal risk. He had to understand why, even if he had no plans to comply with her request.

"I see no harm in listening to what she has to say," Wes ventured.

"I agree," Celesyria said aloud. The others at the table nodded, including Bargren's four sons, who were looking toward Oria's end of the table with apparent interest. Wes couldn't blame them. Life had probably been much more mundane before he'd brought such chaos to their lives.

Oria nodded. "Much has changed since you left Stronghollow. A day before I left for Auranth, assassins entered the city during the night. We have good reasons to suspect that they were elves."

He heard Celesyria suck in a breath.

"Elders Gunnan, Qofi, and Derden were stabbed to death in their rooms," Oria said, tears filling her eyes. "We also found Elder Rahma dead in bed, but he had no stab wounds. He was very old, so we can't be sure if it was a coincidence. Either way, it is a horrifying act. I am sorry to have to recount it, and I am glad I was not one of the servants who found their bodies."

"This is unthinkable," Wes said. "However corrupt those men were, to kill them in cold blood..."

For a couple of moments, no one said anything. The cheerful sun pouring in through the damaged ceiling and the few small windows did not suit the somber mood that had fallen over the table.

High One, have mercy on us all.

"What of the final Elder, aside from Bram?" Alder asked finally.

"Elder Jate has been spared for the moment," Oria said. "He is in Vaevar, though I do not know what he is doing. We sent messengers there to warn him, so if he's smart, he'll go into hiding for the time being."

"Where is Elder Bram hiding?" Wes asked.

"Stronghollow palace. Not a very safe place to stubbornly remain, it turns out. Something like this has never happened before. The people are terrified, and the streets are filled with mobs of people screaming for the Envoy to be captured and forced to resume the sacrifices."

"Did any of the Guardians show up?" Celesyria asked. Wes felt a pang of hurt for his friend's sake. Despite everything that had happened, she still believed in the goodness of her race, and he knew that she was right in her optimism. There were always good people who stood against the darkness, even if they happened to be dragons.

"One remains there, keeping watch over the city, but he did not make it in time to catch any of the assassins."

"By the Dracodei..." Mella said, her voice trailing off as she put her head in her hands.

"In any case, Elder Bram had already been working under Elder Dorold to take over eventually, and now there is no one else to be leader anyway, with Elder Jate gone."

"How do we know that he didn't have the other Elders killed himself?" Kessara asked.

"I considered the same possibility," Wes said, crossing his arms over his chest.

The child did not hesitate in answering.

"You cannot know. You can only trust me. He did not have anything to do with this. I swear on it with my life."

"Oria, do you not recall that Elder Bram forced you to reveal that Kessara was in Stronghollow? He has always treated you like scum on his boot. Why were you willing to deliver this message for him? Why are you defending him?" Wes said, finding that a greater rage was filling his voice with each syllable he spoke.

His head continued to pound, and he felt as though it required a great effort just to focus his thoughts beyond the pain. He did not want to reveal his weakness, but he decided that he had to truly consider going to Mella for medicinal help. He could not lead effectively if he could not even think straight.

"Another very good question," Alder chimed in.

"Another question that is not mine to answer," Oria said calmly, lifting her chin again and sweeping her blonde hair behind her ears. "There is so much you do not understand. Please, if you do not trust Elder Bram, trust me."

"The last time Wes trusted you, you caved under pressure and Kessara nearly ended up in jail as well. If she hadn't been free to break him out, we might not be having this conversation right now," Alder said.

"No one would have ever actually imprisoned the Princess," Oria said. "It was all a ruse."

"But why?" Alder pressed.

"For reasons that you will find out just as soon as Wes meets with Elder Bram."

Kessara cleared her throat, pulling her hand out from under the table and resting it in front of her empty breakfast plate. "I find it hard to believe that she would have been willing to make this trip if she had been forced. She came on her own. She could have fled anywhere between Stronghollow and Auranth, and no one would be able to find her. By the sound of the chaos in Stronghollow, Elder Bram would have few men to spare to track her down, anyway."

Wes sat back in his chair, lost in thought. Kessara had a point.

"I don't think I need to tell you how dangerous it was for me to ride here," Oria agreed. "I narrowly escaped robbery near Briarcroft, and enslavement near the west side of the mountains. Every day, Kaveryth grows more dangerous. I came here because I was the only person that Elder Bram could send."

"For reasons that you can't tell us, I'm sure," Alder said.

She nodded.

"For what little it may be worth, I believe her," Celesyria said in his mind.

He struggled to imagine a situation that could justify any of this madness, but he had to agree that Oria seemed sincere. She had always been clever for her age, but now he could see that she must have been hiding a much deeper intellect as long as he'd known her. She was not an ordinary servant, that much was clear.

Still, he did not trust Elder Bram.

With the chaos in Stronghollow, the chances were high that he'd be captured by Red Army soldiers before he ever made it to the meeting. If he was lucky. More likely, he'd be torn to pieces by a screaming crowd.

"Even if I agreed to meet with him—and I do not—I can't leave Auranth now. We've only just begun to build our own army here. If I leave now, who is to say that King Ursa won't send his army in to uproot the rest of us? We're too vulnerable. We need more time."

"I stand by what I said before," Alder said. "King Ursa's men are stretched thin as it is. With so many civilians supporting us, he'd be a fool to try anything. It's in his interest to pretend we don't exist, at least for now."

"I can't take that chance," Wes said, getting to his feet. "Finally we have the possibility of being able to come out of the shadows. I'm not going to risk jeopardizing that for some meeting with a man who hates me."

"Wes, I am begging you," Oria said, her eyes filling with tears. "Elder Bram is in grave danger. If you wait, it could end up being too late."

"I'm sorry. I do not trust him. If he needs to speak to me, tell him to come here himself. Or he can use his usual methods and have me dragged back to Stronghollow in chains."

There was a long pause. Wes caught Oria's gaze and stared, refusing to blink.

"As you wish, my lord," Oria said, getting to her feet and drawing her hood over her hair. "I suppose I can say nothing else to change your mind. I will pass on the message."

Without another word, or even returning to her room, she strode out of the fortress, her back as stiff and straight as the tall stone walls.

An awkward quiet filled the room, and Bargren's family excused themselves, grabbing the dirty dishes from the table as they headed for the unfinished kitchen.

"That may have been a hasty decision," Alder said once they had gone.

"Then it's a good thing you're not the one in charge of making it," Wes snapped.

"Please don't fight," Celesyria said, gazing wistfully at the door that had closed behind their guest.

"I see both sides," Kessara said, fidgeting with the end of her braid. "Elder Bram is a cruel snake of a man. I've interacted with him enough to understand Wes' distrust."

Wes nodded. "He has finally become head of the Septemvirate, just in time for Silverfell to devolve into complete chaos. Capturing me would be the perfect way for him to regain at least fragile control."

"But I can imagine what Alder is thinking, too," Kessara answered.

Alder grinned. "Right now? I'm thinking that you have pancake syrup in your hair."

"I'm serious," Kessara scolded, swatting him on the shoulder before examining the end of her braid more closely. "If Elder Bram really does have something urgent to speak to Wes about, can he afford not to hear it? What if he is killed by another assassin, taking vital information with him to his grave?"

Wes rubbed at his temples, trying to get the thoughts straight. If there was any chance that the new head of the Septemvirate really was on their side, he should get the chance to explain himself. But even if there was an explanation, could he really forgive someone who had treated him so terribly?

"In any case, it's too late now," Alder said. "Perhaps Elder Bram will seek him here after all, or maybe Wes will change his mind by the time he passes near Stronghollow again. In the meantime, we have other things to worry about."

Celesyria lifted her head, her yellow eyes roving between her friends. "My parents."

"I think it's time you returned to Umrym to seek your

mother," Alder said. Wes nodded in agreement. "Hopefully nothing exciting happens while we're gone."

"We?" Kessara asked, making a face. "Why do you get to go?"

"You're certainly not going," he said, rolling his eyes. "And I have no doubt the wanted posters have reached their cities. Wes would be imprisoned, if he's lucky enough to avoid being slaughtered by elves first. No. It's simple. I'm going with Celesyria, today if possible, and you two can keep things together here."

Wes nodded, his head aching so much that he had no energy to argue.

ALDER

Alder found Kessara near the outer wall of the courtyard.

Alone, of course, out in the open.

He looked around, hoping that no nefarious characters were lurking here outside of the safety of the old forge, but saw nothing.

She was laying in the grass, her blonde hair freed from its braids and spread out like a halo around her head. Her eyes were closed, and there was a hint of a smile on her lips. He was certain that she knew that he was standing there, so he said nothing, only waited.

He hefted his pack off of his shoulder and laid it against the trunk of a tree. It had taken him only a few minutes to gather up his things and to attach the leather saddle to Celesyria's back. The sun was high overhead, and he felt its warmth resting against the back of his neck as he drew closer to the

Princess. It was a perfect day to fly.

"I don't want you to leave," Kessara said, not opening her eyes. She was completely still, aside from the gentle rising and falling of her chest beneath the blue fabric of her dress. Alder sat down beside her, feeling the grass bending beneath his weight as he settled into the shade of the wall.

"And I don't want to leave you," he replied, reaching out a hand and stopping just short of stroking her cheek. She was so beautiful that it almost pained him.

"So stay."

"You know that I can't."

Silence. Alder cleared his throat, gathering up his courage before he continued.

I cannot leave unless I know the truth. I can't do it.

"I heard you and Wes talking last night. Up in the tower."

Kessara did not reply, her face revealing nothing.

"I know that you need to marry him," he started again, unsure of how to find the right words. He was leaning toward her now, dangerously close, unaware of any threats that may be waiting to leap out at them from the woods. He was too intoxicated by her to think. "You must. There's no other way."

"But you want to know if I love him. As though that will make a difference. As though it will hurt less if I am marrying him purely out of duty."

Her eyes were still closed, her expression still unreadable. A long pause stretched out between them. Suddenly he felt pathetic, a lovestruck fool with a longing to be wounded.

She's his. Why am I torturing myself?

Before he could think of a reply, her eyes fluttered open. She did not smile as she reached for him, pulling him down beside her in the grass. He pressed his fingers into her hair, drawing her closer, inhaling the smell of summer grass and rich perfume. She had one hand around the back of his neck, her fingertips brushing gently against his warm skin as she leaned in close.

Discipline.

I can't.

We can't do this.

As his lips met hers, everything else was oblivion. He felt the softness of her mouth against his, the warmth of her body as she pressed into him. The warning bells were sounding in his mind, but he found them easy to ignore as they kissed. It felt like seconds and hours all at once.

Kessara reached for the top of his tunic, her fingers fumbling with the first button.

She deserves better than this.

Somewhere deep inside himself came a voice he had not heard in a long while, a voice usually relegated to his dreams. He caught her hand in his own and stopped her from opening his shirt further, pulling back from her lips. Her blue eyes were filled with hurt.

"Kessara, please," he whispered, reaching out to touch her shoulder.

"Don't touch me," she said, her voice dangerously quiet. "This is your fault. You should have left me alone. I didn't want our first kiss to be like this, to be a promise that we could not keep."

Alder felt a flash of anger. "You kissed me."

"You asked me if I loved him. Even though you already knew the answer, you just had to be sure," she said. She was smiling now, but her eyes were cold. "You don't care that I am being forced to marry a man that I have no romantic feelings for.

You only care to know because it makes *you* feel better."

"That's not true," he said, his words sounding hollow to his own ears.

Kessara's eyes filled with tears. He wanted more than anything to comfort her, to hold her, to tell her that he was the world's biggest fool and he was sorry. But he knew that it would only make things worse, just as the kiss had done

"You need to go," Kessara said, getting to her feet and brushing bits of stray grass from her hair. "Celesyria's poor mother has waited long enough."

Alder watched as she headed back into the courtyard, her face revealing nothing of what they had done. But he knew that somewhere deep within, her heart was just as shattered as his own.

She was right. He was selfish. And it was his fault.

High One, forgive me.

10

Chapter Ten

CELESYRIA

Celesyria looked up at the stars as she flew, lost in the silence of a perfect, clear night.

The past few days had been far less pleasant, especially as they passed over Boneshire. Windstorms had sent the desert sand high into the sky, destroying visibility. When they had finally found a relatively safe place to camp, Alder had spent a curse-word-filled hour helping her get bits of sand out of the creases of her wings.

Having gotten used to the bountiful food available in Auranth, she had felt rather cranky when she had to hunt foxes and even birds to fill her belly. Alder had fared even worse, relying on a large snake for his dinner the night before.

Despite their difficulties, on the whole they had been fortunate. They had managed to avoid any interactions with bandits or wayward elves, and for that she was thankful.

Now, she was hopeful that the final leg of their journey would prove easier than the rest of it.

They had found deer at the base of the mountain near

Claywind that afternoon, so their bellies were full, and the searing heat had finally begun to let up, even during the day.

By night, the inky blue sky was unspoiled by clouds, and thanks to the chill in the air Celesyria found it easy to see the constellations that guided her home.

She felt a pang in her chest.

Home.

I'm not sure I know where my home is any more, but I know it is not here in Umrym.

The Severed Summits were beneath them now, and they seemed to go on forever.

Celesyria could imagine Wes as a young child, making his way through the mountains, the treasures of the people in tow.

He would never have gotten lost. Every Envoy for hundreds of years would have taken a similar path, winding between the stones and shadows, the stamping of boots and deer hooves leaving a great scar across the world.

"Are you alright up there, Alder?" she asked after a while. He'd been uncharacteristically quiet, and though he had assured her that he was fine, she couldn't help but to worry.

"Fine," he said out loud. "I'm still awake."

She gave a small smile that he could not see. He could not yet mindspeak on his own, but she was glad that he was finally able to hear when she spoke to him. It was progress.

"I'm surprised that Kessara was willing to stay behind," she ventured after another long silence. She liked solitude well enough, but she couldn't relax when she could sense that her friend was in distress.

Alder said nothing.

"I hope that she and Bargren and the rest can make some progress with the new army. There is so much that needs to be

done, and time is racing us already."

"The High One will take care of everything. We don't need to worry," Alder said. She could still hear the sadness in his voice, but at least he was saying more than one word. That was something.

"I hope Wes will go to see Elder Bram eventually," she said, hoping that a subject other than Kessara would produce a more fruitful conversation. *"I feel like we're always stumbling around in the dark. There are more answers out there, and we need to seek them, even if there is a risk."*

"If only Wes was as bullheaded as you are. We could be restoring worship to the High One in a month," Alder said, giving her a firm pat on her shoulder scales.

"I am not bullheaded!" she said, raising her wings quickly so that they dropped several feet without warning.

She heard Alder laughing as she righted herself at the lower altitude. Wes would have probably fallen off if she tried a stunt like that, but she knew that the Aridmoorian enjoyed the thrill.

"No, you're just brave," Alder said. "I wish I had your courage."

"You do. Perhaps more."

"Courage and recklessness are not the same."

"No," she agreed, making a more gentle turn to the left. *"I suppose they're not."*

She could not see the glow of sunrise yet, but it would be upon them before long. They had to hurry.

"Do you see that? Beyond that plateau?" Alder asked, leaning forward in the saddle. She turned a bit more and flapped her wings, trying to maintain speed as she flew closer to the flat stone expanse. Sure enough, there were fires on the far side, spread out in a long line..

"A new settlement," she said, flying through a narrow mountain pass at their right. Her bright orange color was not ideal for avoiding detection against the dark sky. *"There will be more."*

As they made their way closer to the great spire and the ruined city that lay before it, she was proven right. It seemed that every bend hid a new group of simple buildings and signal fires. A dozen more had sprung up since the last time she had been here, perhaps more.

"We need to recruit more dragons," Alder said as they circled the top edge of the valley that housed what had once been the underground city of Whitespire. "It's too dangerous to travel by land."

He was right. She couldn't carry him, Wes, and Kessara all at once.

But finding another dragon to help them, let alone two, was going to take a miracle.

KESSARA

"Are you ready, Princess?" Mella whispered in her ear, placing a comforting hand on her shoulder.

Kessara nodded, fearing to speak, as though someone in the crowd might recognize the sound of her voice. She pulled the borrowed purple scarf more tightly across her face as the two women stepped forward in line, filling the gap left by a large woman dressed head to toe in loose black fabric.

"What are you so afraid of?" Mella whispered, adjusting the pin that held her own purple scarf over her hair. "It's not like it is your first time visiting a temple."

Kessara smiled beneath the hot fabric, but she did not answer. It would not be a safe place to announce that her faith in the High One had convinced her that the temples to the Dracodei were built upon lies.

Before Mella could prod her further, the black-clad woman moved past the two female guards that stood at either side of the door. They were next, and she said a brief prayer that she would avoid detection. Nerves simmered in her stomach. It was strange to think that a familiar ritual now filled her with trepidation.

One of the women glanced up and down at Mella, taking in her plump-cheeked face and green eyes. "Thank you," she said, ushering her toward the temple doors.

Here we go.

"Ma'am, I will have to ask you to remove your scarf for a moment," the other guard said, her voice almost apologetic. After all, she wore a scarf that covered her own face as well. "There's been a lot of trouble lately, and temples are always a potential target. We have to be cautious."

Kessara didn't speak as she undid the gold pin at her neck and unwound the soft fabric. To her relief, the woman did not seem to recognize her, waving her through without another word.

She replaced the scarf as well as she could as she walked up the five steps leading into the temple.

As she entered the massive room, she felt a sinking feeling deep in her belly.

It was beautiful here, in a clean sort of way. There were no dragon statues or paintings, as one might expect. Instead, as far as the eye could see were rows and rows of tall white pillars that gleamed in the glow of lanterns that hung from the ceiling. The floor was made of the same stone, so smooth and pale that it reminded her of ice.

Everywhere she looked, she saw women standing before the pillars, leaning forward until their foreheads touched the stone, chanting beneath their breaths. There were no less than a dozen women wearing the same purple scarf that Mella wore, and for a moment she feared that she would never find her. To her relief, the older woman was not among the worshipers, but standing right behind her against the back wall.

"I've spent so many hours here," she said, ushering Kessara toward a back corner where they could speak privately. "And yet, all of a sudden, it feels strange."

"I know what you mean," Kessara replied, thinking back to the first time she'd visited her home temple near Windshear after breaking Wes out of Stronghollow Penitentiary. The same nagging feeling had been there then, though at the time she'd had even less of an explanation for it. When she'd tried to pray, she had felt so sick that she nearly collapsed on the floor.

Now, she understood.

"It's because of the High One. I know that you are not certain what you believe yet, but the same thing happened to me when I began to follow Him, even only part way," she continued, ushering Mella to sit on a tidy wooden bench set against the wall.

She could speak at a normal volume here, confident that none of the women would hear her over the chanting that filled the room. It was an otherworldly sound, almost beautiful, but not quite.

"Ever since you all showed up in Auranth, I've been unable to pray at all," Mella confessed, looking at her feet. "And yet, I keep coming here. Keep waiting for what I've always known to make sense to me again."

Kessara rested a hand on her forearm and waited for the woman to continue.

"Mostly, I think I just come here because I miss it. I miss the way I used to feel when I was honoring the Dracodei. My husband, my sons, they didn't bother with it very much. Oh, they were loyal to the sacrifices. Bargren was generous when the Feasts came along. But outside of that..." she waved a hand.

"I think most people are like that," Kessara said, giving the woman a quick smile. "We do the bare minimum that we must, rather than the greater things that we ought. Though, in this case, I must confess I am glad of that human tendency."

Neither of them spoke for a minute, watching as a new group of women entered the full room and a few more left. Kessara was surprised at how many there were. Auranth had struck her as a very independent sort of city, far from the reach of government and the Septemvirate, and yet here was an outsized display of piety.

"It's busy here." Mella said, answering a question that had gone unasked, her eyes searching Kessara's hidden face.

"I was wondering if you knew why."

"The men of our city have their own purpose. Nearly all of them work in weapon manufacturing, in one way or another. We women are left to raise children, preferably a lot of them."

Kessara tried to read Mella's expression, but she could not tell what the woman was thinking. She had four sons, which would have been a huge number back home in Galeharbor. Here, it was typical.

"Don't misunderstand me, Princess," Mella said with a smile, dropping her voice to a whisper as she uttered her formal title. "Raising children is a great gift, and one I embrace with joy. Most of the women here do."

"But," Kessara prompted.

"But our purpose is... a small one. Yes, that's what I'd call it. We don't try to change the world. We stay close to home, we keep our feet on the ground. Most of it is mending bloody knees and washing dishes."

Kessara smiled. She found the idea of such a life to be appealing, though she knew that it would have seemed a far less romantic notion to someone who had not been raised with servants attending to such menial tasks.

"Worshiping the Dracodei gives us something bigger. We may not forge swords or go to war, but we pray for all who do. We are given a spiritual power that many of the men cast aside. It makes us feel like we're part of something greater, even as we knead bread dough or wash undergarments."

"I understand," Kessara said.

"Now that you know why I'm here, despite my growing doubts, I must ask. Why did you ask me to bring you along?"

Kessara looked over at the nearest row of pillars, where six women had just begun a new round of chanting. Their words blended together into an intoxicating harmony as they pressed their foreheads to the stone.

"A dream," she admitted finally, not wanting to meet Mella's eyes.

"Hmm," she replied.

Kessara thought of Alder, blinking away the tears that threatened to fall if she dwelled on him for too long. He had dreamed of the High One. Perhaps he still did. Despite how furious she was with him, she hoped that he and Celesyria had not forgotten to pray, wherever they were. It could not end the way they had left it. He had to be okay.

"I dreamed that the High One spoke to me," she continued, knotting her fingers in the fabric of her blue dress. "He told me that the force we are building would not be enough, not if those who are a part of it seek only their own self interest. He told me to teach everyone that I could about Him, and that he would give me the words to say."

"And you came here to see what you were up against?" Mella asked, her dimples showing as she grinned.

"Pretty much," Kessara said, smiling. "It's easier to bring someone on a journey if you know where they are starting from."

They sat in a companionable silence for a few moments, watching and listening.

The lingering sick feeling remained, but she could bear it. It was a gift, a warning from the High One of what she had to leave behind. She could never say those familiar words to the Dracodei, never feel the cool stone against her face as she prayed. But he had given her new prayers, a new purpose, a new hope.

Now, she had to find the courage to bring it to others.

She hoped that they would listen.

11

Chapter Eleven

HOLGA

Before

Holga watched as the strange men rode into the village of Rill, the hoofs of their stags kicking up dust as they trotted along the main road. The summer had been long and hot, and all around her the parched ground was longing for the refreshment of rain.

"Who are they?" Gohr asked, looking up from the tunic he'd been scrubbing across a washboard.

Holga did not answer straight away, as though she could hold back the evils she feared if she did not speak their name aloud. She took her own washboard between her knees and began scrubbing at a pair of filthy orange trousers until the basin-water had gone nearly black.

When she was done, she added the article to the growing pile of clothes waiting to be rinsed. They had made good time today. The sun had not yet reached noon-height, and they were already nearly finished with their laundry orders.

"They look like Silverfell men," she answered finally, gesturing to the green cloaks that they wore. They were close enough now that she could see the distinctive swirls of silver thread that ran along the edges of their clothes. "Probably something to do with the summer Feast. Perhaps there are still some people in town who have not offered their treasures yet."

She did not really believe this. As useless as the local administrators in Rill were, they did not take lightly to those who would not give their share to the Dracodei. Even if the Envoy could no longer offer it properly atop the great spire.

"Should we hide?" Gohr asked, knitting his brows together across his smooth brown forehead as the riders rode closer. There were five of them, each riding a neatly-groomed stag gelding. They looked too handsome for their poor little village.

"We've done nothing wrong," Holga said firmly, plastering a smile on her face as the men reached the block where the village laundry stood. "No one knows anything about us."

Gohr opened his mouth as if to ask more questions, but closed it again beneath his older sister's withering gaze. Even if she wanted to run, it was too late now. She had expected the approaching riders to continue past them, but instead they came to a stop in front of the laundry, the man in front climbing off of his horse and walking toward them.

High One, please be with us.

"Holga and Gohr Zahrezain?"

The man stood tall, arms at his sides, every part of his posture indicating that he was someone who was used to being listened to and respected. She gave Gohr a glance that she hoped would convey to him that he should stand still and be polite.

"Yes, sir," Holga answered, putting her soap-scoured hands into her pockets to avoid fiddling with her braids. "Can I be of assistance?"

The man turned to glance at his companions, and she caught a glimmer of silver at his belt. These men may not be soldiers, exactly, but they were certainly armed.

"Our business concerns your younger brother," he said, his voice softening. "We have received reports that he fell very ill with the water-sickness, but then recovered."

She couldn't hold back the smile that rose to her face. She placed a hand on Gohr's shoulder, glad that he was content to let her speak for him. "Yes. The river leading from Redvale remains safe, but being a foolish little boy, he decided that he just had to go and drink out of a watering hole he found behind a stand of cactuses. He was very sick, and our healer warned that he may not make it."

"Praise the Dracodei that he has lived," the man said. He smiled back at her, but it didn't quite reach his eyes.

"Praise the Dracodei," she repeated.

Forgive me, High One.

The man was silent for a moment, and she felt her smile falter. This whole encounter was far too strange. She could trust very few people, and certainly no one who might be linked to the Septemvirate.

"Well," he said finally, clearing his throat. "The news of your brother's miraculous survival has reached the ears of our dear Elders. With the approval of King Kylan Ursa, they wish to bring him to the Academy at Vaevar, in hopes that he will provide a key to curing this strange malady."

Holga's blood went cold. Gohr stiffened beneath her arm, but kept quiet.

"King Kylan Ursa is not the King of Boneshire," she objected, unsure what else to say.

"Nor is he King of Silverfell, only Steward," the man said easily, giving a brief glance back at his companions still on stagback. Holga thought she could see the flash of more hidden knives, but it didn't matter. Even without weapons, there was no hope of physical resistance against so many adult men. "But the Elders have certain prerogatives pertaining to the public good, as I'm sure a bright girl such as yourself is well aware."

She nodded numbly, wishing that they had run after all, though fleeing into the desert would have brought a sure death in any case.

"Holga," the man said, leaning forward a little so that he was closer to her height. She forced herself to meet his dark eyes as he spoke.

The High One is with us. We will not fear you.

She wished that she had the strength to believe it.

"Yes, sir?" she asked when he did not continue.

He smiled again. This was not a cruel man, that much was clear. She had met many cruel men in her life, especially since her parents had died, and she had developed a sense about such things. She was still terrified, but better to be at the mercy of a soldier performing his duty than a sadist indulging his desire.

"Hundreds are dying across Kaveryth. We know where some of the bad water is, but we are finding new sources all the time. Of those who drink it, some never seem ill at all. Others, usually children, have minor ailments that fade with time. But until young Gohr here, there has never been a case where someone has become extremely ill and then went on to live."

He paused, waiting for her to comprehend the gravity of

114

what he was saying.

The sickness of the water had begun to strike Boneshire first. She had watched dozens of people she knew fall ill and die. The village of Rill would benefit from a cure more than almost anywhere else in the Four Kingdoms.

"If the scientists at the Academy are able to study Gohr, they may find the key to curing or even preventing this horrible sickness. His apparent immunity may be the key to saving hundreds or thousands of lives. You must understand why this matter is so important to us, and why my men and I have come so far to find him."

She understood, of course, but she did not want to say so.

She had heard many dark things about the Academy and about those who resided within its walls. They had brought great innovations to the Four Kingdoms, but there were evil designs, as well. The scientists were capable of a great deal, but she did not trust them to know when they had come up to a line that shouldn't be crossed. Nor did she trust them to carry out their experiments ethically.

Before she could find a way to say so, Gohr spoke up.

"I will go," he said, taking a step forward as Holga's arm fell from his shoulder. "I wish to make this sacrifice for the greater good of the Four Kingdoms and all Kaveryth."

She opened her mouth to object, to scream at him if necessary, but when he turned to look at her, she went silent. His eyes were filled with tears and he shook his head.

Ever since they were children, they had always been able to communicate without words, the special language of siblings only magnified after they had lost their parents. She knew what Gohr's eyes spoke.

They are only pretending that we have a choice. In the end, I will go with them. My decision is only whether I go at the end of a sword, or with my head held high.

WES

Wes held the paintbrush in his hand, watching as the lumps of color on the palette transformed into discernible shapes on the canvas. He was not a great painter, not like his mother had been, but she'd taught him enough that he could make the image obey his imagination.

"Fantastic job, Addis," Kessara said, gesturing to a painting that one of the little boys had just finished. She was moving between eight young students, and though Wes was technically helping her to teach, he had gotten lost in his own art for quite a while. In any case, he lacked her aptitude for teaching, and preferred to let her take charge when possible.

He sat back on his stool, examining the canvas on the easel in front of him. He had just added a final stroke at the top of the great spire, which stretched high into a sky filled with dark, swirling clouds. He wasn't sure why the idea for the image had occurred to him, but the details had come together easily on the page, as though an unseen hand helped to hold his thin brush.

"Now, who can tell me who the greatest painter in all of the Four Kingdoms is?" Kessara asked, her voice an octave higher than usual. Wes smiled. She was so good with the little ones, and they adored her.

She will be a wonderful mother to your heirs.

His smile faltered for a moment at the thought as he continued to listen to her lesson. One of the little girls raised a hand timidly.

"Yes, Sareena? Any ideas?"

"In some places they don't even have art. They think that the images offend the Dracodei."

"Boneshire still has art of their own, but you're right, it's different from what we see here in Silverfell," Kessara explained patiently, glancing over at Wes. "They use lots of shapes and text to convey what they wish to look at. It's been that way ever since the war. The elves do not like to see depictions of people, or animals, or places, and I suppose it stuck with the people they left alive."

As the Princess fielded more questions from the curious children, Wes found himself lost in his own thoughts. Not long after he'd met Celesyria for the first time, he had rescued two young children, Holga and Gohr, from a band of slavers who had captured them.

Now, Alder and Kessara had learned that the girl was secretly heir to the House of Noctua, and therefore the rightful ruler of Boneshire. The family that had adopted her were from a long line of tapestry makers, most of them wiped out along with their forbidden art.

She and her brother were alone in the world, and now they would soon learn of an even larger burden that they must carry. Wes was struck with sadness on their behalf. He knew better than most that those who were chosen were not called to be served, but to become servants. Holga's life was only going to get harder.

"Okay, my dears," Kessara said, clapping her hands. Wes returned his attention to her along with the little ones. "Now, it is very important that we answer my question. Nevermind the greatest in the Four Kingdoms. Who is the greatest artist in all of Kaveryth, and the whole world?"

She lowered her voice to a whisper, looking between each

child with a look of excitement on her face. They sat rapt before their messy paintings, each glancing at one another, eager for someone else to give the answer.

"Perhaps Wes knows," she said, smiling at him.

"I'll give you a hint. It's not someone you would expect," he began, leaning forward in his chair, drawing out each word. The children looked about ready to leap up and tackle him if he did not come out with it.

"The High One is the true God of all Kaveryth. He can paint anything, just by thinking of it! He painted the ground we walk on, the blue sky over our heads, the grass, the horses, and each and every one of us."

Kessara gave him an approving smile. Perhaps he was better at this task of teaching the little ones than he thought.

Ever since Alder and Celesyria had left for Umrym, Kessara had thrown herself into the task of bringing more people in Auranth to the truth.

He had been nervous about it at first—after all, trying to tell followers of the Dracodei about another God had landed him in jail once already—but he could see the necessity of the task. The High One had brought them this far. If they were faithful to Him, he would move mountains that stood in their way.

Working with the children seemed to be good for Kessara, too, after days of moping around the fortress since Alder and Celesyria left for Umrym.

It was not a mystery that she and Alder had feelings for one another, but Wes figured that something more specific must have happened before he left that had driven her into melancholy. He had tried to talk to her about it more than once, but she had refused to admit that anything was wrong. He didn't dare to hope that she would talk to him now that she was in a better mood.

I'm the last person she wants to talk to about her romantic feelings for Alder. It's my fault that she can't act on them in the first place.

"Could the High One make a chocolate cake?" one of the children asked, interrupting his thoughts.

"Did the High One make the High One?" asked one of the older girls. Her brown eyes glimmered as she glanced over at him, a teasing smile on her lips.

"Okay, class," Kessara said, clapping her hands again to call for quiet. "Wes and I have some things to discuss about our next art project, and your mothers will be looking for you for lunch. Run along."

The children gathered up their palettes, paint cups, and brushes and brought them to a small table near where Kessara stood, thanking her and making her promise that they would get to bring home their paintings once they dried. Finally, the older girl appeared, plunking her supplies down on the table with a smirk and heading out of the fortress without another word.

"We need to get her on our side," Wes said, shaking his head with a laugh.

"That's the second time she's tried to make me look foolish. The other day she asked me why the High One allows so much suffering."

"That's a good question."

"Sure," Kessara replied, picking up a handful of the nearest paintbrushes and sliding them into a storage tube with a bit too much force. "Too good. Too good for someone like me to adequately answer it."

"You're doing a great job," Wes assured her, taking hold of

two of the nearest easels and lining them up along the wall. "The High One already knew of your limitations when he called you to share His truth with the people. He will give you the right words to say when they are needed."

She said nothing for a couple of minutes as they moved the remaining easels into place. A lot was going on in this large open room, and until they had a dedicated space for art class, they would need to keep things tidy or risk the wrath of Bargren's wife.

Mella had already pulled together a sewing club that met near the firepit, composed of local women who volunteered to help provide their new recruits with proper uniforms. Wes had not been allowed to see the design yet, but he supported the idea wholeheartedly. Already they had two dozen men and older boys ready to stand and fight, and there would hopefully be more coming. The least they could do was to treat the soldiers well, keeping them in good clothing, food, and drink.

Finally, the last of the paint supplies had been tucked neatly away. Kessara turned to leave, no doubt ready to rush off to her next task, but Wes reached out and placed a firm hand on her wrist.

"We need to talk," he said, the words tumbling out rather less gracefully than he'd envisioned.

"So talk," the Princess said, giving him a mirthless smile. Wes released her arm and she let her fingers fall to her side, knotting in the blue fabric of her dress.

"I'm worried about you."

"I'm fine."

"You're fine when you're busy," he corrected her. "You're fine when you're taking care of everyone else."

"So I should sit around all day? Let this new army build

itself?" her eyes flashed with anger.

"No," he said, trying to keep his voice gentle. "I'm thankful for everything you've done. You're the whole reason that I'm beginning to believe this crazy idea might actually work."

Kessara glanced around the room, saying nothing. Everyone else was busy with their own work, paying them no attention, but he lowered his voice. He had no interest in embarrassing her.

"Anyway," he continued. "I fear that you're pushing yourself so hard because you are trying to run away from something. Something that you're not telling me about."

"I'm right here."

"Did something happen between you and Alder?" he asked before he could stop himself. He'd wanted to approach the topic tactfully, but he was growing impatient.

Of course, he did not expect that Alder had done anything untoward, but he feared that something as simple as a kiss may have been enough to dredge up traumatic memories that the Princess was no doubt trying desperately to bury. Especially since Alder had not stayed around to pick up the pieces.

"Why? Are you jealous?" Kessara spat.

For a moment, he almost started laughing.

"That's what you think I'm worried about? That you might prefer to be with a funnier, stronger, more handsome man than me?"

She shook her head, saying nothing.

"Don't worry, Kessara," he said, forcing himself to smile. "I'm not jealous. Like I said, I'm worried about you. You have a lot on your shoulders."

"So do you," she pointed out.

"True enough. But at least I have nothing to lose by marrying you. You're being asked to give up much more."

"I'll be fine."

"I know you will. But if I'm going to be your husband eventually, whether we like it or not, you need to be able to trust me. Let me be your friend."

"You are my friend. I trust you with my life. But there are some things that you can't fix."

"I never said I could fix it. I said I would listen. But that means that you need to let me try."

Their eyes met, and a few seconds later when he held out his arms for a hug, Kessara collapsed into his chest. He could feel her tears dampening the front of his simple brown tunic.

"We kissed, before he left," she said, her voice muffled against his chest. As suspected, he felt no pang of jealousy at this admission, only concern.

"Did it... upset you?" he asked, unsure how to approach the topic of her attempted assault without her finding out that he knew of it.

"Upset me?" she asked, pulling away from his chest. She looked up at him, her blue eyes bright, a hint of a smile touching her lips. "It was wonderful. I never wanted it to end. Time stopped. It was like I had been lifted up into the clouds, floating high above all of these worries below. It was magic."

Wes paused, rubbing at his temples. All of this sentimental-ity made him feel rather off balance.

Her face fell.

"I'm sorry," she said. "This is why I didn't want to talk to you about this. Even if you're not jealous, I'm your future wife, and here I am fawning over Alder."

"You do realize that you may as well be speaking Vilzanian

with all of this mushy stuff, right? I want to listen, but I'm sure Celesyria is more eager to hear more about the softness of his lips than I am."

Her cheeks went red. "True enough. I'm sorry," she said again, stumbling over the words.

He smiled at her then, pulling her close for another quick hug. "I'm just relieved that he didn't hurt you."

"He'd never hurt me."

"Of course he wouldn't. Not on purpose," he said.

"Well, he hurt me when he left," she continued, the short-lived smile falling from her face. "He pulled away, and we got into a fight. About you, in fact."

"Me?"

"He asked me if I had feelings for you. I told him that he already knew the answer, he just wanted to hear me say it because it made him feel better."

Her knuckles were white as she balled up the fabric of her dress in her fists.

"Anyway, you were right. He left, my heart is broken, and I've been trying to escape it since. It's easier when I'm busy. As soon as I get a few minutes to think, I feel him kissing me. I imagine myself yelling at him, more or less pushing him onto Celesyria's back and away from here. I wonder if he still hates me."

"He will forgive you," Wes said, though part of him wanted to say, *he deserved a far worse dressing-down for being such an insufferable lout.*

"If anything happens to him out there, I will never forgive myself," she said firmly.

Before Wes could attempt to argue with her, a familiar voice called out to them from across the open space. They both turned.

Their old friend Moorn stood at the front door, waiting to be invited in, one hand raised in greeting.

12

Chapter Twelve

KESSARA

"Please, come in! I think lunch is going to be served soon," Kessara called to Moorn, adjusting her skirt and heading across the expanse of stone. Wes followed behind her without a word, and by the look on his face, she assumed he was rather surprised to see him.

She was not.

She'd had a feeling that he would make his way here eventually, however annoyed he was at the fact that the last time she'd seen him, she had traded places with Wes and ended up in the prison cell he was supposed to be guarding.

Even though he'd joined the Red Army, she had continued to hope that he would have the courage to defy the Steward of Silverfell when it counted. It seemed that her instincts had been right.

"Moorn," Wes said as they shook hands. "What a blessing to see you alive and well, my brother."

"And hardly a guarantee, in these days," Moorn said, not quite returning Wes' smile. "But the same to you."

"Hello, Moorn," she said as he bowed to kiss the hand she proffered. "Welcome to Auranth."

"I hear that you are raising an army of your own," he said, ignoring her and looking over at Wes. Kessara pushed aside a flash of annoyance. Perhaps he was still upset about the whole prison thing, and she would just have to wait for him to forgive her.

Wes nodded. "The way we see it, we can't afford not to train our own men. King Ursa's army will defend the Four Kingdoms from Nox as long as it suits his purposes, but I do not trust him to do more than that. Until now, his men have continued to act as armed goons for the Septemvirate, still demanding treasures from our people as they suffered. I doubt he's a true believer in the Dracodei, but if worshiping them ultimately helps him to shore up more power, he will continue to make sure that the people do it."

Moorn nodded. "Even after the assassinations in Stronghollow, it seems that the autumn Feast of Offering will continue on as planned. Without the Envoy, of course."

Wes smiled. "Anyway, in the short term, our goals align with King Ursa's. We seek to offer protection from the elves, and anyone else that wishes to bring our people harm. Most importantly, we wish to restore worship to the High One across Kaveryth, and we see no way to do that if we are relying solely upon the Red Army. Eventually, of course, we hope that our army will help to free Silverfell from the tyranny of our so-called Steward and restore rule to the House of Cervos."

Kessara's breath caught in her chest at how matter-of-factly he'd said it. Wes was beginning to sound nearly as practical as her father, which was a rather troubling thought.

"So, my Princess, are you going for this High One business

as well?" Moorn asked.

"I believe in Him, yes," Kessara said. "It is my hope that those who join our force—and those in the support roles that undergird it—will eventually share in that belief."

There was a pause for a moment as Mella swept into the room, asking them and their guest if they were going to be ready to have their lunch shortly. Moorn nodded politely and assured her that a decent meal would be most appreciated after his long trek across the plains and through the mountains.

"Things are changing," Moorn admitted once the woman had moved out of earshot. "Even since the summer Feast. I'm not sure that I know of anyone who openly believes in this strange God, but my brothers in the Red Army speak of His name. It is strange to think that less than a year ago He would be dismissed as myth and legend. I suppose for some of us, the High One does still fall within that category, but it would be foolish to dismiss the impact that you and the rest of your friends have had on Kaveryth."

"Why did you come?" Wes asked. "I'm glad you're here, but I suppose that you do not come as a believer."

Moorn chuckled. "No. Though perhaps I'm less dismissive than I once was. I came because my mother received a note addressed to me, and I found its contents compelling."

He glanced over in Kessara's direction, and she met his eyes.

"I'm glad to hear it," she said, ignoring Wes' questioning look.

She had sent several such letters to men that she knew back home and in Silverfell, men that she thought she could trust, asking them to join their new force in Auranth. In any case, the secret of their location was already out, so she figured it would do more good than harm.

"I almost ignored it, after I saw who it was from," he said, his face darkening. "You two got me into a lot of trouble, my Princess. I was beaten badly for letting you escape."

Kessara felt sick. She pressed her hand to her lips, unsure what to say.

O High One, why did you not protect him? I was so sure of my plan, and yet I put an innocent man at risk.

There was a long and awkward pause. Somewhere in the background, Kessara could hear humming and the clanking of pots as Mella cooked.

"You're a terrible liar," Wes said matter-of-factly after a while, punching Moorn playfully on the arm.

She stared dumbfounded for several seconds before their visitor burst into laughter.

"Sorry, Princess. You should have seen your face. No, it worked out exactly as you planned it. I told the guards that I'd gone along with the escape to ensure your safety, and the worst thing I endured was a rather cranky lecture from Elder Bram."

Setting aside for the moment her confusion over whether Elder Bram was friend or foe, she walked over to him and gave him a half-hearted smack on the chest.

"That wasn't funny," she said, though her relief had bubbled over and she couldn't help but smile.

"Oh, but it was," he replied, dodging as she attempted to punch him again. Wes nodded, and within moments the two men were pretending to fight, kicking and punching each other as they skittered about on the damaged stone floor.

The scene reminded her of Alder, and her smile grew forced.

After a few minutes, Kessara declared Wes the clear winner, and the three of them headed for the empty dining table and sank into their chairs.

"Anyway," Moorn said, taking a glass of water that Mella had offered. "It was not just a chance to stand up against King Ursa that motivated me to come here."

"What do you mean?" Kessara asked, troubled by his expression, which had suddenly gone dark once again.

"I got another letter recently, from a friend of mine, a navy soldier in Galeharbor. He was on duty in Windshear on the day of the first Blackmask attack. I believe you were there as well."

Kessara nodded.

Blackmasks.

She had heard the name around Auranth, but she supposed it was being taken up across Kaveryth. Not the most original, she supposed, but it got the point across.

"Anyway, in the letter, he told me that King Manta has ordered the navy to prepare to head for the West Strait, near Nox."

Oria was right. My father has caved already.

She didn't want to believe it was true, but it made sense. King Ursa had been pressuring him for a while already, and she knew that a threat to the safety of their people was something her father never dismissed lightly. She was still furious, but she tried not to let it show on her face.

"I see," Wes said.

"It gets worse," Moorn said, sounding rather apologetic. "The fishermen along the coast of the North Sea have been reporting disturbing sightings as of late. The men in Kingsvier Landing are so spooked that they refuse to go out onto the water at all."

"Dwarf boats?" Kessara guessed, furrowing her brow.

"We've spotted those before."

Moorn shook his head. "Those were concerning enough, but we haven't seen a single one in several weeks. Perhaps a little longer. No. This time, it is something else. There is a strange shadow in the deep, just like in the stories of old."

Wes looked perplexed, but Kessara knew immediately what he spoke of.

"The Gorok," she whispered, looking over her shoulder to be certain that Mella was still in the kitchen.

Moorn nodded. "I hope we're wrong."

"A sea monster? Like the one from my favorite storybook as a child?" Wes asked, sounding incredulous.

"As the Codex Veritatis has proven, it is often the passing of time that creates legend, not falsehood," Kessara pointed out.

"I fear that Kingsvier Landing will be just the beginning of the fisherman's strike," Moorn said. "Even those who continue to fish have moved further down the coast, leading to clashes with the Vilzanian fishermen over the use of their local waters."

And my father is planning to let them fight it out, I suppose, with our navy gone. Brilliant.

"This won't help the food shortages across the Four Kingdoms," Wes said, running a hand over his thick brown curls.

"What's being done about it?" Kessara asked.

"I know only the gossip, my Princess," Moorn said.

"It will have to do."

"Very well. Supposedly, the King is ignoring the pleas of the fishermen entirely. Says it's all superstition and nonsense."

She swallowed. If she spoke now, she feared she would let something slip about her father that she would regret later.

"So what do we do?" Wes asked.

"I did come here in hopes of joining your army," Moorn said carefully, fiddling with a little wooden pendant that he wore around his neck. "But I also came to ask that the Princess return to Galeharbor. Your people are in need. Perhaps the King can be made to see sense."

She caught Wes' eye.

The fishermen are telling the truth. The elves are here in Kaveryth. Is it any surprise that evil would follow them?

ALDER

As they swept down the steep mountain walls that formed the valley, Alder blinked quickly, hoping that his eyes would adjust to the sudden darkness. The moon was somewhere out there, hiding behind the endless gray stones, but they could not see it.

The light was of little use to them now, down here amidst the Whitespire ruins.

"So, I assume that you have a brilliant plan to actually find your mother?" he asked Celesyria, his voice sounding a little bit more cross than he'd intended.

They had been flying all day, and now that the ground was so close, he longed to plant his feet upon the steady rock. Getting a few hours to sleep would be even better, but there was no point in thinking about that at the moment.

"I've been calling out to her in my mind since we arrived. I had hoped..." her voice trailed off.

You had hoped she was still nearby, close enough to guide us. But she isn't.

"Anyway," she continued, taking another banked turn as they approached the far end of the valley, away from the tower. "I just hope she's alright. I will find her somehow if she is alive."

Alder wanted to reassure her that her mother, Sharsi, was fine. But he couldn't be sure, and he couldn't bring himself to lie to her, however small the lie was.

"Do you ever feel like the spire is watching us?" he said instead, staring out at the great stone height.

Celesyria chuckled, and he could feel the rumbling sound of it beneath the saddle. "That's what Wes always said. He said he can never tell if it's a good place or an evil one, only that it scares him straight through to his bones."

Just then, Alder spotted a flash of yellow toward the eastern edge of the valley, along the base of a particularly steep mountainside.

"I see it," Celesyria said in his mind before he could point the spot out. He grabbed hold of the leather straps of the saddle just as the dragon dropped into a stomach-churning dive. A few seconds later, she pulled up, unfurling her wings and slowing down until she was nearly hovering in midair.

"Or rather, I see her," she corrected herself. The yellow had been the wing of a small dragon, perhaps half of Celesyria's size. She was watching the larger dragon, her huge green eyes looking as though they were about to pop out of her head. Alder held on again as Celesyria landed, raising a hand in greeting.

A look passed between the two dragons, lasting so long that he began to feel almost awkward.

What are they saying? Who is she?

He had so many questions, but instead he thanked the High One. She seemed to be a friendly face, and that's what they needed most at the moment.

He watched as the yellow dragon lifted her front claw and extended her arm toward the north, still staring at Celesyria. A few moments later, she leapt up from the ground and took off over the remains of the city, dodging huge broken entrance-buildings and pieces of stone that had been blown straight up into the sky before falling again.

"*That's Meraxes,*" Celesyria explained, stretching out her back, neck, and wings as she spoke and nearly sending her rider tumbling to the ground. "*Her parents are Guardians, and her mother is on the other side of the mountains, patrolling the valley borders, though of course she missed us.*"

Alder made a face, though of course she could not see it. "That's a strange name for a dragon."

"*It is,*" Celesyria agreed. "*She came to Whitespire and was reunited with her family when she was 66 years old. She was raised—and presumably, named—by a human girl from some village in the south of Galeharbor, though how her egg came to be in the child's possession in the first place, I have no idea.*"

Alder waited patiently as Celesyria stretched her ankles as best she could, the heavy metal manacles clanking against her orange scales.

"*Anyway,*" she continued finally. "*She told me that many of those displaced here were sent north, to Skanden. She doesn't know if my mother is among them.*"

"How far?"

"*We can be there by dawn.*"

Alder looked around the valley, squinting against the dark. Despite his efforts to adjust, he still struggled to see. He was glad that dragons possessed much better eyesight than humans did. "Are there more settlements on the way?"

"*I asked her,*" Celesyria said, taking a few long strides along the ground before pushing off with her back legs and leaping into the air. Alder took a final glance at the ground, any hope of getting a few hours of sleep fading away. "*She said that they would be no threat to us, anyway. The elves have been swarming over the mountains, but no violence has been reported whatsoever. They've been ignoring the dragons and the dwarves entirely."*

Alder clenched his hand more tightly around the leather holding strap.

"This appeasement will be the downfall of your race," he said as they flew higher, glad to be back at a height where he could see by the light of the moon. "They're invading your land, and no one is even trying to stop them."

"They're afraid. There are not many of us anymore. Less treasure is coming into Umrym, as well, and I'm sure it's led to hardship for many within the cave cities."

Alder chose his words carefully, not wanting to come off as entirely heartless. Even he understood the temptation to stand down when faced with a battle you couldn't win. But it was not the answer, and he hoped that the dragons and dwarves would realize it in time.

"Still. Appeasing those who want to destroy you is as foolish as feeding an Ironwolf in hope that he will eat you last."

KESSARA

"It's not safe, Kessara," Wes said, pacing around outside of her room as she shoved clothes into a trunk and hunted for her riding boots. Moorn had headed off into the back courtyard with Mella in search of a barrack tent, but Wes refused to leave her side, trying with increasing desperation to convince her that she could not return to Galeharbor.

"I know it isn't," she replied through the old wooden door, taking the blanket from her bed and trying to fold it small enough to fit in her saddlebag. "But I have no idea how much time we have, and I'm planning to leave at dawn. If the Gorok

134

really is out there, I doubt it's going to be content with only scaring people. It will attack, and not only will people die, but entire fishing fleets could be destroyed. My people could starve, especially if King Ursa ever stops selling us Aridmoor's grains."

Wes said nothing for a moment, but she could hear him continuing to pace, his boots thumping against the stone floor of the narrow hallway. She finished packing, but still he didn't reply.

She set her saddlebags and pack beside her narrow cot. Perhaps she could ask one of Bargren's sons, or one of the new recruits, to make sure that the gelding that she had come to the city on was ready for her to ride as soon as the sun rose. She was still a little nervous to ride the huge animal again, but she had to admit it would make her feel much safer knowing that her mount could stomp a bandit to death if she needed him to. With a sigh, she headed for the door.

"I'm coming with you," Wes said as soon as she emerged into the dim hallway, his arms crossed firmly over his chest. "As your future husband, I am responsible for ensuring your welfare, even if you insist on chasing calamity."

She suppressed a chuckle. "How many times did you rehearse that?"

The shadow of a smile crossed Wes' face. "Seven. Anyway, I mean it. I'm not about to leave you to ride across the world yourself. You know what could happen–"

He stopped suddenly, looking at his feet.

He knows. He knows what happened in High Keep, and there's only one person who could have told him.

"I know what could happen, but it didn't happen, and I'm fine," she snapped. "I've somehow managed to survive my entire life before you and Alder declared yourselves my protectors."

She had grown up surrounded by palace guards, but she figured that was beside the point. She was tired of them acting like she had no right to an opinion on her own life.

Still, before she could stop them, thoughts of that night rose in her mind. She couldn't stop the memories. All she could do was stand up to them and refuse to be afraid.

"Anyway," she said, glad that Wes had not attempted to argue. "The entire point of us marrying in the first place is to protect your kingdom, and mine. You can't do that if you're not in Auranth, and I can't do that if I am here."

Before Wes could respond, she noticed a shift in the lamplit hall behind him, toward Alder's empty room. She froze, and he spun around, hand on the sword at his belt just as a figure emerged from the depths of the shadows.

It was an elf-woman, her silvery skin seeming to glow from within beneath her smooth black hair. "I see you're just the same as I remember, Wes Cervos," she said, taking a few steps toward him, her movement as graceful as water. "Chivalrous to a fault."

Kessara stood there for several seconds, panic rising in her chest until she finally found herself able to speak. "Bargren!" she cried, glancing behind her, wondering if she'd be able to make it to her room and out through the window. "Someone, help—"

Before she could say more, Wes was there, clasping her shoulders. "It's okay. Don't worry."

Too dumbfounded to argue, she watched as the elf walked over to Wes and gave him a quick hug. He did not shy away.

"Hello, Aelrie."

13

Chapter Thirteen

CELESYRIA

As the sun rose over Skanden, Celesyria tried once again to reach out to her mother in her mind, but there was no reply. She did not want to give up hope, but she was struggling to push away the gloom that had settled over her.

"There's still hope, Celesyria," Alder said as they looked down at the city from the sky above, not wishing to announce their presence before they had to.

"I know," she replied, watching for any sign of movement below. She had flown over the city once or twice before, but it looked nothing like she remembered it. All across the ground, between the scattered stones of the nearby rockfall, were huge canvas tents.

"I guess dragon refugee camps are not so different from ours," Alder said as she felt him leaning over in the saddle, probably trying to get a closer look.

"I've never seen one before. But I suppose it makes sense. Skanden is not very big, and certainly not big enough to absorb

the entire population of Whitespire within its caverns."

They were both silent for a moment as she took a sweeping curve to the east, trying to spot a good place to land. These mountains were even steeper than those that surrounded Whitespire, and she was nervous to fly low between them without knowing where the dark passes led.

"There. I see a plateau, next to that gash against the stone," Alder said. She squinted in the harsh sunlight, able to make out a flat stretch of rock just big enough to land on.

"That'll work."

As she descended, she kept waiting for someone to call out to her, but no one did. The sky was empty, as were the crags and pathways that wound through the mountains. She wondered how long it would take for the elves to build settlements here, spreading over every inch of Umrym like a dark cloud.

Would the dragons ever stand up to them? Would the dwarves? Or would the fate of her land rest upon the shoulders of men?

"Careful of that jagged spot," Alder said as she circled a final time in the tight space. She landed without incident, though her ankle had never healed perfectly and still ached a little when she put sudden weight on it.

For several seconds, they caught their breath, watching as the sun rose higher, the shadows dissipating bit by bit.

O High One, please let my mother be down there. Please let her still be alive.

"So," Alder said, reaching into his pack and grabbing a piece of dried meat. "I assume I'm handling this. I see a way down where I'll be mostly hidden, and once I get to the camp they won't know my face."

She shook her head.

"I'm sick of cowering in fear."

"You're not cowering. You're being smart."

"They have my mother. You don't even know what she looks like! Even if we find her, why do you think she'll be willing to leave with you?"

"Hey now, I thought you always said that I was charming," he said between a mouthful of desiccated beef, placing a hand on his chest in mock horror.

She grimaced at him. "You're in danger here, especially alone. We don't know where the elves are, and that's assuming the dragons don't give you trouble."

"Your friend said that the elves tended to leave everyone alone, which seems to make sense."

"You can't trust them. They're not going to remain peaceful forever. They're waiting for their numbers to build, otherwise they don't have a fighting chance of being able to defeat the Guardians," she said, glancing up at the sky. Not so long ago, it would have been filled with powerful dragons, watching over those below.

In those days, not a single elf would dare to step foot within the mountains.

"They also know who you are," Alder said, swallowing the last of his food and taking a drink from his waterskin. "I can blend in."

She snorted. "Sure. Just as long as there aren't any dwarves to stand beside you."

"Celesyria. You don't know where the surviving members of the council ended up. They told you their secrets thinking that you'd be dead by now, but you escaped. They're not going to let you get away a second time."

She said nothing for a moment, thinking back to the secret

meeting she'd been dragged to. One of the elves, Falloren, had been willing to indulge her curiosity, but just after he'd informed her that elves and dragons were once allies, they'd been interrupted.

She dragged her claws across the ground, forming thin gashes in the gravel, trying to think.

I was so close. So close to knowing the real truth about Kaveryth's history. If Gramnok had only pulled off his rescue a few minutes later, perhaps things would be different now. As it is, we are nearly as blind as we were before, and now there is even less of a chance we will ever find the full Codex Veritatis.

Not to mention the fact that a good dwarf is now dead.

"No, they won't," she said at last, scuffling her marks out with a flick of the end of her tail. *"Though I'm sure the council members will be underground rather than in some human-style tent with the rest of the riffraff."*

"Which means I, the riffraff, should be relatively safe," Alder added.

Her eyes met his. For a long moment, she debated the matter within herself. Perhaps it would be better for her to go instead, or for her to at least go with him, but she couldn't think of a reason why. No. He was the logical choice.

She could only pray that she wouldn't have to leave behind another dead friend when she left these mountains.

She leaned her head down until her eyes met his.

She managed a nod.

WES

Evening was approaching, and all around the fortress, people were busy. Wes and Aelrie sat in the courtyard, watching as six men carried a large iron cannon toward a back corner.

Bargren followed behind them, shouting orders, a look of unmistakable satisfaction on his face as the men obeyed his commands.

Wes felt a smile tugging at the corner of his lips, but Aelrie sat expressionless. She was looking in the direction of the new weapons being brought in, but he could tell that her thoughts were somewhere else, far beyond the walls.

"It's strange to be out in the open," he said finally, unable to bear the silence.

Aelrie nodded, sitting up straight so that her back pressed firmly against the stone wall. Ever since she'd snuck up on him and Kessara a couple of hours earlier, she had been fidgety, like she wanted to escape, and yet, if she did, why had she come? And why didn't she just leave now?

Wes had forced himself to set those questions aside, instead directing his energy toward helping her feel at home, but he was growing more impatient by the minute.

"I'm used to hiding. But being here, taking a stand, it makes me feel like I'm following the path that the High One wants for me," he continued, trying to stare at her face without making it obvious, though he was sure that her elven senses would expose him immediately. "I just wish that I knew where the path led from here. I see this whole force coming together, and it's surreal. It's even more surreal to imagine that we might actually wind up on the battlefield, fighting back against..."

He froze, wanting very much to smack himself on the forehead. *Very smooth. I'm sure talking about killing her people will make her feel comfortable here.*

To his relief, she smiled. It seemed to light up her whole face, dispelling her weary expression like a breeze shifting away a stormcloud.

"It's okay. I want to fight them, too. But I'm still not exactly sure about the High One."

"Most here are not. My friends and I have seen enough to trust that He's looking out for us, but it has taken time. The young woman you met, Kessara, has been focusing on teaching the younger children and some of the women about the High One. It's not easy, especially since we only have so much to go on from the fragments of the Codex Veritatis in our possession, but I'm hopeful that great faith will be born here in Auranth."

They watched as a long line of men burst through the back gate, carrying dozens of long swords and wooden shields to the makeshift armory in the corner.

"A holy army that does not yet believe," Aelrie said, smiling again. Wes couldn't look away from her when she smiled. She became otherworldly, gleaming from somewhere deep within.

She's so beautiful. I could look at her forever.

The thoughts surprised him, and he felt a blush rising to his cheeks, horrified that Aelrie would somehow know what he was thinking.

"My lord! Where do you want the battle axes?" came a shout from across the courtyard.

"Oh, er, ask Bargren," he stammered, having no idea whatsoever about the efficient organization of weaponry, but thankful for the interruption. Aelrie's face looked pensive once more, and he found himself longing to see her smile again. Preferably at him.

"Are you okay?" he asked after a moment, hoping that his blush had disappeared.

"I want to believe in Him," she said, not meeting his eyes. "I want to, but I don't, so I'm here. Is that absurd?"

"No," he said, a little too quickly. "Actually I'd say it's a normal response when you hear that there is a true God, and that He wants you to believe in Him. You're caught between a desire for what He promises, and a fear of what you will have to give up in order to be made worthy of it."

Aelrie went quiet again, seeming to consider this for a while before she spoke again.

"You can't imagine what it was like to grow up in Nox, Wes," she said, a sad shadow of her usual intoxicating smile passing over her face. "All my life, I saw the reality of the darkness that surrounded me, but I was helpless to stop it. I was insane, and everyone else was normal. I wanted to be like them, just so I didn't have to be so alone. Even though I hated what I saw."

"I feel like that sometimes," he said, hoping she would not take offense. "It's not like what you experienced, of course, but I think everyone who follows the High One feels it to some degree."

"I'm sure that's true," she said.

They paused for a moment as a group of filthy teenage boys, several with minor wounds, filed past them, headed for their barrack tents. Mella would be ringing the dinner chime soon, and she would expect them to be dressed decently at her table even after a combat practice.

"When I met you, I asked you if you were innocent," he said finally, hoping that after all this time, he would finally understand. "You said you weren't. So why are you here? What changed?"

"Nothing changed," she said, looking up at the darkening sky. "And everything did. I came here because I'm not innocent. I came here because I needed forgiveness, and I trusted that you would be the person who could help me to find it."

She smiled, and Wes felt the butterflies dancing in his stomach again. The headache that had plagued him since he woke up seemed to clear at the very sight of her face.

A part of him wanted to reach out to her, to embrace her and to assure her that he forgave her for whatever she had done, however terrible. But that wasn't the forgiveness she sought, nor could he rightly offer it even if it was. She needed to trust in the High One, and the best thing he could do was pray that He would bring her home to Him.

ALDER

The inside of the tent felt very small. Alder pushed his way between dragons and dwarves as he tried to figure out whether or not he was even in the right place. To his surprise, no one paid him much attention at all, even though he stood easily two feet taller than even the tallest dwarf in the entire camp. For a moment, he wondered if the High One was providing him with some sort of special protection, but then he shook his head, chuckling to himself.

No. I'm not that special. These people and dragons are just too concerned with their own present needs to ask why a human is prowling around.

He wondered how busy the underground city of Skanden must be for this overflow area to be so full. Everywhere he looked, he saw nothing but the crush of bodies. It seemed there had been some early attempt to separate the two races into their own sections—dragons given nests made out of blankets, dwarves provided with proper cots—but there were so many refugees that they mostly just found space to lay where they

144

could.

He felt a pang of guilt pass through him. Gramnok had been the cause of this, and even though his intention had been to save Celesyria, he had gone about it in a despicable way.

Alder felt as though he should regret the dwarf's actions, but found himself unable to do so. Had Gramnok not done what he did, Celesyria would almost certainly be dead, likely Wes as well, and the portion of the Codex he had found would be in Elder Dorold's hands.

The ends don't justify the means.

He could almost hear Kessara's snootiest voice in his head. He wished that he could kick himself for leaving things so badly. She'd eventually forgive him, but the feelings that they had for one another would take even longer to fade. He couldn't let anything like that kiss happen again, not ever. He had to be strong.

He bumped into a large dwarf standing nearby, interrupting his thoughts. He apologized, trying to make his way in the other direction along the tent wall, but the man hardly seemed to have noticed. Finally, he found the next opening in the canvas and made his way through it.

There were several tents connected together, and there did not seem to be any coherent organization system, nor anyone in charge who might know where Sharsi was. Celesyria had said that she looked like her mother, which was of some help, as not many of the dragons he saw were orange, but he had only explored a small section of the huge camp.

Finally he gave up, and caught the eye of a pleasant-faced dwarf woman who was sweeping the floor in her little section, mostly inhabited by other dwarves.

"Hello, ma'am," he said, giving her a half-bow.

"Can I help you, sir?" she asked, her voice as cheerful as her face. She stopped sweeping, resting on her broom.

"I hope so," he said, unable to stop himself from smiling back. She beamed at him. "I'm looking for someone. A dragon."

"We have a lot of dragons here, but I'm afraid they're not for sale," the woman said, laughing at her own bad joke.

"Her name is Sharsi. She has orange scales and yellow eyes."

All at once, the laughter ceased.

"Oh, my dear boy," she said, rushing over to a stack of tall wooden boxes and resting the broom against them. "Follow me at once."

"Is she here? Is she alive?" he asked. His words hung in the air as he waited for an answer, hoping against hope that Celesyria would not have to face such a crushing loss.

"She's in the medical tent," the woman said, half-shoving her way through the crowd of dwarves and past several dragons, who raised their claws to make a clear path for her. He followed, nearly smacking his head against their scaly feet.

Please, High One. Let her be alright, at least well enough that we can get her to Auranth.

He wondered if this explained why Celesyria had not been able to speak to her in her mind. Perhaps their mindspeaking abilities were weakened by physical illness. He tried to call out to her himself, considering that he was now much closer, but alas it was no easier with her than with Celesyria to master the skill of speaking rather than just listening.

Finally, after what seemed like a dozen twists and turns, they reached another passage between tents, though this one was closed off with great curtains of canvas. The dwarf woman reached for the flap of the door, but before she could pull it open, a dragon stuck out its claw, blocking their path.

14

Chapter Fourteen

KESSARA

Kessara woke before the sun. She had struggled to sleep very much anyway, and she figured that she may as well get on with her journey just as soon as she could manage it. Aelrie's arrival had been unexpected, but it served as a distraction for Wes, and she was thankful.

If she was lucky, he would not miss her at all.

With a final glance at her cot, she left her bedroom, leaving the door unlocked in case someone else wished to take up residence indoors while she was gone. Aelrie would be a logical choice, but she hadn't had the chance to ask if she was planning to stay long.

Ever since she'd arrived, Wes and the elf had been lost in their own world. If she hadn't known better, she would have thought that perhaps there was something more than burgeoning friendship between them.

Nonsense. Humans do not associate in such a manner with elves. We all know how well that turned out in the early days of Kaveryth, Dracodei help us.

She did not wish to think of the other reason that Wes was not an eligible bachelor. Even though she was furious at Alder, her mind refused to let her ignore him. He was always there in the background of her thoughts, taunting her from across the mountains, reminding her that love could be a curse if you weren't careful.

The main hall was still very dark at this hour, and she was glad that she had brought her lantern with her. She listened for the sound of snores, but heard nothing. The old forge felt strangely lonely without the sound of Celesyria's usual sleepy rumbling, and she found herself sad to leave it. In the short weeks that she had been here, the place had begun to feel like home. It was no Windshear Palace, but it was wonderful in its own way, filled with the beauty of old forgotten things brought back to life.

She made her way to the front door and slipped through it, not daring to look back. She didn't want an excuse to wait around, to risk having to say goodbye.

Wes did not want her to leave, and she understood why, but it was something she must do.

As she began walking down the path toward the village, she resolved to pray for Aelrie that she would come to find the truth. Even elves were not beyond the power of the High One to save. She could only hope that the seeds of faith she had begun to plant here would continue to grow in her absence.

After walking for several minutes, she reached a rise where she could see the West Strait, smooth and gray in the distance. It was flat and empty, without so much as a dinghy in sight, but she knew that meant little. The elves could decide to row across at a moment's notice, swarm into Kaveryth, and make their way inland.

They can't get in along the cliffs of Umrym. They can enter only over the Black Beach, or along the edge of Auranth.

The thought didn't scare her. The people here were strong, and she was confident that the High One stood with them.

If that dark day ever came, they would stand and they would fight.

The stars were beginning to fade in the sky, blinking out one by one as the inky darkness softened into shades of dark blue. Behind her, she knew, the sun would be beginning its ascent up over the mountains.

It did not take her long to reach her destination, nodding at the handful of guards she saw as she went. Most of them were out beyond the city walls, watching over the paths that led between the trees. In any case, there were few now who did not know her face.

Near the entrance to the town gate was a little river with a quaint stone bridge stretching over it, and standing on the bridge was Bargren. He did not see her as she approached, his fishing rod cast over the railing, his eyes focused on the shallow water below. She knew that he hunted for a certain kind of fish that preferred to feed under the stars, and she couldn't blame the creature. The night was beautiful. It almost pained her to know that the sunrise was near.

"Hi, Bargren," she said after a silent moment had passed, stepping off of the dirt of the path and onto the stone. "I have a favor to ask."

"Princess?" Bargren turned to face her, nearly dropping his pole over the edge of the bridge in surprise.

"Sorry to startle you," she smiled, a twinge of nervousness pressing against her chest. She hoped that he would understand.

"That's alright. How can I be of service?"

"Forgive me for the early hour and the short notice," she said, gesturing to the still-dark sky. "I do not wish to be burdened with goodbyes. I plan to leave straight away, for Galeharbor."

Alder would return from Umrym any day now, and that goodbye might prove impossible. She couldn't take the chance that he'd convince her to stay.

Bargren waited for her to continue, resting his fishing pole against the stone wall.

"I am in need of escorts. Preferably two men."

She did not need to explain to him why two was better than one, even setting aside the matter of extra protection. Traveling with Alder had required her to feign marriage, and she did not wish to cause any scandal now, especially once she arrived in her homeland where many more people would recognize her.

"My two eldest sons would be happy to assist you, my Princess," he said without hesitation, smiling broadly, as though it was a great honor to send his boys off across the world before dawn. "Vard and Viggo."

"The mission may prove dangerous," she said, meeting the man's eyes.

"My sons are the bravest in all Auranth."

"I don't doubt it for a moment. But they are dear to you, and you should know that they will be accepting potentially fatal risks if they agree to aid me."

bargren considered this for a moment. She felt rather guilty when she said the words aloud, even though she knew it to be true. She was a Princess, and soon enough a queen. Her duty did not include death at the end of a sword. It was not a pleasant reality for those who served her, but she saw no use in denying it or brushing it away.

"My sons are old enough to choose."

"The Gorok has been sighted in the North Sea," she added, wishing for him to know the entire truth of the threats that lay ahead. "My father does not believe the reports, but I do. I must do what I can to protect the people of the coast."

The usually cheerful weaponmaker paled, and his eyes grew wide for a moment before he composed himself. "Not something we hear tell of every day, is it?"

She shook her head, relieved as he broke into a smile. "Anyway, as I told you all before, if King Ursa is allowed free reign any longer, I will lose all of my sons to his Red Army. I would rather see them die in your service than in his."

"And I will do everything in my power to make sure that they don't die at all," she said firmly, reaching over to clasp his outstretched hand. He shook it.

"Deal. They slept in town tonight, I will go and ask them to meet you at the stables as soon as they can dress. I assume you will be taking the two plains horses that you and Alder arrived on?"

"Yes."

"Regrettably, I don't know if there is a third anywhere in Auranth, but Vard has a well-bred stag of his own that he can ride, a gift from a merchant. A fellow from Briarcroft."

"That will be fine," she said, shifting from foot to foot. She had already taken her supplies out to the stable late the night before, after everyone had fallen asleep, and she hoped that the stableboys would not attempt to tidy away her packs and saddlebags before she got there. "If they will not agree to come, please send any other man from your Guild or elsewhere who you believe to be fit. I will defer to your judgment."

"They will agree."

"Thank you, Bargren," she said, trying to smile through the sudden nerves that bubbled up in her stomach.

"It is an honor," he assured her, looking as eager to leave as she was.

"Before you go, there is one more thing."

"Anything, my Princess."

"Please tell Wes that I'm sorry, but I have to do this."

He nodded, taking her small hand in his perpetually soot-covered palm and closing his fingers gently around it. There was so much more that she wanted to say. So much business that she was leaving behind half-finished. But her people needed help, and she could very well be the only person capable of offering it.

With a final wave goodbye, she made for the stables, holding up her skirts as she raced the rising sun.

ALDER

"Who are you?" Alder asked the orange dragon, taking a couple of steps closer to the door until she lowered her claw.

"My name is Jaconial. I'm one of the Guardians entrusted with the security of this camp."

It took him a couple of moments to place the name, but then the memories of conversations with Celesyria fell into place. He tried to reach out to her in his mind, but was not surprised when it didn't work. Even if he could mindspeak as well as Wes could, it would be difficult from such a distance.

"I'm here to visit a friend," Alder said quickly, hoping that his face had not registered the fact that he recognized her name. "If you permit me to do so, I will gladly lay down my weapons."

He pulled his sword-sheath from his belt for emphasis, moving to lay it at the door flap of the medical tent.

He felt a rumbling fill his chest as the dragon chuckled. "Your weapons are useless here. I could kill you in an instant if I wished."

Alder noticed that the kindly dwarf-woman who had escorted him had disappeared somewhere in the crowd. No one was paying them any attention at all. For several seconds, neither spoke, and a far-away look filled Jaconial's eyes, though he was sure that she could easily kill him just as she said if he tried anything.

"I was informing another guard that I am heading into the medical tent," she said, narrowing her eyes at him. "Look, Alder Cadogen. I know who Sharsi's daughter is, and I'm sure she's close by. If I wanted to kill her, I would have headed over to do it by now."

He tried not to let his face register his shock. She smiled, her reptilian lips curling up over her jagged teeth.

"This way," she said, gesturing toward the tent. Without looking back, Alder stepped inside, feeling Jaconial's hot breath at his heels. Several questions raced through his mind, but for the time being, he wanted only to find Sharsi. If the dragon was planning to harm him, there was little he could do, especially without his sword.

The medical tent was full, but at least those who were sick had a little more living space. Each patient rested in his or her own section of the tent, separated by great canvas curtains that hung from the ceiling. This area seemed to house only dragons, though the staff was composed entirely of dwarf-women as far as he could tell.

"There," Jaconial said, raising a claw and pointing ahead of him, toward a section at the far corner of the room. Alder could see the tip of an orange tail poking out from behind the curtain, and as he stepped toward it, he called her name as gently as he could, hoping he was not waking her.

"Come in," came a girlish voice that reminded him immediately of Celesyria.

As he pushed through the curtain, he only just managed not to cry out in horror. Sharsi's flank was marred by a deep gash surrounded by crushed scales, and across the top her crest had been ripped off entirely. One of her back legs was held in a sort of metal brace, and he could see that it too was covered in dozens of smaller cuts.

The worst, however, was her front left claw, which was entirely missing, cut off at the wrist.

"Can we have some privacy?" he turned to ask Jaconial, glad to have a moment where he did not have to glance at the carnage before him.

"I am not permitted to leave her unattended."

Her tone did not make it clear whether or not this was a policy applying solely to Celesyria's mother or to the occupants of the medical tent generally, and he did not dare ask. Instead, he said a quick prayer to the High One that He would protect them from any wicked plans that had been laid.

For whatever reason, Jaconial was acting like an ally, or at least as someone who was willing to turn a blind eye. He didn't trust her, but he had no choice but to speak freely in her presence. He doubted they would get another chance to rescue Sharsi.

"How are you feeling?" he said to the dragon, who had been staring at him with an amused expression, waiting patiently for him to state his business.

"I'm told that my injuries are severe, but I'm stable," she said, giving him a pained smile. "Hard to feel stable with a leg encased in metal and an entire claw missing."

"I'm sorry," Alder said, wishing that there was anything else he could say. Gramnok's choice to free Celesyria by way of an explosion had damaged so many lives.

"Thank you."

Alder cleared his throat, glancing up at Jaconial, who was looking off at the corner of the ceiling, as though she could choose not to hear the conversation so long as she didn't watch his lips move.

"Celesyria found somewhere safe to stay, and she wishes for you to come with me right away so that I can help you get there," he said in a whisper, holding his breath as he waited for some objection from Jaconial.

"Thank the Dracodei she's alive," Sharsi said, her voice cracking. "I was so afraid. I didn't see her after the collapse."

"She sustained a minor injury, but she has recovered well," he assured her.

"What about my husband?" she asked, her eyes pleading.

"He's still in Nox. We are trying to get to him, but we need to be careful. It's going to take more time."

She looked down at the stump of her missing claw. "I should have gone to him myself when I had the chance," she said flatly. "He was right all along. I thought that if I went along with those in charge, if I did what they said, I would be safe. But I should have stood up to them. We all should have. It's only getting more difficult now that they've sunk their claws in."

She glanced at Jaconial, who was watching intently now. Alder wondered if unseen words were passing between them.

Before they could say anything else, one of the dwarf nurses burst into the room, wheeling a cart with a huge shoulder of what looked to be deer meat resting upon it. Sharsi hardly glanced at the food before addressing the woman.

"I am leaving today. I will need assistance removing this brace."

The woman looked at her, confusion spreading across her thick features. "Sharsi, you are not strong enough to fly yet. In any case, I understand that your daughter is wanted by the administration in connection with the very bombing that wounded you in the first place. This boy here could be one of her associates. No. There is no way I can release you without permission from my superiors, and even if I did, there would be surveillance for your own safety."

Alder forced himself to breathe slowly. The woman spoke with such matter-of-factness that her words sounded even more cruel. Sharsi was right. Her husband had stood up to these people early on, and it had cost him dearly, but now she risked paying an even higher cost to follow behind him.

Before Sharsi could argue, he heard Jaconial clear her throat. "Actually, Gzarinna, she has already been given permission. I was assigned to assist her in leaving Skanden."

The dragon spoke with such confidence that even Alder almost believed her. He knew that lying was wrong in the eyes of the High One, but at the moment, he could not find it in himself to correct her.

"Oh," said Gzarynna, her face turning rather red. "Forgive me, Sharsi, Jaconial. I must not have received word of these orders, or perhaps I neglected to read my patient notes well enough today. As you can imagine, there is a lot of work for me here at the moment."

"I understand," Sharsi said, her voice sweet.

"No need at all to apologize," Jaconial said with a small chuckle. "Try as we might to remain organized, this entire camp is chaotic at the best of times."

With a few more pleasantries exchanged, the dwarf nurse removed the metal brace and led them to the door of the little makeshift room, holding aside the flap so that they could pass.

Alder felt the whisper of Jaconials breathing at his ear, but the words sounded inside his head.

"I will help you to get Sharsi away from here. But you must allow me and one other to follow."

WES

Wes' bedroom at the old forge was not as opulent as his palace chambers back in Stronghollow, but Mella had done a great deal to make it lovely. The broken bits of stone in the walls had been repaired neatly. Thick rugs were laid across the jagged cobbles of the floor, which he knew would also bring much comfort when the cold months of winter arrived. His cot was fitted with a quilt that she had made herself, with the aid of her sewing society.

Fit for a forbidden king, as she would say.

His bed was now so comfortable that he often found it difficult to leave it in the morning. The sun was shining through the small window near the top of the wall, and though his stomach was rumbling with hunger, he felt too relaxed to care.

After a few more minutes of blissful half-sleep, his mind not yet molested by the worries that plagued his waking hours, he got to his feet and went to his washbasin.

It was then that he noticed the envelope on the floor near the door.

He strode over and picked it up, tearing it open gently as he could, and began to read.

"I am sorry that I could not say goodbye. You might have convinced me to allow you to join in my mission, and I could not allow that to happen. Auranth needs you.

I will send news of the Gorok, if the rumors turn out to be true, and I will send a report regarding the Galeharbor Navy's location in any case.

I appreciate that you wish to protect me, and I assure you that my safety is in good hands, as you will surely find out at the breakfast table.

Thank you for caring for me, and please pray to the High One that I will succeed.

Tell Alder the same.

– Kessara"

He stared at the neat handwriting, the words losing more of their meaning the longer he stared. He knew that she had been planning to leave, but just as she predicted, he had hoped to get another chance to convince her to let him join her.

And then Aelrie showed up, and I half lost my mind.

He rubbed at his temples and opened the drawer of his night table, placing the letter inside. There was enough on his mind without thoughts of the elf. He would see her at breakfast, of course, and would likely have to explain once more that she was not the enemy, at least, not any more.

In any case, he was glad that Alder was far away in Umrym at the moment. He was certain that the Aridmoorian would rip his head off when he found out that he'd let the Princess get away under his nose, and he could hardly blame him. The last time that Kessara had gone off on her own, she had almost met with disaster of the worst kind. He could only hope that she had indeed taken proper security precautions.

Before he could wonder further about who it was that he would be getting answers from at the breakfast table, there was a knock at his door.

Standing there was a boy in too-big armor, his face flushed with excitement. He looked very young, too young to become a soldier, but Wes remembered that Alder had joined King Radagar Ursa's forces when he was only fourteen. At least this boy was a few years older than that. War would come, and they needed every man that they could find. Sentimentality about the innocence of childhood was a luxury they could not afford.

"There are dragons in the sky, approaching from the south!" he announced. "I was told to summon you to the courtyard immediately."

Just then, he heard a familiar voice sounding in his mind.

"We're home, Wes. We have my mother. And the High One has provided us with allies in our time of need."

15

Chapter Fifteen

CELESYRIA

The people of Auranth stood along the outside of the city walls, dozens of men, women, and children staring up at the sight above. Celesyria felt as though a great weight had been lifted. Not only had she been able to rescue her mother, she had found a place to belong, where she no longer had to hide in the shadows. The citizens had welcomed their new army, and now they cheered as three new dragons made their way toward the old forge.

"Are you alright?" she asked, watching as her mother drew up beside her. Her wounds still looked terrible, but thankfully, her wings had not been damaged and she had managed the long trip from Umrym without further incident. Still, Celesyria could see the exhaustion on her face. *Just a few moments more, and she'll be able to rest.*

Sharsi nodded and beat her wings a couple of times until she had gained a little height on her daughter.

"Lead the way."

Celesyria pulled up ahead. Jaconial and her betrothed, Nazzan, took up the rear. She stole a glance back at them as they reached the trees that stood near the south wall of the fortress. As usual, they were flying close together, and could imagine them speaking sweet words in their minds to one another.

She felt a surprising pang of jealousy as she forced herself to watch where she was going. Nazzan had been her second guard when she had been dragged to the mysterious meeting of dragons, elves, and dwarves deep in the caverns of Whitespire.

When Alder had returned from Skanden with not only her mother but Jaconial, she had been nervous. When she saw the third member of the party, she'd become angry. The two dragons had participated in her kidnapping, and even aside from that, as far as she knew, Jaconial had always hated her.

Now, as they had made their way back home to Auranth, they had come to an uneasy peace. Nazzan had been especially nice to her, seeming to possess few of Jaconial's more difficult personality traits, and she found it difficult to dislike him.

In fact, she found herself wondering why someone as prickly as Jaconial had found such a handsome mate while she had always been alone.

As she flew over the wall and circled over the courtyard, she forced those thoughts from her mind. She was thankful that the High One had softened the hearts of someone she found difficult, and Nazzan's service would also be useful. With time, she hoped that they would all become friends, just as she, Wes, Kessara, and Alder had. Celesyria refused to sully things by holding a grudge.

"*Alright, mother, you land first,*" she said, taking another wide circle around the top of the open courtyard. She did so, coming

162

to rest gently in an open grassy area near the barrack tents. The rest of them followed, making sure not to snag any claws on the tents that filled the space.

She could hardly believe how the place had changed. Before they left, it had been almost empty. Now, dozens of men and several women filed over the grass, talking to one another and ducking in and out of their canvas shelters.

A moment later, Wes emerged from the fortress door, rushing over to hug her as best as he could manage. Relief flooded her chest. Even though it was relatively safe here in Auranth, there had been no way to know for sure that her best friend was alright while she was gone.

In any case, she missed him. They had been through so much together, and she could no longer imagine a life where he was not her best friend.

"I'd like to introduce you to my mother, Sharsi," she said, gesturing to her older dragon with her snout. Already, Mella was directing three local herbwomen who were applying various salves and bandages to her wounds. *"Mother, this is Wes Cervos, Envoy of the Four Kingdoms."*

Her eyes were filled with suspicion as she looked him up and down, her gaze roving slowly over his beat-up clothes and unruly curls.

"The Envoy, and yet you're dressed like a vagrant! By the Dracodei, all children really are the same," she said aloud, shaking her head.

"Forgive me," Wes said, giving a half bow. "But it is an honor to meet you nonetheless."

Celesyria snorted. It seemed that her mother had perhaps changed less than she would have expected.

"Anyway, you are very ill, mother, and you had best go inside and rest," she said, speaking aloud for Mella's benefit. "I've made my nest in the main hall near the fire, but there's a private walled area on the far end that I thought would suit you and the others."

"I've already gathered up comfortable blankets for all of you," Mella said proudly, shooing the herbwomen away as she began to lead Sharsi in through the main door, which was only just big enough to accommodate her. "And it was no small feat, let me tell you."

When they had gone, Celesyria turned her attention to Wes. Bargren had already introduced himself to Nazzan and Jaconial and directed them to enter the main room through the more comfortable hole in the ceiling.

"Where's Alder?" Wes asked, looking around the tent-filled space.

"He probably went inside with the others, in search of Mella's cooking. He had to resort to eating squirrels for his last three meals," she said, grinning. "Where's Kessara?"

Before Wes could answer, a beautiful elf-woman came through the back gate, carrying a bouquet of pink flowers in her silvery hands.

The elf from the mountains, the one who became stuck amid the stones. It has to be.

"Aelrie!" he called to her, gesturing wildly with his hands. Celesyria thought he looked ridiculous, and she had spent enough time around him and Alder to know that when men began to act like fools around members of the opposite sex, trouble was never far off.

WES

Wes sat at what was now one of four long breakfast tables

next to Aelrie, feeling uneasy.

Alder had already demanded to know where Kessara was and who the elf was, and he'd only just managed to convince him that his questions would be answered after breakfast was finished.

Aelrie gave him a nervous glance as Alder sat back in his chair across the table, sipping at his mug of coffee, watching in silence.

Ever since the elf had arrived, the two of them had spent a lot of time deep in conversation, but he could sense that there were still secrets lingering beneath the surface, secrets that she was not ready to share with him or with anyone else. His instinct was to make demands of her, to find out what she hid, but he knew that it was foolish. He would have to allow her to open up when she was ready. There was no way to rush the process and maintain her trust.

Finally, most of the dishes were cleared away, and one by one, the soldiers who had been eating with them began to make their way back outside, attending to their own duties.

Celesyria, Nazzan, and Jaconial, who had been eating outside in the courtyard, stood as close to the table as they could. Wes had assumed that this would be a private meeting, but if Celesyria was choosing to trust their new associates, he was willing to follow her lead.

"So," Alder said, setting his empty mug down in front of him with a slight thump. "Where's Kessara?"

Wes glared at him, saying nothing.

After a long and rather awkward pause as Alder fiddled with the lip of his coffee mug, he finally extended a hand in Aelrie's direction.

"Forgive me. I said hello to Jaconial and Nazzan when they

arrived, but I suppose we haven't met properly. I'm Alder Cadogen, of Aridmoor. High Keep, to be more precise."

Aelrie smiled at him, though Wes noticed that her hand wavered a little as she gave it to Alder to shake. Alder, for his part, sounded almost nervous, though Wes couldn't tell if it was his distrust of the elf or the intoxicating effect of her beauty.

"I'm Aelrie. It's nice to meet you."

"Likewise. Did Wes tell you that you're actually the second elf we've met who has sought the High One?"

Relief flooded his chest. He should have mentioned the man they had helped to her earlier. It probably brought her comfort to know that she was not as alone as she thought.

"No. But I'm glad you seem willing to accept that even members of my race have a chance at finding favor with Him, however few of us are willing to try," Aelrie said.

Jaconial cleared her throat. "At least you have a soul, unlike us dragons."

"She's right," Celesyria added. "It seems that the High One is drawing the most unlikely creatures to Himself. Even those of us who do cannot hope for the promise of rest in the Eternal Lands."

Nazzan nodded in agreement. Wes wanted to remind Celesyria once again that the High One still loved all of His creatures and that she need not fear being sent to the Farplace when she died, but there were more pressing concerns at the moment. All he could do was be grateful that the High One seemed to be blessing their mission here in Auranth, just as he'd hoped He would.

"The High One calls upon who He will," Alder said, catching Wes' eye. The former Protectorate soldier knew this truth well. The High One had called on him from within his dreams, and against all probability, Alder had been willing to give up everything to follow His words.

Murmurs of approval filled the air, and Wes drew a long breath.

"Now that we've all met and eaten, there is another matter to discuss," he said, shooting Alder a warning glance. "Princess Kessara chose to flee Auranth early this morning, making for Galeharbor. I tried to convince her to wait for your return, or at least to allow me to go with–"

"Why?" Alder interrupted, leaning back in his chair so abruptly that it scraped against the stone. "What would possibly impel her toward such a foolish act?"

Wes did his best to recount what Kessara had heard about the Gorok, and explained that the King was apparently planning to offer his navy ships to the Red Army, who were amassing their numbers along the West Strait.

Jaconial and Nazzan shared a glance.

"We've heard talk of this monster, as well," Nazzan said. "Back in Umrym. Some of the dwarf traitors used to take boats out along the coast of the North Sea, spying and thieving and whatever else their elf masters demanded of them. But now, the rumor is that they've all been called back. I guess the elves believe the rumors."

"They would, I suppose," Aelrie said, her voice barely above a whisper. Everyone at the table turned to her. For a moment, she didn't continue. Wes could hear her beside him, breathing slowly, and drawing up his own courage, he placed his hand gently on her back.

"You can speak openly," he assured her. "No one will blame you for the actions of your people. But your knowledge of their ways is incredibly valuable to us."

She nodded. He hoped that he was right to trust the newcomers, but he saw no other choice. If they were going to ride these dragons into battle or on other missions, they were going to need to be a part of the new army's inner circle.

"The rumors are all true," she began, tapping her fingers silently on the wooden table in front of her as she spoke. "The Gorok is indeed the beast from the scary stories you all heard as children, with tentacles big enough to drag a merchant's ship down into the sea with ease. It has been dormant for hundreds of years now, perhaps longer. It has certainly not ascended from the deep in my lifetime."

Wes felt flustered for a moment, having forgotten that though Aelrie looked a year or two younger than he was, she was likely in reality at least as old as Celesyria.

"So why is it here now?" Celesyria asked.

"Because it has been summoned."

"Summoned by who?" Jaconial demanded, nearly shouting. Wes felt his own headache—which had been rather tolerable this morning—begin to intensify.

Nazzan pressed his snout against the side of Jaconial's head, no doubt mindspeaking to her and asking that she calm down.

"It obeys only one person. Meira Daeleth."

Aelrie's voice was no longer shaking.

There was a pause, followed by a cacophony as everyone at the table began to speak all at once. Wes could not think of anything to ask, his head was pounding so badly now that he could scarcely think at all.

"Everyone, please," Nazzan said, loud enough to make the remaining mugs and extra butter knives clatter against the wood. After everyone had gone quiet, he turned to face the elf, lowering his green snout so that his huge eyes met hers. "The Regent is still alive?"

Aelrie nodded, her face solemn.

Finally, it was quiet enough that Wes could gather his thoughts. The others seemed to be doing the same.

Meira Daeleth was Regent of the Elf-Queens, and had been ever since their exile to Nox, perhaps longer. The Queens themselves could not die, not with their dark magics, but they were not truly alive, either. They needed a Regent to handle the rule of Nox in their place.

During the Boneshire wars, however, a Guardian called Salazin was said to have sacrificed himself to kill her, leaving Nox in anarchy, ruled directly by the capricious magic of the Elf-Queens.

Apparently not. And now she's brought forth her horrible demon pet.

"It's fitting, in a way," Celesyria said aloud after several moments had passed. "We learn that one who can never be queen lives on, just as one who can never be king seeks to fulfill the prophecy of the thousand years. It seems that the High One's plans have unfolded rather poetically."

Jaconial snorted. "What in the Dracodei are you talking about?"

"Watch your tone," Alder snapped at her. Celesyria shrank back, saying nothing, as Nazzan prodded his betrothed with his snout once again.

"Forgive me," Jaconial said more gently. "I suppose we have missed a lot. I feel rather like I'm in over my head."

"I can imagine," Celesyria said. "I'm sure Wes felt that way when I ambushed him in the desert and declared to him that everything he thought he knew was a lie."

Wes smiled, and the dark cloud that seemed to hover over the table began to lift. He was thankful that Celesyria tended toward graciousness rather than grudges.

"You're certainly in good company," Alder added. "None of us were prepared for this."

"Which is why I firmly believe that the High One has chosen us," Celesyria said firmly. "All of us. But I do think it might help if Jaconial and Nazzan tell us a little more about why they have come."

The others nodded in agreement. Wes was glad that Aelrie was spared telling her own story for the moment, though he hoped there was more she could tell them about the Gorok and Meira Daeleth.

Nazzan spoke first. "Ever since we learned of the secret council that was meeting in Whitespire, we began to have our doubts, though it took a while for us to confess them to one another."

Jaconial nodded, continuing. "The Guardian commanders claim that we must remain true to our oath of protecting Kaveryth, and yet they and the dwarves are permitting elves to wander all over the mountains."

"Such a thing was unthinkable before, even well within my lifetime," Nazzan added.

"So why are they allowing it?" Alder asked. "And why did it take you so long to leave, if you knew that they were saying one thing and doing another? It seems that all of the Guardians must realize by now that something is wrong."

"It's not so simple," Jaconial snapped. This time, Nazzan did not seek to calm her, so far as Wes could tell, and he could hardly blame her for her reaction. Tact was not one of Alder's virtues.

"We did question the orders," Nazzan said mildly. "But when our commanders ignored our concern, we assumed that we had to be wrong somehow. The oath compels us to fight the elves only if they attack us, and though their behavior is threatening, it has not been violent. At least, not in a direct way that everyone could see."

"Anyway," Jaconial continued. "It was not as though we knew what was going on in every inch of Umrym. We were trying to continue as we always had, serving the Dracodei. Everyone else around us was doing the same thing. You must understand."

Wes glanced at Alder, who folded his arms over his chest and said nothing, though some of the hardness seemed to have gone out of his expression.

"Most in Umrym are not trying to do evil. They are caught up in their own sufferings, especially since the Envoy decided to abandon the sacrifices," Jaconial said, shaking her head. "I understand why you did it, but it has negatively impacted my race and the race of the dwarves. The Septemvirate has continued to collect treasures, but the people are not going above the minimal requirement, knowing that their hard-earned coins are not going to be properly brought into the sacred cave."

Wes narrowed his eyes, and though he could understand intellectually what she meant, his sympathy for the Guardians was hardly improved.

Perhaps a system built on extracting unearned wealth from others deserves to fail.

"You must understand," Nazzan repeated. "If even the mock sacrifices were to cease entirely, we would struggle to feed ourselves. Our economy relies upon the treasures of the

Four Kingdoms. None of us realized just how much until now. We trusted that our leaders had things under control, but it was all an illusion. So yes, Alder Cadogen, we were cowards to continue to follow orders, but we had our reasons."

"I can understand that very well," Aelrie said, her voice reminding Wes of the windchimes that his mother used to hang over the back door that led to her favorite garden.

For some reason, probably not an entirely fair one, sympathy for the elf came much more easily.

"So why did you change your minds?" Wes asked.

"Initially, before the cave-in in Whitespire, we had planned to join King Ursa's Red Army," Nazzan said. "According to relatively reliable gossip, Elder Dorold was speaking with a few of our most esteemed commanders before he was killed. Supposedly he had been sent by the King and charged with bringing some of the Guardians into his unified force, in preparation for a violent attack by the elves."

Wes felt the ache behind his eyes beginning to intensify again as he tried to untangle this latest development. He didn't trust Kylan Ursa as a rule, and certainly not Elder Dorold, but if this gossip was true, it seemed that they were not on the side of the elves, at least.

He caught Alder's eye, and the former soldier nodded his unspoken agreement.

Wes thought of Elder Bram and Oria's urgent request that he meet with the new head of the Septemvirate, wishing that he had perhaps done so when he had the chance. Elder Bram would likely be able to shed more light on what Elder Dorold had been planning before he died, and certainly he would understand what the Septemvirate's connection with the Red Army was.

172

Do they intend for the Septemvirate to retain any power at all? Or will all control fall to Kylan?

"I suppose it makes sense," Celesyria said at last. "King Ursa has a lot of men, but without dragons they would be at a strong disadvantage when fighting elves."

"Especially if they have more Gorok-like pets to attack us with," Alder said dryly.

"Oh don't worry, they do," Aelrie said. Her voice was grave, but Wes could see the laughter in her eyes, and it made him smile.

Perhaps in time she and Alder would get along just fine.

"So why did you turn to Alder instead of to the Red Army soldiers?" he asked Jaconial.

"Before Whitespire was destroyed we... heard of something terrible that took place nearby," she said, stealing a glance over at Nazzan. "We realized then that even if King Ursa gained control of the entire continent and expelled the elves, he wouldn't put a stop to it. It is clear that he cares about power above all else. Everything else is negotiable. When I saw Alder—a human—in Skanden, and realized he was looking for Sharsi, it was obvious that he had to be with Celesyria. I decided that this was our sign, that it was time to fight alongside someone who would no longer tolerate the rot and evil that fills Kaveryth."

"Even if it meant becoming my ally? You must have seen something truly terrible," Celesyria said, her voice teasing. Nazzan chuckled, and even Jaconial cracked a sharp-toothed grin.

Wes wondered about what the terrible thing was, but did not wish to ask. Like Aelrie, he was sure they had reasons for their silence. At the very least, he couldn't blame them for not wanting to speak of some dark foulness in the cheerful morning light.

In any case, it's not like I don't have my own secrets.

He rubbed his fingers against his temples, awaiting the next wave of pain that always came sooner or later. A time would come when he would have to tell them about the headaches, and would have to grapple with what they might mean, but he was not ready yet.

A moment later, they all turned their heads to look as the heavy front door swung open.

Three teenage soldiers came rushing in.

"Excuse us," the oldest one said, giving Wes a half-bow and walking over to the table. "There is a company of dwarves approaching on foot. They told the Auranthian city guards that they were looking for whoever was in charge of the new army."

Alarmed, Wes stood, bumping his knee into the table and setting the remaining coffee mugs to rattling.

"Sir," the boy said, chuckling. "There's no need to hurry. They're here because they wish to enlist."

16

Chapter Sixteen

DROHMA

Captain Drohma followed at the King's heels, narrowly dodging a tree branch that stretched out across the hallway. He glanced down at the floor in disgust, watching as King Ursa's boots trampled upon dead leaves, dirt, and even a few live bugs. He had never seen Stronghollow Palace in such disarray, but the King did not seem concerned.

"I'm receiving new reports every day about the situation in Auranth," he said, quickening his stride as they moved closer to the outer area of the palace. He could hear the crowds already, even through the walls. He had to make him listen.

"Yes, I know," the King replied, not slowing his pace. His red cape whipped behind him as he took a turn down a side corridor, and Drohma struggled to keep up.

"The Envoy is there. The dragon, too, and several other traitors."

"I'm aware of it, Captain," the King said mildly.

So why am I still standing around here stepping on beetle shells!

Drohma cleared his throat, suppressing the urge to tell his superior that he was acting like a complete bonehead.

"My King, are we going to send a company to capture them?"

"No."

Drohma placed his hands in his pockets and balled them into fists until he felt his fingernails biting into his palms.

"May I ask why, my King?"

"Because the Septemvirate has effectively been destroyed. Elder Jate is up in Vaevar, where he will probably remain hidden until he's dragged out, and Elder Bram scarcely leaves his study. I'll be lucky to be able to drag him out to oversee the autumn Feast."

Drohma opened his mouth to speak, but King Ursa pressed on.

"Silverfell is falling apart. The people are restless. Now that the Septemvirate is no longer a real concern, I will be able to take control of it. Of my new Kingdom," he said, turning back to glance at Drohma, a grim smile on his lips.

"I see," he replied, though he still thought that Wes Cervos and the others needed to end up in prison, whatever else the King had planned.

"The last thing I wish to do is to split my forces. Our intelligence is limited by the fact of distance. It's difficult to ascertain how many allies the Envoy has amassed at any point in time, and it may take a large effort on our part to secure their fortress."

"But what will you do if their army continues to grow?" Drohma asked, shaking his head. However difficult it would be to rout them now, surely it would only become more difficult with time. "If I may give my own opinion, my King, wouldn't it be better to defeat the House of Cervos for good while we have the chance?"

"Captain Drohma," King Ursa said, stopping short and turning to face him. Even though Drohma was the taller of the two men, he couldn't help but find the King intimidating. His face was handsome, but there was no softness to his features. Every line was hard and serious, somehow, like he had been hewn from stone.

He forced himself not to fidget under the King's gaze.

"I assure you that I have thought this through, Captain."

"Forgive me, my King," Drohma stammered. "I know you are not a man who leaves decisions to whim or chance."

The Envoy and that dragon will never face justice. Can he not see that so long as Wes Cervos lives, his power will always be at risk of being lost? If not now, then another day, when he finds a woman to make queen?

They reached the door that led to the courtyard. As soon as the King pushed it open, the swelling sound of the furious crowd assaulted Drohma's ears.

"I do appreciate your concern," the King said, pausing to look back at him once more. "But my objective is to rule, not to indulge in petty vengeances."

"Of course, my King," he replied, giving him a tight smile as he followed him out toward the courtyard. "Such is a wise way to lead."

Though the weather was mild, the entire courtyard looked as though winter had already swept through it. The huge potted trees, once the pride of the city, had been burned by the mob, their leaves gone and their trunks blackened. If he looked carefully at the ground below, he could see bloodstains where the crowd had turned on one another, or where soldiers had used severe force. He could see dozens of their guards from where he stood, stationed here day and night lest the crowds breach the palace itself.

The people continued to scream and to throw rocks and other detritus toward the King, and Captain Drohma exchanged glances with one of the Protectorate guards standing nearby. The man shook his head. He was certain his fellow soldiers had advised the King not to stand so near to the crowds, but clearly he had not wished to listen.

He wishes to show them that he is not afraid, and will not cater to their tantrums.

At the moment, he could not decide if it was noble or stupid. He settled on both.

"My dear citizens," the King said, nearly shouting to be heard. Much of the crowd went quiet, most likely curious as to what he would say, but Drohma noticed many rocks still clasped carefully in beefy hands.

"Will the autumn sacrifice be canceled?" a woman screamed from near the front, two soldiers raising their swords at her in warning.

The crowd began to shout again, but the King held up an arm for silence, and the people mostly obeyed.

"I know that you all have been through a great deal as of late. I wish to assure you that under the leadership of Elder Bram, the Feast of Offering will take place as planned."

"Will you even have time to gather the treasures?" a man's voice asked from somewhere in the press of bodies.

"None of us could have anticipated the tragic assassinations of our dear Elders, but I assure you that your treasures will be brought to the great spire in time."

178

Cheering and heckling blended together into an ugly sound that reminded Drohma of barking dogs.

"You are correct to assume that gathering the treasures will be difficult this season," the King continued, smiling at the crowd. "We wish to ask for the help of volunteers. Men and women will be needed for various tasks. Please speak to a Red Army soldier as soon as possible, if you are able to offer assistance. Time is short."

The crowd continued to shout and to cheer, but he did not say another word, turning on his heel and heading back toward the palace. Captain Drohma followed behind him, his feelings as mixed as those of the crowd.

KESSARA

The North Sea was perfectly calm. There was no wind to cause ripples in the water, and the full moon cast a gentle sheen upon its surface. But there was not a single boat to be seen.

The grassy plain that rested before it was yellow and dead, most of it eaten by the swarm of late summer insects.

The winter snow will bring healing, and by spring it will be green again. Nature is resilient. If only it were as natural for us humans to rise from our despair.

Kessara pressed her fingertips against the railing of her bedroom balcony, wishing that she could collapse into bed. The journey to reach Windshear had been long and exhausting, even with the pleasant company of Bargren's sons. Worse, they had passed through a good portion of her Kingdom, and riding past the insect-ravaged farmland had made her heart ache for her people. If Galeharbor could not produce its own food, it was a certainty that her father would have to do

179

whatever King Ursa demanded.

She turned aside from the balcony and entered her bedchamber, rushing over to the dressing cabinet and finding a clean dress more suitable for a princess than a peasant. There would be no rest yet.

A couple of minutes later, she heard a knock, and her mother's voice calling from behind her door. She opened it to find both the King and Queen, who embraced her in a nearly suffocating hug.

"You nearly broke our hearts when you ran away like that," her mother scolded, patting at the back of her blonde hair.

"You didn't need to leave a note, Kessara," her father said, his voice hard. "You should have spoken to us directly and told us what you were planning. You could have been killed."

He said more, but she scarcely heard him as she rested in her mother's comforting arms. No matter how old she got, there was nothing quite like the consolation of a mother's touch to calm her troubled heart.

I could not have told you I was going with Alder. You'd have locked me up.

She did not dare say any such thing, however. The deed was done, and she would offer no apologies.

They all sat down in her parlor, and she caught them up on recent events as best she could, leaving out her attack in High Keep. Her parents shared their own news. Most of it was depressing, but at least their people were holding on, and she was thankful to have a home to return to that had not met the fate of Stronghollow palace.

"Kessara," her father said finally, his voice serious. She shared a glance with her mother, who only shook her head. "I know that we have spoken before about this matter, but I have commanded our navy to head to the West Strait to guard against an elven invasion."

She knew that the words were coming, but they still hit her like a blow to the stomach.

"Even the men who rely completely on sailing to feed their wives and children will not venture into the North Sea," she said, trying to keep the shaking out of her voice. "Not only have the insects returned, but now another food source has been decimated. Father, you are mad if you do this! We must deal with this threat at our own shore."

"Don't speak to your father that way," her mother said softly, placing a hand on her wrist. Kessara clenched her fists, willing herself not to lash out further, but her father waved a hand at his wife.

"It's alright, Jinna. This is politics," he said, giving them a grim smile. "I care for your opinion, Kessara, but I have been ruling this Kingdom for a very long time. Our soldiers will go to the West Strait, do what must be done, and then return. If this Gorok nonsense turns out to be real, it will be dealt with when time and manpower permits it."

"And what if they are too late?" she asked, ignoring her mother's warning glance as she raised her voice. "If they leave, and the Gorok rises from the sea, we will be defenseless. Entire ports and coastal villages will be thrown into the waters. Thousands of innocent people will die. And in the meantime and perhaps a while after, people will starve."

Before her father could argue, her mother cut in.

"Errol, I think that perhaps we should evacuate the villages, at least, in case Kessara is right. Just until our navy can return."

The King did not hesitate.

"Done."

"It isn't enough," Kessara said, wishing that she could stomp her feet against the ground like a child. "Even if the people are safe, assuming that the Gorok does not go for an early strike, the loss of fish from the sea is intolerable now that the insects have destroyed the land crop."

"I am seeking to compromise. I do so out of respect for both of you–" her father nodded at her and her mother "–but I have not forgotten that no evidence of this monster has been presented other than the fearful tales of fishermen and ancient legends of a great beast."

Kessara sucked in a breath, trying to calm her nerves.

"Why are you so determined to give our navy, the pride of this Kingdom, to Kylan Ursa?" she said.

Anger flashed across her father's face.

"Because we have no choice! You've seen the fields, and it's exactly as you say. We desperately need to be able to purchase food from Aridmoor and Silverfell."

"If we could still catch fish, we would not be so desperate," she pointed out, trying to stop herself from raising her voice to match his.

"That's not the only concern," he snapped, pacing back and forth against the far wall. Her mother said nothing, watching the proceedings with a look of bored neutrality, a practiced expression that Kessara often employed herself.

At the moment, it infuriated her.

"If we refuse to offer our men to the Red Army, King Ursa has warned me that he will be forced to withdraw protection. They are not like the Guardians. No oath binds these men. If bandits attack again, or—Dracodei forbid—elves, it won't be just the coast that we have to worry about. Our entire Kingdom will face the possibility of destruction."

No one said anything else for a long breath, the sound of her father's yelling still ringing in her ears. Finally, her mother turned to her, knitting her brows over her softly lined face.

"Your father is right. We don't have enough men to protect our people."

"So the solution is to give them all to King Ursa? We can't trust him!"

"Diplomacy is not about trust," King Manta said, shaking his head. "Diplomacy is about power."

"Is that really what you believe?" Kessara asked, incredulous.

"It's what King Kylan Ursa believes," her father snapped. "I don't have the luxury of naive idealism. I must work with what we have."

Kessara laid back in her chair, playing with the soft blue velvet with the tips of her fingers. She wished that she had a greater trust in the High One's power. It was difficult, especially when it seemed He was not listening. After all, He had permitted these evils to infect His creation. Perhaps He was fulfilling the thousand year prophecy, but in the meantime, she, too, could only work with what she had.

"It is not just the power of King Ursa you must consider, Errol," her mother said finally. "The elves are wiser than he is. What if they are trying to bring all of the forces of Kaveryth to the West Strait so that they can be more easily destroyed?"

"That may well be. But if there is a better course of action that I have not yet thought of, I'm open to hearing it," her father said, getting up from his chair.

He paused for effect, and Kessara glanced at her mother, who gave her head an almost imperceptible shake.

"Every choice a King makes is an acceptance of risk. My orders will stand."

Kessara watched as her parents left her chambers, trying to contain the anger that threatened to boil over. Raving at her father, the High One, or anyone else would not do any good. Instead, she reached into the drawer of a nearby desk and found a paper and pen.

Trying to stop her hands from shaking, she began to write, trying to be clear as well as brief.

A few minutes later her letter was complete, and she ducked into the hall to call for a servant.

"Please set aside your tasks and ask Viggo and Vard to meet me in my chambers," she said to the young girl who arrived carrying a large basket of dirty sheets. "They're two Auranthians. You'll find them in the guests' quarters."

"Straight away, my Princess," the girl said, dropping the washing and taking off at a near run. Kessara stood there in the hall for several moments, leaning against the molded ivory wall, deep in thought. Bargren's sons would be faster to return to Auranth without her slowing them down, but would the strength of the horses hold out?

She felt a knot of anxiety forming in the pit of her stomach. Pulling her friends from Auranth would leave it weakened, she knew, even with Bargren, Mella, and the other soldiers staying behind.

If only the Guardians still roamed the skies. Things would be so different.

She could not deal in what-ifs and fantasies, she knew. Her father was right. Every choice that she made had a cost. She could only pray to the High One that she was making the correct one.

17

Chapter Seventeen

ALDER

"Spread your legs out, Glokken!" Alder shouted at a tan-skinned boy, gesturing with his wooden practice sword.

The boy was not quick enough to obey, and his opponent–a younger Aridmoorian boy whose name Alder had forgotten at the moment–shoved him in the chest and sent him sprawling to the ground. Before Glokken could register what had happened, the wooden sword was pressed against the front of his neck.

"Match!" a loud female voice called out, and Alder turned to see Celesyria standing near the makeshift practice field that lay just outside the courtyard wall.

"Good fight, men," he said, extending a hand to help Glokken to his feet and clapping the younger one on the shoulder. "Work on the stances that I showed you for next time."

They were not men at all, of course, but he didn't want them to be reminded of their boyhood. They could not afford to doubt their purpose, especially on the battlefield. Any lack of confidence, any weakness they perceived within themselves, could lead to disaster. Alder sought to teach them confidence along with humility, which was a difficult line to walk, and one he himself had hardly mastered.

The boys scurried off toward the courtyard gate, no doubt hoping to grab a snack from Mella's kitchen, and he went to sit near Celesyria as the next group of fighters moved into the field. This time, Wes was among them, standing on his own and practicing stances with his favorite curved sword.

"I'm glad he's working on his skills," Alder said, settling down in the dry grass and leaning against the dragon's flank. "He's actually not as bad as he thinks he is."

"No. More confidence would do wonders for him," Celesyria agreed. Alder was glad that she had chosen to speak aloud. Though he was getting better at listening to her in his mind, it was still very tiring compared to just having a normal conversation.

They sat in companionable silence for a few minutes as one of the other soldiers, a man in his thirties who Alder recognized from the nearest butcher shop, coaxed Wes into a sparring match with him. The sounds of clashing wood filled the air as they fought, but Alder was no longer watching them.

Along the side of the field, near the tall courtyard wall, he could see Aelrie speaking with a group of several soldiers in their new practice tunics. She held her elf-made bow in her hand, the lower limb resting against the grass. She looked more animated than he had ever seen her, and he hoped that she was educating the men on elven battle tactics as she had promised.

She'd already been dedicating several hours each day to teaching basic archery to the men, many of whom had never held a bow before, and he appreciated her assistance. If the men could become even novice archers, it would help a great deal. Still, he could not help but to feel a certain level of worry about her presence, and the fact made him feel guilty.

"Do you trust her?" he asked Celesyria, keeping his voice low, although he doubted anyone could hear them over the clacking sound of the practice swords.

"Wes does," Celesyria said. "That's enough for me."

He wished that he shared her confidence. He held Wes' opinion in high regard, but still, Aelrie was an elf. He wanted to believe that she earnestly sought the High One and wished to stand with the forces of good, but the reality was that none of them knew her well. She could be a spy, or something worse.

He felt a shudder ripple through him at the thought of the attack in Stronghollow that that left several of the Elders dead. It would not be difficult for Aelrie to do the same thing here.

He voiced these concerns to Celesyria, but she shook her head. "I think you're paranoid, but I suppose I can't blame you. Everyone is on edge right now. The autumn Feast is approaching."

He didn't need to be reminded. He could tell that many of the soldiers had been acting strange, especially those who had not yet shown interest in being taught about the High One. They were likely here because they believed King Ursa to be corrupt, or because they needed financial security for their families, and not because they believed in the broader cause of fighting to restore worship to the High One.

He himself was on edge because Kessara had not yet returned safely, but he doubted that the other soldiers paid that fact very much attention.

"I think many of them are still true believers in the Dracodei," Alder admitted. He did not enjoy saying such things aloud, but for the moment, it seemed to be true. He could only hope that with time they would see the truth. "They're unsure if they're fighting for the correct side. They must feel that their loyalty to their gods is in conflict with what they believe is best for their people."

Celesyria nodded. "I can empathize with them. It's a hard choice. Do they follow King Ursa, who will leave their worship alone but seeks power over every inch of Kaveryth? Or do they follow Wes, who is forbidden from taking power himself and only wants to restore a balance to their land?"

"And if they follow Wes and we are successful, they know that eventually, the Dracodei will cease to be worshiped," he added.

"Exactly."

He watched for a moment as one of the smallest boys he had been training managed to win his match. He felt pride bubbling up in his chest and he cheered from where he sat, not caring if he looked foolish. He'd never imagined that he would enjoy working with the younger trainees. When he was in the army, the task of working with new recruits was seen almost as a punishment. But here, things were different. Or perhaps he himself had changed.

They were making real progress, one soldier at a time, and he was thankful to be such a central part of it.

They watched for several more minutes as one of the other boys sparred with Wes in hand-to-hand combat, followed by Aelrie matching up with three other soldiers and beating them easily. Finally, she and Wes strolled over to where Alder and Celesyria sat, collapsing on the grass nearby and drinking greedily from their waterskins.

The sun was finally hidden behind a cloud, but the day was still hot, and Alder was happy that he had remained in only a coaching role for most of the afternoon.

"Good work," Alder said, hoping to ask Aelrie for a one-on-one sword match later that evening once the sun had begun to set. At least if she turned on him then, he'd already have a sword in his hand, and he wanted to see how his training would fare against her inborn abilities.

"Bargren's youngest son told me to tell you all to stop in to see him before dinner," Aelrie said, tightening the cap on her waterskin and setting it in the grass. "It's about Kessara."

Alder jabbed Celesyria with his elbow as he got to his feet. "And you're just telling me this now?"

Wes swallowed a gulp of water, raising a hand. "He just told us."

Alder stalked off toward the gate without another word, only just restraining himself from breaking into a run. He could no longer think of sparring, dinner, nor the success of his trainees. He had to know if Kessara was alright.

A few minutes later, he burst into Bargren's makeshift office near the main bedroom hallway and slammed the door behind him. His friends may have been following, but for the moment, he didn't care.

Bargren dropped several of the papers he had been holding onto his desk. "Alder," he said, fumbling to put the documents back into order. "A-are you alright? You startled me."

"Kessara. Is she alive?" he demanded, placing his hands on the wooden desk and leaning forward until his face was inches away from Bargren's.

"By the Dracodei, boy, she's fine!" the weaponmaker nearly shouted, thumping his fists against his desk and letting out a

189

string of expletives.

Alder had no interest in apologizing. He shrugged. "I was told you had something to tell us. Where is she? Has she been injured?"

"She's in Windshear, just as we expected," Bargren said, saying each word with deliberate slowness. "Her letter made no mention of any harm."

Before Alder could demand to see it, Bargren reached into a drawer and pulled out a thin white envelope with "Please entrust to Bargren or Mella" written on it in regal handwriting that he recognized immediately.

He opened the flap with fumbling hands and read.

A few moments later, with a quick apology to Bargren, he emerged from the office and found his friends waiting in the main hall.

"Kessara believes that the Gorok is going to attack, and she has asked that we make our way to Windshear immediately," he said, thrusting the letter into Wes' hands.

As the others began to bicker and to plan amongst themselves, Alder strode toward the large fire pit and sank into a nearby chair, suddenly exhausted.

High One, please take care of Kessara until we can get there. Please keep her safe.

He didn't care what the rest of his friends did. He would be setting out just as soon as he caught his breath, even if he had to go alone.

Finally, he began to understand why she had been so angry with him. She was right. He was selfish. He did care about himself more than he cared about her, much of the time.

But now, he felt something different.

He felt no jealousy, no rage.

Even if he was killed on the way to Galeharbor, he did not care if Wes or anyone else took his place.

He just needed her to be okay.

WES

Wes was tucking a pair of trousers into his pack, noticing too late that they were his least favorite pair, when there was a knock at the door of his bedroom. He moved to answer it, expecting Alder, or perhaps Bargren. When he opened the door and saw Aelrie standing there, tucking a lock of her raven black hair behind a pointy silver ear, he felt a rush of embarrassment.

As usual, his bed was unmade and pieces of clothing were scattered across the floor.

Even back home in Stronghollow palace, he'd always been a bit messy, but it was much easier to conceal when he had servants to assist him.

Of course, back in Stronghollow and even here in Auranth, manners typically dictated that men and women seek to avoid such unnecessary intimacies in the first place. Elves, it seemed, had a different understanding of propriety, but he did not wish to make her feel uncomfortable by mentioning it.

"Aelrie," he said, staring at her, one hand pressed against the doorframe.

She knows her own name, you dolt.

"Er, come in," he added, backing aside so that she could pass through.

"Forgive me for intruding like this," she said, standing there near the door, twisting her fingers together and not quite meeting his eyes.

"You're not," he said firmly, making a half-hearted attempt to straighten his quilt so that they could both sit on the bed. "You can sit," he added, gesturing toward a clear space that

191

was a safe distance from where he himself sat.

"Thank you," she said, giving him a small smile. As usual, it was enough to turn his insides into Mella's homemade blackberry jelly.

For a moment, neither of them said anything, and it was Wes' turn to fiddle stupidly with his hands.

"This is a nice room," Aelrie said finally, glancing around at the mess. Wes refrained from letting out a snort.

"It's a disaster," he said, chuckling.

She shrugged. "We're leaving. The only reason my room isn't a mess is because I've already packed everything I own."

"Mine was messy long before we decided to go to Galeharbor," he admitted, kicking at a small pile of dirty socks that lay just under the edge of the bed.

"Fair enough," she said. "But I still like this room. It feels like the kind of place where you can rest and read a book and forget about the chaos outside."

He considered this. It was by far the nicest room in the fortress, and the fact that Bargren and Mella had insisted it be given to him was a constant source of personal discomfort.

All his life, he had defined himself not only by his role as Envoy, but by the role he could not take. Until the day that they were killed, he'd watched his father rule as King of Silverfell, and his elder brother preparing to take up the role in his place one day. It was a role that never would be his, whether he wanted it or not.

And yet, here he was, the closest thing that these people had to a king.

He had managed to escape the burdens of being Envoy of the Four Kingdoms, only to have new responsibilities thrust in his direction. He was more certain now than ever before that he had no desire whatsoever to be the leader of any sort of movement, and yet, it did not seem that he had much of a choice.

The master bedroom, and all of the duties that came with it, was his whether he wished for it or not.

"What was your home like, back in Nox?" he said after a while, clearing his throat to break the silence. In truth, he was curious. Most of his knowledge of the elves had come from his schooling, and he suspected much of what he had been told was nonsense.

"There will be time to tell you all about it later," she said. He tried to ignore the feeling of disappointment that crept over him.

She smiled at him as she spoke, and it was as pretty and otherworldly as ever, but he could see that she was sad.

"I hope you get the chance," he said, before he could think about how morbid it sounded.

"Are you afraid? Of the Gorok?"

"Absolutely," Wes said, smiling at her, glad for an opportunity to lighten the mood. "I think I speak for most of us in saying so. Alder is probably the sole exception, and I'm not sure that's a compliment. He's been moping around here for too long and I'm sure he's itching to use his real sword rather than a wooden one. If he can unleash his fury on a sea monster rather than a human being, so much the better."

"I've met many fearless men in my life," Aelrie said, shifting her weight slightly. "But I have only met a few truly courageous ones."

Wes felt his breath catch in his chest as he realized he was sitting a couple of inches closer to her than he had been before. He shifted back slightly toward the headboard, hoping she would somehow miss his nervous scrabbling despite her superior elven senses.

"I'm sure there is little that elf-men fear."

"Which is exactly why they don't impress me," she said, giving him a half smile. "It's easy not to be afraid when you know you're going to be able to overcome the things that step in front of you. It's a lot harder when you have something to lose."

Wes pondered this, but before he could say anything, she continued, speaking more quickly than usual.

"I guess what I'm trying to say," she said, tripping over a few of the words. "Is that I really admire you for what you have done here in Auranth. I think you are one of the truly courageous ones, in a way that Alder cannot compare to."

He felt heat rising to his cheeks again, and he knew he was powerless to stop it, so he tried to smile in spite of his embarrassment. "Thank you. It means a lot to me that you would think so," he managed.

"You're welcome," she smiled back.

For a moment, Wes thought about telling her about the headaches, about how heavy his limbs often felt, about all of the things he had been hiding from his other friends. How could he let her go on thinking that he was brave when he was keeping such secrets?

Before he could work up the courage, the moment passed.

Aelrie spoke again, and this time, her expression was grave.

"For what it's worth, I'm afraid, too," she said, her voice small.

"Why?"

"The Gorok is not merely a natural creature. It's something worse, something dark and full of hate," she said, worry lines crossing her pale gray forehead. "I have no idea what will happen if I get close to it. It's possible that Meira and the Elf-Queens will know that I am there, fighting against them."

Wes felt a chill ripple through him.

"If going near the beast will be a risk to you, you should stay here, where you can be safe from the darkness."

Aelrie shook her head. "I fear that you will need my help to defeat him."

"We have three dragons," he pointed out.

"But they do not understand this enemy as I do. No. I will come with you to the shores of Galeharbor."

Her words left little room for doubt. Wes caught her gaze, and he could see that there was a fire within her eyes, a determination that he would be foolish to try and break.

"Besides," she said after a moment, her voice lowering to a near whisper as she gave him a gentle smile. "I'll feel the safest being near you."

Wes did not dare to speak.

His heart was racing now, and all of a sudden he was even more aware of the short distance between his fingertips and hers.

"I can't run from the evil of my race," she continued. "I need to face them. But I know that I will be stronger if I can draw upon your courage."

He tried to smile back at her, but he was sure it came out as an awkward grimace. He couldn't seem to figure out how to position his mouth properly.

He got up from the bed, guiding her out of the room on the pretense that they both needed a good dinner before they left in the morning.

She went on ahead down the narrow hall, and he took a

moment to catch his breath, watching her go, her silky black hair falling in a single braid to the small of her back.

I can't feel like this, not about her.

It is forbidden.

It is unthinkable.

18

Chapter Eighteen

CELESYRIA

The glow of the setting sun stung at the dragon's eyes as she flew toward the gleaming white city of Windshear. In the distance, she could see the rippling mirror of the North Sea, orange and pink and gleaming beneath the changing light.

Everything else was ugly and gray and dead, every bit of greenery eaten by the swarms of insects that had visited not long before.

The surrounding desolation made the beauty of the capital city seem almost obscene.

"Just in time for supper," Alder shouted from Nazzan's back, several feet to her left.

"Sounds lovely," Aelrie added from her other side as Jaconial rolled slightly to the right, avoiding a particularly rough stream of air that buffeted her a moment before.

"If I can hold anything down," Wes called from her back, clinging tightly to the crest of her neck along with the saddle straps as she followed Jaconial's tilting path.

Celesyria tried to suppress a grin. Wes had hated to fly from the very moment he'd first tried it, and she'd once held onto hope that he would learn to love it with time. That day did not seem to be coming anytime soon.

Even she was growing tired of it now, after so many days and nights spent in the air, crossing the vast distance from the very north of Kaveryth all the way to Galeharbor in the east. The journey had been pleasant enough—no longer did she fear being spotted from the ground, especially with two other dragons accompanying her—but worry about what they might find at the end of it had kept everyone on edge.

"Look!" Nazzan shouted. Celesyria glanced at his back and saw Alder pointing toward a group of three soldiers in Galeharbor blue that were coming into view at the base of the city walls. They held two huge flags aloft, the blue points fluttering toward the east, where Celesyria knew that the palace lay.

"They're expecting us," she said, relieved. Even without a messenger, Kessara had known that they would answer her call for aid.

They flew lower, and Alder gave the men a salute as they passed over the top of the city wall. Below them, the white buildings seemed to glow from within, the fading sunlight glistening upon the intricately carved buildings. It would be even more beautiful beneath the moonlight.

"This place is incredible," Jaconial said, sounding more pleased than Celesyria had ever seen her. "Look at the little shells and anchors carved into the top of that building!"

Nazzan agreed, declaring that he wished they had time to circle over the place a few more times to get a good look at everything.

"It's a lot prettier without Blackmasks swarming all over it," Wes pointed out within her mind. She had to agree.

The last time that she, Alder, and Wes had been here, the city had been under attack. Many had died, and civilians had been taken into slavery. She still planned to help the captives somehow, if she could. The thought of them suffering somewhere in Boneshire—or worse, in Nox—was almost too much to bear. For the moment, however, her immediate duties were all that she could manage.

As they drew closer, they saw another group of soldiers bearing the big blue flags. This time, they seemed to be gesturing toward a large courtyard that stood at the northern edge of the palace. With another salute from Alder, they flew over the short wall and circled low. From what she could see, the paved area looked only just big enough to accommodate the three dragons.

"Let's land," Celesyria said to the others, taking a final pass above the walls before landing, touching down first on the smooth white stones.

The others followed suit, and she took a moment to get her bearings. The facade of the huge palace of the House of Manta lay to one side, and in front of it stood a group of six soldiers in blue uniforms. Directly across from them, near where Jaconial stood with Aelrie still sitting in the saddle on her back, there were at least twice as many Red Army men.

She swallowed the fear that seized her throat. They would not dare touch them. They were here under the Princess's orders.

At least, she hoped that they wouldn't.

"Please wait," one of the Galeharbor guards said, gesturing toward the large metal grate that rested over the palace door.

"I wasn't planning on breaking in," Celesyria heard Jaconial mutter under her breath.

They waited for what felt like a very long time. Wes, Alder, and Aelrie climbed out of their saddles and got to the ground, stretching their stiff legs and pacing between the two rows of soldiers. Nazzan and Jaconial laid down on the stone, curling up next to one another, no doubt engaged in a conversation that no one else could hear.

Finally, as the final rays of sunlight dipped below the walls, casting the courtyard in dusky shadows, they watched as the door's gate rose away. Alder rushed forward as the palace door opened, but to his surprise, it was not Kessara who appeared to meet him.

"Cadogen," King Manta grumbled as Alder nearly plowed into him, raising one eyebrow and stepping past with a curt nod.

"My King," Wes said, bowing low as the King reached him. Celesyria could see the resemblance to Kessara in his deeply tanned skin and graying blonde hair, but that was all. He walked with a slightly off-kilter gait that made her wonder about just how many years he had spent striding along the tilting deck of a ship.

"My King," she echoed, and the other dragons followed suit as he went to greet each one in turn. When he reached Aelrie, he paused, looking her up and down as though he had never seen an elf so close before.

Perhaps he hasn't. Not a living one, anyway.

"Where is Kessara?" Alder asked, his usual deep pitch rising to a near squeak. "My King," he added quickly as the old sailor glared at him.

"The Princess is safe inside the palace," he said, scratching behind one ear. "She begged me to ask Captain Drohma and his men to permit you safe passage here, and to leave you unmolested once you arrived. I agreed."

Celesyria saw Alder tightening his fists, his knuckles going white, but for once he was wise enough to keep his mouth shut. She knew that her friend had a low opinion of his former Captain in the Protectorate, and she, Wes, and Kessara shared his distaste. She was certain that Drohma would be most eager to imprison them all, especially Alder, who he saw as a traitor of the worst kind.

"Now, if you and the Envoy would please follow me, we have certain matters to discuss," the King said, nodding to Alder and Wes before turning on his heel and heading back inside without another word. The two men followed with an apologetic glance at their friends, and soon the gate was replaced behind them.

"I'm sorry," Wes said in her mind from somewhere within the palace walls. She assured him that she was not offended. "Are you always left out of such things?" Nazzan asked her, nudging her shoulder gently with his snout.

"Pretty much," she said, smiling at him. "In King Manta's defense, I'm not sure any of us could actually fit through the door."

"Fair point," Jaconial said, standing up and stretching out her wings as best she could without bumping into the still, silent soldiers. To Celesyria's surprise, she was actually smiling.

"If anything, it's Aelrie who has really been left out," Nazzan said. The elf smiled.

"It's quite understandable that he should not trust me yet. I wouldn't trust me either."

She sank down to sit against the wall, ignoring the soldiers that stood watching at either side. A few moments later, she had closed her eyes.

Celesyria felt like pacing, but she refrained. There wasn't enough space.

Instead, she watched Jaconial and Nazzan as they stood side by side, lost in another secret conversation, not seeming to notice her at all. She could not help but to admire the handsome male, and though she did not feel specifically jealous of Jaconial, she did feel a more general longing to have what she had.

What would it be like to have someone to stand beside me, to face all of these evils knowing that I wasn't alone?

She reminded herself that she had Wes, Alder, Kessara, and perhaps even Aelrie, Nazzan, and Jaconial. She said a quick prayer to the High One, asking for contentment with the friendship that surrounded her.

She was not alone.

But as she stood and waited, her legs going numb beneath her, she couldn't help but to wish for something more.

WES

The halls of Windshear palace were just as beautiful as Wes remembered, but he wondered how long such opulence would last.

The gleaming floors required servants to polish them. The dainty, oceanic statues needed to be dusted. Tapestries needed to be struck clean. Beauty only seemed effortless. There was always sweat and blood hidden beneath.

He and Alder followed King Manta deeper into the palace, saying nothing as he led them around turns and through doors, all three of the men lost in their own thoughts.

The last time that they had been here, the two of them had found themselves stuffed in his study closet as all Wrathlands broke loose outside. This of course had happened after Wes had endured a lecture about the importance of him marrying the Princess.

Every time the King cleared his throat, he expected him to bring it up once more, which would be especially awkward in Alder's presence, but mercifully he said nothing as they made their way toward their destination.

Despite everything, Wes could find a lot to admire in King Manta. It was clear that he cared for his people, and he respected the views of his daughter more than many a king would. He could only hope that, this time, he would see that she was right to be concerned about the Gorok.

Finally, they reached a broad hallway that looked familiar, and Wes' memories fell into place. They were approaching the throne room, and as they crossed the threshold of the door, he met Alder's gaze. It was here that they'd fed the fallen elf the bread of hope, or at least attempted to. Guilt flickered within his mind. He had promised to pray for the fallen man, but had forgotten to do so in recent weeks, too preoccupied with his own fears to pray about much of anything.

As they entered the room, he noticed even more guards, most of them Red Army. Before he and Alder could reach the seating area that the King gestured them toward, however, the Princess was darting out of her father's study, skirts flying as she ran over to give him a hug.

He felt warmth spreading through his chest as she paused in his arms, noticing that her hair smelled much nicer than it had back in Auranth. He could almost picture her as a child again, running around the forest with him and Roven instead of sitting at some stuffy charity dinner with their parents.

O, High One, thank you. Thank you for keeping her safe.

When she pulled away, there was a terrible moment when he thought she might not hug Alder at all. He knew that they had left things very badly, and perhaps she was still angry.

He watched with a mixture of relief and trepidation as she finally stepped toward him, tears filling her eyes. She and Alder's gaze was locked upon one another, but he could see King Manta staring at them both, eyes narrowed.

"I'm sorry," he heard Alder say.

"You should be," Kessara said, but she was smiling as she closed the distance between them, accepting his embrace.

Wes was glad that they had reconciled, but it pained him all the same. He knew that every touch, every smile, every hope that somehow things could be different between them was a false hope that would only bring them more pain in the end.

Perhaps even hate would be easier than friendship.

When they parted, Wes noticed that several of the Red Army soldiers shared the King's murderous expression. He wondered if perhaps some of them had served with Alder in the past, back when they were only a normal Aridmoorian force, before they had spread across Kaveryth like a bloody fog.

"My King," Alder said, stepping away from Kessara. "Is it truly necessary that we invite half of the Red Army into your throne room for a simple diplomatic meeting?"

"Captain Drohma wished that they be present outside," the Princess said quickly, her usual composed expression returning to her face. "We can speak privately in the study."

The men glanced at one another, but said nothing. Fortunately, Captain Drohma was nowhere to be seen, but Wes was sure he must be somewhere close by. He would be waiting for any opportunity to arrest him, Alder, and Celesyria, he was sure of it. He could only hope that Alder would keep his temper, and his attitude, in check.

King Manta looked furious at the whole exchange, but said nothing as he ushered them into the study. Wes found his silence even more terrifying than his temper, but still he hoped that the promise of being overheard by the soldiers outside would keep him from exploding too badly.

To his surprise, Queen Manta was already present, relaxing in a chair beside the liquor cart, a tumbler of brown liquid in her hand. Wes suppressed a laugh at the thought of the dainty Queen drinking some vile sailor's spirit, but he supposed she might desire the stress relief at the moment.

He and Alder walked over to kiss the Queen's hand. She directed them to sit, but finding a place turned out to be difficult. The King had clearly been hard at work with various bureaucratic tasks that had flooded his office with piles of parchment and paper. Finally, Wes settled on resting against the wall, his arm pressing uncomfortably against a tall stone support beam.

"Well," King Manta said finally once everyone was sitting still, giving his daughter a quick nod "Best to get on with it."

Kessara stood near the door, her hands held behind her back, chin forward. Wes was almost surprised to see her dressed in a proper regal outfit rather than the plain, peasant-like gowns he'd become accustomed to seeing her in. Her ability to fit into whatever role was thrown at her was rather impressive.

"So," she began, clearing her throat. "Despite my attempts to convince him otherwise, my father has decided that the best course of action was to send our navy to the West Strait, in order to assist King Ursa in preventing an invasion from Nox."

She waited a moment, as though to let her words suffuse thoroughly. Wes was not surprised, of course, having heard Moorn's gossip, but when he glanced over at Alder, he noticed the tightness of his jaw and the stiff posture of his back. Perhaps for once he had been the naive one, holding onto hope that the King's decision might have been different in the end.

As she spoke, the Queen got to her feet and began to light a few candles that sat in stands around the room. The sun had set, and the moon was still too low for its light to come in through the small, high windows that rested near the ceiling. In other circumstances, the study may have looked cozy, but at the moment Wes felt as though he could scarcely breathe.

"As much as I understand my father's reluctance to defy Kylan Ursa's commands, I too must do what I believe to be right for our people," the Princess continued.

"Do not be rash, Kessara," her father interrupted. Wes watched in silence as the Queen rested a hand on his forearm, but he shook her off, his cheeks red with anger. "You are still a child. There are still things that you do not understand."

"Certainly you are correct, father," Kessara replied. There was no anger in her voice. If anything, she sounded almost aloof, as though she was about to rattle off a list of unimportant tax figures. "I cannot understand all of what is going on here. But what is clear to me is that I cannot and will not leave the citizens of our coastal cities defenseless. My friends are here, and it is my plan that they will assist me in offering protection and, if need be, other aid."

The King chuckled at this, and Wes shot Alder a warning glance. Kessara was handling this as well as could be expected, and any input from them would no doubt make matters worse.

"Surely if this Gorok does exist, your friends would present little challenge to the beast. You would sacrifice their lives to prove a point to me?"

Kessara let her arms fall to her sides and took several steps closer to the desk where the King sat. Her eyes seemed to burn from within. "I would be willing to sacrifice my life, if the High One demands it of me. The others will make their own choice."

She stared at Alder and Wes expectantly. Both of them nodded, giving each other a shrug as soon as her attention returned to her father.

"In any case, the odds are better than I feared. I did not expect two more dragons to join this cause."

Wes had not expected Jaconial and Nazzan to come either. At first, he had resisted the idea, thinking that they would be better off staying behind and guarding Auranth. But the townsfolk didn't yet trust them, and ultimately they had all decided that if the Gorok did appear, the strength of dragons would be their only chance to stop it.

Our only chance aside from Aelrie.

The thought chilled him. He hoped that somehow they could prevent her needing to be near the creature at all.

"You will not put yourself at risk, Kessara," King Manta said, his voice dangerously quiet. "Is that clear?"

"I'm at no risk, father. Scary stories and legends cannot draw blood."

With a sweep of his thick arm, the King sent several papers and a half-empty tumbler flying off of the end of his desk. The glass shattered mere inches from Alder's foot, but he scarcely seemed to notice, his eyes trained on the furious King.

For a terrifying second, Wes thought Alder might leap over the desk and strike him. He watched his friend's fists, clenched tight against his thighs.

"Errol," Queen Manta pleaded, staring down at the floor as pungent brown liquid began to pool between the cracks in the stone. "If you wish for her to be safe, help her. Tell King Ursa that he's on his own. Bring our navy back to our own shores."

"Nothing has changed, Jinna," King Manta said, settling back in his chair, his voice gruff. "I love you, Kessara, but I must think of all of my subjects."

"Fine. But I will be there at the coast."

A look passed between them for several tense seconds until finally King Manta gave a short nod.

"We will protect the Princess, my King," Alder said, his voice wavering with barely-suppressed rage. "Wes and I will not leave her side. In any case, the dragons are strong. She will return in good health when this is all over. I promise."

"I request that you ask Captain Drohma to go to Kingsvier Landing, and to inform the rest of the Red Army men there that we are to be left alone," Kessara said. "If we have any Galeharbor soldiers to spare, I would appreciate their aid, even if it is only a few men."

"Of course, darling," the Queen said, but the King shook his head and raised a hand.

"You would deny her a guard?" Alder snapped, ignoring Wes' pleading glare.

"It is not so simple, Cadogen," the King said, his voice rising once more. "My instinct as a father is to send every soldier in Windshear and their brothers to protect my daughter."

"So do it!"

"No!" King Manta shouted, pounding on the table again.

Wes glanced down at the floor where the spilled liquor had spread nearly to the door along the smooth white stones. "I cannot allow King Ursa to believe that my loyalties are divided. I've already asked him to refrain from arresting three wanted fugitives.

"Because you are still the Princess, I will order a small personal guard from among our palace men to escort you to Kingsvier Landing. I will also permit that Drohma go and deliver an order of continued immunity for you and your entire party, including the elf and those dragons. But that is all."

The Queen looked over at him, her mouth opening and then closing again. After only a brief moment of hesitation, Kessara got up and walked over to the desk.

"Thank you," she said quickly, leaning over and giving her father a peck on the cheek.

She turned to Alder next, tugging at the sleeve of his tunic and pulling him toward the far end of the study. They spoke for a moment with hushed voices, and Wes looked at the ground, desperate to avoid any awkward questions from the King and Queen about their closeness. He had no answers to give them, at least, none that would bring calm to the situation.

Without another word, Alder strode to the front of the desk, bowed to the monarchs in turn, and headed out of the study.

Chapter Nineteen

ALDER

Though Alder had told them that he knew the way, two of the palace guards insisted on escorting him back out to the courtyard. When he finally emerged beneath the starlight and walked toward his friends, he was relieved to see that most of the soldiers who had been standing on both sides of the courtyard had finally retired for the night.

Only two palace guards and four Red Army soldiers remained, with two of the latter four seeming to be nearly falling asleep on their feet as the guards who had escorted them gave them their new orders.

Captain Drohma would have whipped me and my men for such laziness.

"Where is everyone?" Jaconial demanded without a word of greeting, getting up from where she had lain next to Nazzan, poking at him with her snout. He grunted something unintelligible.

Aelrie, who did not seem to have moved from where he'd last seen her sitting against the wall, opened her eyes. The male dragon got to his feet slowly, stretching out his neck toward the sky and giving a yawn loud enough to shake the stone walls.

Alder glanced up at the moon. It was not yet very late, but it was later than he thought. He was tired, but sleep would have to wait.

"Kessara had to speak to Wes alone," he said, hoping that he sounded nonchalant. She had not told him what she wished to discuss with his friend, and though he knew that he had no right to any such emotion, jealousy continued to plague him.

He tried to hold onto the memory of when she had hugged him hello, but already the brief passage of time was beginning to blur the details. He could still remember the smell of her hair, though, and the feeling of her head pressing against his chest.

"Hello, are you there?" Jaconial said, cocking her head to one side as she stared at him. She had lowered her head until she was mere inches away.

Get ahold of yourself. There are more important things to worry about than private conversations between a Princess and the man she is bound to wed.

"We are to make for Kingsvier Landing, a small fishing city that sits along the coast. Immediately."

Aelrie seemed to pale, but she said nothing, and the others waited for him to continue.

"If anyone wishes to leave and head back to Auranth, they must do so now. If the Gorok is indeed out there, we are going to be fighting it on our own."

"Will we have enough men?" Celesyria asked. "Or drag-ons?"

"We already took everyone that we could," Alder reminded

her, glancing over at Aelrie. Despite the feelings of distrust that never quite went away, he knew logically that bringing the elf had been a wise decision. She was stronger even than he was, and they would likely need her, despite Wes' warning that letting her get too close might harm her. "If Auranth is attacked while we're gone, at least they will still have a chance, even without the dragons. It's the best that we have."

"I know," the orange dragon said, but Alder could hear the fear in her voice.

"Everything is going to be fine," he said, forcing a smile. "We have three of you dragons, and an elf."

He wanted to mention that they also had a decorated soldier with advanced knowledge of general battle tactics and exceptional skill with a sword, but for once, he refrained. He was not as nervous as they, but something about the calm, dark waters of the North Sea made him uneasy. Even he could tell that it was no time for overconfidence.

"What are Wes and Kessara going to do?" Aelrie asked, not returning his smile. He glanced over at the soldiers, who were now wide awake and listening from their posts.

"The Princess and the Envoy have decided to travel on stagback with a small royal guard," he said, glaring at the Red Army soldiers. They could hear every word of their plans for all he cared, so long as they obeyed King Manta and left them alone. "It will likely take them all night to get there, even if they ride fast."

We will arrive first. Perhaps the Gorok will attack us before they can even get to the coast.

It was a small hope, but it urged him forward. He still worried for Kessara, traveling by night, alone amongst men. He trusted Wes, of course, but even the palace guards were not

212

beyond his suspicion.

No. The High One will protect her, even when I cannot. Nothing is going to happen.

"Are we free to leave?" he asked the Red Army guards, his tone a little harsher than the men likely deserved.

Without a word, one of the men raised an arm, and the others headed for the courtyard gate, raising it within moments.

"We must hunt before we fly for the coast, but it will not be long," Celesyria said in his mind as the dragons took off, their huge flying forms disappearing behind the walls of the courtyard within seconds.

He found himself alone with Aelrie as they made their way through Windshear. It was quiet now, with most of the citizens retiring to their homes once night fell. In any case, he was glad to see that the place seemed to be largely free of street criminals, let alone bandits or slavers.

Aelrie said nothing for a long while, content to follow him as he led the way through winding streets, past shops and taverns, and toward the city gate. After a couple of minutes arguing with the guards posted there, they let them through. Once he was sure they were a sufficient distance from prying eyes, he sat down on a patch of dead grass near a thin, leafless tree.

His stomach was growling, and he opened his pack, glad that they had brought more than enough provisions. Aelrie did likewise and they chewed on their dried meat and fruit in silence, looking up at the constellations in the dark sky overhead. To his surprise, sitting here with the elf on his own wasn't quite as awkward as he'd anticipated.

Celesyria's voice sounded in his mind again, assuring him that the dragons would be on their way before the moon reached its peak height. He could not respond, of course, but he appreciated the information nonetheless.

Finally, as she took her last bite of meat and a final drink from her waterskin, Aelrie stood.

"There's something I must do," she said, her voice so quiet that for a moment he was sure he'd heard her incorrectly.

Alder nearly dropped the remainder of his own food. "Now? The dragons are returning. We have less than an hour!"

"Please, don't ask questions," she said, her eyes pleading with him. "Don't wait for me."

Long-suppressed anger rose in his chest as he got to his own feet, letting the final bits of dried apple fall onto his boots. "Why should I trust you?"

Dark imaginings filled his mind.

She could be planning to assassinate Kessara. She could be planning to warn the Gorok of their approach. We never should have welcomed an elf, as though they were just like us, able to truly turn to the High One and do right. This is madness.

"Please, Alder," she continued, pacing in place, her long black braids whipping in the breeze that had swept up from the sea. "I am quiet, and faster than any human. I need to watch over him."

Despite the worries that filled his thoughts, he could feel something else as her eyes met his. Within their strange, alien depths, he saw reflected there something that he knew, something that he had been trying to run from ever since he'd first laid eyes on the Princess.

He knew that perhaps it could be some kind of elven trick, some manipulation of his mind, but he didn't believe it. The High One was with him now, deep within his soul, telling him that he could trust her. That she cared for Wes just as he cared

CHAPTER NINETEEN

for Kessara, despite logic and reason screaming at them both to stop, to run away before they destroyed everything.

She was not a danger.

The opposite was true. She'd die for Wes if she had to.

"I will protect her, too," Aelrie said softly, her gaze never wavering as she looked into his eyes. "I promise."

KESSARA

Kessara stood beside Wes on the small balcony that led off from her room, waiting, her eyes upon the sea.

As soon as their small guard could be found and their stags prepared, they would leave, on their own, and make for the site of the most recent Gorok sightings.

The water was still calm, but she knew that a maelstrom could arise in an instant, changing everything. She understood it perhaps better than most. She had been there from nearly the beginning, when a dragon had met an Envoy and set the world on fire. There was no turning back, and there would be no return to the old ways. They had to keep moving forward, however large and frightening the threats may be.

"Do you see the ships?" Wes asked, pointing toward the western part of the horizon. She nodded, and they both stood in silence again, watching as Galeharbor's navy made for the West Strait. They were already too far away, nearly to Vilzan if not within their territorial waters already.

"My father made his choice. We are making ours."

Her voice did not falter, but inside, she felt like weeping. She wished desperately that her father was the one riding to battle, huge and menacing on his own stag, sword raised as he led a whole company of their best men toward the coast.

She wished that she was remaining here with her mother,

215

safe and cared for. How easy it had been to fall back into her own life, even in such a short time.

How easy it is to be a Princess when one knows what it's like to be a peasant.

Another wish flitted into her mind. She felt guilty, but she could not help but think it, to turn it over in her head. She wished that she could still worship the Dracodei. It was easy for her to give treasures. That was all that the dragon gods really demanded, with perhaps an extra trip to the temple now and then.

The High One was different. He wanted her to sacrifice herself, and that was a much more difficult thing.

She swallowed hard, trying to remove an imagined bitter taste from her tongue.

He's demanded everything from me. Everything that makes me happy, everything that makes life worth living.

"Do you still believe that the High One is with us?" she asked Wes.

"He is here now. I know He is," Wes replied without a moment's hesitation.

"How do you know?"

"Because I'm afraid, and I'm not running away," he said, giving her a sad smile.

She moved closer, resting her head upon his shoulder. He did not pull away.

She knew that being here in her chambers alone with him would lead to gossip, but at the moment, she could not bring herself to care. She was thankful that he was with her.

She felt the bitterness fade away, replaced by a warmth that seemed to spread from her head to her toes. He was right, about all of it. The High One did ask a lot of them, but He would not forsake them. She trusted in that, even when the fear told her something else.

"Do you think that more of our people will turn to Him, given time?" she asked, her timid voice filling the silence.

"I do. It has begun already. So many of them have lost their trust in men. I heard it every day back in Auranth. They know that their interests have been cast aside for so many years, all in favor of greed and power."

"And you think they believe that the High One and our army are merely offering them a better deal?"

Wes chuckled. "Probably. That's not the right reason for turning to Him, of course. Truth is the right reason."

"Not to mention the fact that the High One demands even what the Dracodei and the Septemvirate do not," she added dryly, returning his smile.

"The High One knows how to meet people where they are, not where they should be. I was conflicted about it, at first, but now I understand that we must do the same. These people are doing the best that they can with what they know. If their hearts are open to truth, they will not stop where they are."

"I wish we had more portions of the Codex," Kessara said, drawing a slow breath.

There was more she had to say to him, and little time to say it, but she could not bring herself to hurry. It was much easier to discuss what other people should do, how other people should be so noble as to follow the truth for truth's sake.

I am a hypocrite. Maybe we all are.

Wes nodded. "I wish we did, too. But you have done a great job teaching the people what you could with what we have. It is clear that Mella believes, and I have no doubt she has taken over teaching the children, at least, while we're gone."

"I hope to continue," she said, surprising herself with how fiercely she meant it. Whatever charms and ease palace life offered, she did not desire it. Not really, not in her heart, not where it counted. Even the dress she wore now felt suffocating in its luxury, even though it was the most practical clothing that she owned here in Windshear.

"You will," Wes said firmly. "You're going to return to Auranth, because you're going to be fine."

She said nothing.

She did not fear that she would die here. She feared that her duties as queen of Silverfell would take her away from such projects as educating children.

Wes said nothing else for a moment, and she took another long breath, trying to find courage from a well deep within that had long since run dry.

Somewhere within her mind, she saw the grassy plains of Aridmoor, with great warhorses riding across the hills. She saw little children, several little boys, all with stark red hair, tumbling about the flowers, laughing together.

Their skin was tan. Their eyes were blue.

"Wes," she said, swallowing. She wanted to close her eyes, to make the images go away, but she knew that they wouldn't. Instead, she focused on the face of her friend. He had grown so handsome. His once chubby cheeks were gone, replaced with firm cheekbones. His unruly curls were neatly combed, a couple of loose tendrils falling into his kind brown eyes.

He was beautiful.

She loved this boy with all of her heart. She could do this.

"Is everything alright?" he asked, sounding alarmed.

"Yes," she said quickly, forcing a smile. "But there is more I must say to you, and I'm not sure how to begin."

He waited patiently, leaning against the balcony railing, his eyes filled with concern. "I suspect that the remaining copies of the Codex Veritatis are buried beneath the rubble of Whitespire," she started, thinking of no better place to begin.

"Probably."

"My father agreed to allow us to delay our marriage because there was still hope of finding the Codex. I convinced him that perhaps with enough evidence from other fragments we had not yet seen, we would be able to convince the people that the Dracodei were impostors."

Wes did not meet her eyes as he nodded.

"I thought that if we could cease the sacrifices for real, we could weaken the Septemvirate, making it easier for me to rule as Queen of Silverfell. My father saw the sense in this. If we married too soon, Elder Dorold and the others would have gotten in our way. The Elders would have continued to rob the people of their treasures, leaving them weak and open to King Ursa's power grab," she said, speaking with more confidence now as she raced toward the terrible conclusion.

She took a moment to catch her breath. She had hoped Wes would speak, had hoped he would preempt what she had to say with some brilliant counterpoint she had not thought of, but he remained quiet.

"Anyway, the Septemvirate has been severely weakened now. Even if Elder Bram and Elder Jate survive, they will have a difficult time regaining control of Stronghollow, let alone the rest of Silverfell. And that's assuming that Oria was lying. It may turn out that Elder Bram is on our side after all. In any case, without an Envoy and without the Septemvirate, it is unlikely that the sacrifices will continue for much longer. The people will resist their treasures being taken from them."

She wanted to ask him about Elder Bram, ask if he planned to speak with him soon, if they made it out of Galeharbor alive, but there was no time to worry about it.

She was here now, approaching the truth, and she could not afford any excuse that might lead her away from saying what needed to be said.

She glanced over at Wes, but still he did not meet her eyes. She saw the twitching of a muscle beneath his eyebrow, his skin gleaming slightly blue in the moonlight, but otherwise he was completely still.

"As you have probably figured out by now, all of the obstacles that I used to try and convince my father to support me in delaying our marriage have faded away."

"Is he forcing your hand?" Wes asked. His voice was calm, but Kessara knew him well enough to know that a dangerous anger burned beneath the surface of his words.

"No. He has remained mercifully silent on the subject since I arrived, but I can tell he's waiting for me to ask. He will be ready to marry us straight away, in a simple ceremony, as soon as we agree to do it."

He said nothing for a long while.

"I see."

She placed a hand upon his shoulder until he looked over at her. She saw the hurt within his eyes, but there was a determination there, too. He was strong enough. She had no doubt of it.

"Wes, it's time. I've known it ever since the destruction of Whitespire, but I was not ready to face it, and I knew that you weren't either."

"What changed?" he asked, his eyes searching her face.

"Everything that I've told you."

220

He shook his head. "No, that part I understand. What is it that gave you the courage to be ready to go through with this marriage?"

"I know now that I am in love with Alder," she said matter-of-factly, before she could talk herself out of it. He deserved the truth.

So do I.

"I tried to talk myself out of it. I tried to push him away, but I've never quite been able to manage it. And now that I've accepted that it is not a feeling I can change, I believe I can work through it and love you as you deserve. That is, if you will aid me."

"I'm glad that you're being honest with me," Wes said, reaching out to give her hand a squeeze. "It will be easier for us if we can lean on one another through our difficulties."

For a moment, she thought that he might have a confession of his own to utter, but he said nothing, and she did not ask. One broken heart was enough to bear for the day.

"I hope that the people of Silverfell will trust me to lead them. I wish to command their remaining forces to ally with our men in Auranth, and to draw back as many as I can from King Ursa's army. My father is wrong to cower to his demands, but he's right to fear for the safety of our people. They need more protection that we can currently give."

"And with Silverfell's men, you should be able to protect both Kingdoms," Wes finished, letting out a sigh. "Hopefully, anyway."

For a moment, she did not respond. She watched the North Sea, which was just as peaceful as it had been a few minutes before.

At any second now, a servant or a soldier would knock at her chamber door, telling her that it was time to leave for Kingsvier Landing. Soon, she would have to face Alder again, and would have to decide when to tell him that her marriage was near.

She would not tell him that she loved him. That was a cruel weapon that she could not bear to wield.

Not unless she absolutely had to.

She closed her eyes and leaned against the railing, enjoying the soft breeze as it brushed against her skin. "Do you ever think about surrender?" she asked.

"Sometimes."

"Kylan is a power-hungry, greed-ridden snake, but he's not completely evil. Sometimes I wonder if we would all be better off under his rule, assuming he could keep the elves and bandits from destroying Kaveryth," she admitted.

"A big assumption."

"I tried to talk sense into him, once," she said, shaking her head. "I went to High Keep looking for him, thinking that if I could just get past his guards, I could convince him to do the right thing. I never got the chance, but it was naive, anyway. It's going to take more than human words to get through to him."

She paused for a moment, pressing her eyes more tightly shut as memories of that night swept over her. No matter how much she tried to skirt around her terror, she could not. It lurked there, somewhere deep within her mind, threatening to paralyze her.

"Are you alright?" Wes asked, his voice gentle. She felt his hand against her shoulder, and she forced herself to take a breath and open her eyes. She had to face it.

Tears begin to pool in the corner of her eyes. Her throat ached, and she swallowed the sob down before it could escape.

She would tell him what had happened, before they wed. But there was no time now.

"I'm fine."

"Is it about Alder?"

"He's the cause of most of my problems, but no, this time, it wasn't his fault," she said, smiling. Her heartbeat was slowing. She only had to keep breathing, and she would be alright. "Anyway, King Ursa cannot be trusted, and I have to believe that we are making the right choice in opposing him."

"King Ursa will allow the false worship of the Dracodei to continue," Wes reminded her. "The fact that he does not even seem to believe it himself only makes this fact worse, in my eyes. We must remember that we oppose him not because he's illegitimate, even though he is that, but because he seeks to continue to suppress the worship of the High One."

Kessara thought about this. She knew that her own desires always tended to taint whatever she did, even things that were good. Wes was wise to be on guard.

"I'm not going to surrender," she assured him. "It's just a foolish wish. A dream, when reality becomes too painful."

"I never in a thousand years thought that you would."

"I'm still afraid, Wes."

The sob spilled out this time before she could stop it, and without another word, Wes took her in his arms, holding her close. For one impossible moment, she forgot the sea, forgot the balcony beneath her feet, forgot the stars.

She was with Roven again, standing in a forest clearing near Stronghollow, saying yes. Promising to marry him, to love him until the very end, whatever evils may come. His arms were strong around her and his chest was warm. She never wanted to be anywhere else.

I never thought I was capable of love like that again. Until I met Alder.

She pulled away from Wes, feeling suddenly very much like she wanted to throw up.

"Kessara, are you okay? Did I hurt you?" Wes asked, his face a mask of alarm.

No. I've hurt you, I'm still hurting you, and in this marriage, I will hurt you even more. You deserve so much better than I can give.

She opened her mouth to speak, but a sob got in the way.

"It's alright, shh," Wes said, raising a hand to comfort her again before letting it fall.

"Will you pray with me?" she asked, each word aching against her throat as though she was swallowing glass.

"Of course," Wes said, his voice husky. She could tell that he wanted to cry, but unlike her, he found the strength to hold back his tears. She was so proud of him. She hoped that somewhere in the Eternal Lands, Roven and his parents could see the man that he had become.

Wiping fresh tears from her eyes, she knelt beside him on the cool white stone, their heads pressed against the railing, facing the sea. Wes began to pray aloud for all of their needs, and she closed her eyes, letting her silent thoughts join with his words. She pleaded for strength. She begged the High One to remind her that love was not merely what she felt, but rather what she chose, one day at a time.

Somewhere in the distance, she heard the cry of gulls, laughing together as they danced in the skies, unaware that the world below them was being torn apart.

Just moments after Wes asked a final blessing, there was a knock at the door.

CHAPTER NINETEEN

The royal guard was ready to leave.

20

Chapter Twenty

AELRIE

Aelrie sat upon the roof, waiting for Wes and Kessara's voices to fade away before daring to move. Finally, when she was certain that they were gone, she began to climb down, landing on the balcony with scarcely a sound.

The decorative stone designs that covered most of the palace made easy work of scaling the walls, and within a few minutes, she found herself back at ground level, wandering into the labyrinth of tall hedges that rested beneath Kessara's chambers.

The garden was large, and she pressed deeper into it, almost hoping that she would somehow manage to get lost.

Somehow, the palace staff had managed to keep the locusts from entering beyond the garden walls. It seemed even more green and lush in light of the lifeless vegetation that surrounded it.

She passed by late-summer flowers and merry bees working

by moonlight, but she hardly saw them. She didn't want to think, not even about anything so mundane as the stars or the gentle swishing of trimmed green grass against the soles of her leather boots. Not yet. Not here.

Finally, she reached the destination she had not known she had been looking for.

There was a recess in the hedge wall here, where a massive stone statue of a mer-woman stood. Aelrie was just small enough to fit beside it, her entire body hidden deep within the shadow.

She began to cry. At first, the tears came in slow trickles, sliding down her cheeks and into the side of her mouth, the taste of salt touching her tongue. But soon, she couldn't stop them, couldn't stop the choking sobs that made her gasp. She pressed a hand against her mouth, terrified that she would be heard, but unable to get ahold of herself.

She went on like that for several minutes, the trimmed branches of the hedge stabbing at the back of her head, damp dirt staining the back of her dress.

She thought of the others back in Nox. What would they think of her now? Sitting here, hiding in the dark like a common thief?

She let out a bitter chuckle, startling a nearby bird who flew off into the night.

They would not care about sneaking around. They do their best work that way, slitting throats when the humans are too weak, too surprised to fight back.

No, that wasn't it. She knew what her shame was, though she couldn't figure out why it still felt shameful to her, even now that she had gotten away from her people.

I love a human.

Worse, I love a human who already has a human girl he is bound to marry.

She shook her head, as though she might get the idea out of it by sheer force. The attraction alone was unthinkable, both to her people and to his. Even if the Princess was not involved, such a thing could never be. So why did she feel it? Why did the very sight of the Envoy send such pangs straight through to her heart?

She slammed her fist against the statue, feeling a crunch that might have been her own bone. Blood ran over her silver knuckles, dripping onto the grass.

I could go back.

The thought came fast, determined to cut through the noise of her pain.

I could return to the others, tell them that I was a spy all along, that I was gathering information on the new human force. They would believe me. Perhaps I'd even be a hero. I could slip back into the crowd, another silver face among many.

Her stomach churned, but still, the thoughts continued. The more that she tried to chase them away, the more she wanted to dive into them, to explore their facets, to unravel her own secrets.

I was not happy there in Nox. I walked through life in a haze. There was no joy, never, which is probably why Wes Cervos could so easily make me feel it.

But there was no pain, either.

She could not feel the sting of her scraped knuckles. The pain of her shattered heart was so big that it engulfed everything else. She'd never felt pain like that in Nox, not ever, not even when—

Another thought. A painful one, but one that she knew was

228

true, that was sane, that was hers.

She took hold of it, trying to focus.

I can still hear those sounds I heard in Umrym. Those terrible sounds of death. I should have told Wes. Perhaps he could have found a way to stop it, eventually. At least I wouldn't have had to bear the darkness alone.

Another bird landed on the statue, a big black one, who looked down on her with huge dark eyes. He cawed, as though asking why she was there.

Why am I here?

I can go to him. I can tell him everything. And I can keep my promise to Alder to watch over the Princess.

Within seconds she was on her feet, wiping the blood from her fingers on a nearby patch of soft blue flowers. She rushed through the labyrinth, glancing up at the sky every few moments to find her way, glad now that elves found getting lost nearly impossible.

Soon she was out in the open again. A few months ago, she would have found a stag or a horse and manipulated it into accepting her onto its back, but she couldn't bring herself to do it now. No. She wanted nothing to do with the darkness her people used, not anymore, not even to beguile a weak-minded beast.

She ran on foot, toward the sea, smelling the salty air as she raced beneath the stars. The thoughts of going home—Nox was never home!—were gone.

She would continue to love Wes, and it would continue to hurt. But she would do everything she could to keep him safe. She would not betray him. She would not go back, not ever.

High One, help me to believe.

Help me to hope that you could love someone like me, even if no one else can.

CELESYRIA

Celesyria flew across Galeharbor, thankful that navigating toward the sea did not require her to think very much.

Ever since she was a child, she'd loved the stars and the constellations, and wanted to learn the way to every corner of Kaveryth, even places that she might never get to visit. Now, she struggled to focus on their gleaming patterns in the inky blackness.

She thought of her mother, back in Auranth, trying to rest and to heal.

At least she was safe. Her father was still somewhere in Nox, assuming he was still alive.

I'm coming for you, papa. If my friends will not join me, I will go alone, and the High One will be with me.

"Do you see anything out on the sea?" Alder called from Nazzan's back, his voice nearly engulfed by the wind that rushed through their wings.

"No," she called, shaking her head. "Nothing."

Waves were beginning to form, but she could not see even a single fishing boat. There was certainly no sign of a huge monster.

It was strange to see Alder riding on Nazzan's back rather than her own. It was nearly as strange to see Jaconial flying without a rider, after she had carried the elf all the way from Auranth to Galeharbor.

"I hope that Aelrie makes it in time," she said, staring down at the sparse trees below.

Jaconial snorted. "In time for what? I'm still not convinced that this monster is even real."

Celesyria felt stung by her harsh words, and was glad that the dragon could not see her face. Though it seemed Jaconial had made peace with her as best she could, she was beginning to fear that a general prickliness was simply part of her personality.

"We should trust the eyewitness accounts of those we have sworn to protect," Nazzan said gently.

"Just because I'm here doesn't mean I'm sure about every-thing, alright?" Jaconial snapped at him. "Just let me figure things out on my own."

"I know how you feel, you know," Alder said, shouting to be heard. *How much easier it would be on his throat if he could speak to us in our minds!* "My journey to the High One was not something I planned. Just let Him help you, even if you don't want to open up to anyone else."

Celesyria thought she heard another growl from Jaconial, but she said nothing else as she adjusted her altitude and banked slightly to the right.

Alder was right. Their friendship had been impossible. She had been in prison, and he had been put in charge of guarding her. Until then, he'd been a loyal servant of King Ursa's Protectorate, never daring to disobey an order. But the High One had done something extraordinary, speaking to him in a dream and urging him to change course.

High One, if you can work miracles for Alder, you can do the same for Jaconial and Nazzan, as well. Please speak to them in whatever way they most need to hear Your voice.

As if coming from nowhere, the approach to Kingsvier Landing was beneath them.

Celesyria looked down as the grassy edge of a vast plateau fell away, revealing a massive stone cliff that stretched nearly as far as she could see before shoring up into a steep hill of broken black rocks.

She heard Alder trying to speak, but the wind had picked up and she couldn't make out the words. Below them, running back and forth along the cliff face, was a staircase leading down to a large cobblestone courtyard of sorts. From the courtyard, streets branched off to either side as well as straight down toward the seashore.

She expected to see Red Army men or at least Galeharbor soldiers swarming the town, but there only seemed to be a few men wandering here and there. She hoped that meant that King Manta's message had made it ahead of them, but it was also possible that the city's protection was simply not a priority in the first place.

How foolish, considering the dwarf boats that had been spotted in the North Sea.

As they flew over the main part of the city, she noticed that despite how old many of the buildings looked, they were tidy and well-maintained. It seemed to be a place that people took pride in, likely inhabited by families of sailors who had lived here for generations.

She bowed her head in sorrow as she flew.

To destroy a palace or a capital was evil, but to destroy an old village, a place filled with the memories of an entire people, was unthinkably cruel. Which is exactly why she did not doubt that the elves would do it if given the opportunity.

I will not let your city fall, even if your own King does not see the need to protect it.

As they reached the port, she noticed that the waves had almost doubled in height. They came in rapid succession, long white lines that extended into the darkness on either side of her vision, rolling toward the shore with an incredible swell of noise before finally breaking.

The mist was thrown so high into the air that her wings began to feel damp. She glanced over at Nazzan and nodded. Following her lead, they made for a large stretch of empty beach and lighted down upon the sand as water rushed toward them again and again.

As soon as Alder climbed off of Nazzan's back, Celesyria noticed three Red Army soldiers walking toward them from a nearby fishing dock. The one in front looked familiar to her, but she couldn't quite place him. He had the red hair of an Aridmoorian, and his tunic had some sort of gold filigree around the neck and wrists that the others did not.

Before she could urge him to wait, Alder was crossing the beach toward the man, his boots leaving a neat trail of prints in the wet sand.

"I expect that the King's message has reached you," Alder said.

The man stepped closer, his face filled with rage, and Celesyria felt her chest begin to tighten. She planted her claws firmly where she stood, refusing to back up even a single inch.

She felt water droplets landing on her face, but they had not been thrown by the sea. Rain was coming down now, hard and fast, soaking straight through her scales.

"Yes, Cadogen. You will not be harmed by my men, as His Majesty has requested."

"Good," Alder said, his hand resting on the pommel of his sword. "I expected nothing less, Captain Drohma."

WES

The ground was thick with mud. Trees swayed in the wind,

and if the insects had left any leaves upon their branches, they would have surely been torn off and carried off into the night. As it was, most of the trees were already bare.

Wes rode beneath them when he could, even if the protection they offered from the driving rain was mostly imaginary. More than once, smaller sticks had broken off and hit him or his stag in the face, but still he preferred their shelter to the wild openness of the plain. The pressure of the storm made his existing headache much worse, and he hoped that it would not continue for very much longer.

He could not see the moon nor the stars now. Clouds had raced in not long after they left Windshear palace, great gray sheets that covered every inch of the sky and pelted them with seemingly infinite raindrops. Still, he hoped that he was right that they were making good time. He was eager to reunite with his friends, and he certainly did not want to be up here exposed to the wind any longer than he needed to.

Then again, even though it would be somewhat protected from the winds, Kingsvier Landing would face the wrath of the North Sea's waters. He shook his head, wishing that he could at least worry with Kessara rather than by himself, but it was far too noisy to be able to talk.

As promised, the King had given the Princess two of her own royal guards, and they rode ahead, just close enough to see through the mist and sheeting rain.

Kessara was beside him, just a few feet away, looking very much like a Princess despite the misery of the weather. She sat in the saddle with her back straight, her head held high even as the wind and rain buffeted her pretty face.

My future wife.

The thought did not bring happiness, exactly, but much

of the dread seemed to have left him. Mostly, he felt numb, resigned to a fate that was inescapable however he felt about it.

He stared toward the coast, though he could not see the waters of the sea through the storm, and wondered how Aelrie was doing.

He knew that she could keep herself safe, and that Alder and Celesyria would help her if it came to that, but he couldn't help but to feel a hint of unease when it came to Jaconial and Nazzan. He was of course thankful for the help that they had offered so far, and did not wish to reveal to them his distrust. It would fade with time, he knew, and until then he would treat them with as much kindness as he could.

Alder would be even more cautious than he himself was, which brought him some level of comfort in regard to the safety of Aelrie and Celesyria.

He tightened his grip on the reins and stole another glance at Kessara. He was certain that she was worrying about Alder every moment, and he was probably losing his mind, especially now that this storm had rolled in. Their connection was so strong, so clear to everyone even when they sought to hide it. It made him angry for Kessara's sake.

Though he could not deny that his feelings for Aelrie were growing, he at least had the assurance that being with her was an impossibility whether he married Kessara or not. The marriage of elves and men had caused their present mess.

However his heart ached when he was near her, he could take comfort in the fact that his feelings were only an illusion. He could care for an elf as a friend, he could minister to an elf as a fellow servant of the High One, but he could not ever take an elf as a bride. That sort of love was impossible.

But for Kessara, it was different. She had loved Roven, had promised herself to him, and he had been taken from her. Now she loved Alder, a good man who treated her well who would also be a worthy king of Galeharbor. Wes suspected that even King Manta would come to treasure him as a son-in-law if given the chance. But that love, too, was denied to her.

Instead, she had to marry Wes.

He pressed his fingertips against his pounding temples, certain that the pain within was going to tear his skull apart.

He had changed so much since the spring feast.

The mirrors assured him it was true. The gestures of loyalty and respect from those in Auranth and even throughout Kaveryth confirmed it. But here in the dark, his trousers soaked through to his underpants, sweat and rain mingling along his back, he felt like he had not changed at all. He felt like the same pudgy, weak, pathetic boy that he had always been.

Kessara would never love him, and he would never blame her. They would simply have to endure it.

"Contact Celesyria," she shouted through the rain, the sudden intrusion of her voice shattering his thoughts. "The guards say that we're close."

He looked ahead, and sure enough, both men were gesturing ahead. He could see little, but he gave them a thumbs-up, and they turned back toward the sea.

There was no time now for broken hearts. Their friends needed them, and so did the people of Kingsvier Landing. He couldn't be sure the Gorok would show up, and even if it did, it might take longer than they feared, but he had no way of knowing.

It's not like we can wait here forever. Celesyria's father needs us. Auranth needs us.

He shook his head, struggling to focus on mindspeaking through his headache and the distractions. They would have to answer those questions when they were asked, not before.

"Celesyria?"

It was difficult to project even a single word. Whether it was the pain in his head or the intensity of the storm, he did not know, but he was relieved when Celesyria's voice poured into his mind.

"I'm here, Wes. No monster yet," she said, sounding far more cheerful than he felt. He smiled in spite of himself. It was hard to believe that he'd only known the dragon for a few months. It felt like she'd been his best friend for years. These days, being around her was the only time that he felt truly balanced, like the world actually made sense.

"Is everyone alright?"

"Everyone's fine. Can't say the same about the weather. The sea is angry."

"So is the sky."

"So is Jaconial," Celesyria said, chuckling.

Wes glanced over at Kessara to ensure she was still looking toward the sea, though of course she could not hear him.

"Is Aelrie alright?" he ventured, no longer caring what forbidden feelings his words may reveal. He was sure Celesyria knew everything anyway, even things he had not told her. She always did.

For a moment, she said nothing, and fear gripped his heart.

"You should know that Captain Drohma is here, though there are relatively few soldiers. I see only him and two of his men in Protectorate uniforms, the rest are Red Army and Galeharbor fellows. In any case, Alder spoke with him and he promised to

uphold the King's decree, which fortunately made it here ahead of us."

He supposed it was the best that they could hope for. In any case, if the Gorok attacked the city, he still had faith that many of the soldiers would defend their people, even if it meant standing side by side with fugitives and rogue Guardians.

"What about Aelrie, Celesyria?" he asked again, nerves churning in his stomach.

"I don't know, Wes," she said after a long pause.

He sat back in his saddle so quickly that he accidentally pulled on his stag's mouth, making the animal slip in the muck for a moment before righting himself. Kessara glanced over, alarmed, but he had already recovered his seat.

"What do you mean?" he asked Celesyria, dozens of terrible possibilities screaming in his mind.

"She's not with us. She told Alder that there was something she had to do. Made him promise that we would not wait for her."

"Okay," he said, trying his best to breathe. *"We will be there soon, I think."*

Celesyria said something else, but he did not hear it. He wanted to tell Kessara what the dragon had said, but he felt too exhausted to yell to her over the rain.

They walked in silence for several minutes until they reached what appeared to be the edge of the world.

Up ahead, their guards were climbing off of their own stags, motioning for them to do the same. The top of a staircase was peeping out over the cliffside, just visible amid the mist. They had reached Kingsvier Landing.

21

Chapter Twenty-One

ALDER

Alder stood alone at the top of the lighthouse at the far end of the beach, staring out through the thick glass windows into the storm. The massive lamp behind him burned bright, making it difficult to see through the rain, but if he squinted, he could just see a few of the last navy boats making their way into Vilzan.

He tightened his fists, feeling very much like smashing something, but fortunately, there was little here that could be damaged even if he did lose control.

A lighthouse keeper had once lived here, somewhere below, but now the structure lay abandoned, filled with broken dishes and shabby blankets.

Still, the lamp shone.

"What a pity to watch our best hope disappear beyond the horizon," a voice said behind him. His sword found its way to his hand, a process as automatic to him now as remembering to breathe. He whipped around to find Aelrie standing in the gleam of the light. He swore before he could stop himself.

"Forgive me," she said, her expression unreadable. "I did not mean to startle you."

Was she telling the truth? Or had she been a traitor all along? Images of Kessara and Wes back in Windshear, dead at the hands of this elf, made his gut clench.

He gripped his sword more tightly, but said nothing, choking down his morbid thoughts.

"Wes and Kessara have arrived safely," she said calmly. "They are walking toward the shore now."

He nodded.

There was sadness in her eyes. No doubt she could sense his distrust, but he could not bring himself to let down his guard.

"They plan to marry. After the fight. I regret eavesdropping on them at all, but now I know, and I suppose you probably deserve to know too," Aelrie said, stumbling over the words in her rush to get them out.

Alder felt like he had been struck in the face. He had known that such a day would come, but now? This soon?

He glanced at Aelrie's expectant face. She looked hopeful, as though there was something he could say to ease her own pain. He felt foolish.

There is no treason. There is no plot. There is only a girl with a broken heart.

He shoved his sword back into its scabbard.

"You're certain of what you heard?"

"Yes."

"Why did you think that I needed to know? What business is it of mine?"

Aelrie shook her head, a sad smile on her lips. "I need not make use of any elven senses to know the truth, Alder," she said. "You love the Princess... just as I love the Envoy."

He wanted to deny it, but he had told enough lies in his life. Instead he shrugged, leaning toward the glass again and staring out into the darkness. He supposed Aelrie had not kept her secret much better than he had.

The signs had been apparent, but he had chosen not to see them, or rather, to deny that they meant anything. Surely the elf knew that her desires could never be anything more than a silly fantasy.

He looked over at her, standing in the light. She was beautiful in a way that Kessara's humanity would never allow, but it was a dangerous beauty. A beauty that from childhood he had been conditioned to hate. Wes had learned the same. And yet, here she was, following the Envoy in the darkness like a shadow, wanting something from him that he could not give.

But was it something Wes wanted as well?

With a silent movement, Aelrie stood beside him, her forehead pressed to the glass. She placed a hand on his forearm, and to his surprise, he found it comforting.

"I'm sorry," she said, not taking her eyes off of the sea. They were filled with tears.

For what felt like the first time, he really looked at her.

She was not so different from him. Was his longing for a Princess any less foolish than her longing for a human? Both of them were walking through life with their chests torn open, hearts beating for someone that could never mend their wounds.

"Thank you for keeping her–them–safe," he said finally, eyes trained on the water.

Through the rain and the mist, he saw a ripple off the coast that did not quite fit the pattern of the waves. His pulse quickened.

"I do not condemn you for your feelings, however unrealistic they may be."

She began to thank him, but he cut her off as he saw another swell of water rise out of place.

There.

"Come," he said, moving for the door without explanation.

He pulled the hood of his cloak over his head as he raced down the spiraling staircase, taking the steps two at a time. He could feel Aelrie close at his heels.

There was never any hope for either of us. It's time we faced the truth, and the beast.

KESSARA

Kessara had not visited the city of Kingsvier Landing in several years, but it looked exactly as she remembered it. It was not the kind of place where people enjoyed bringing change for the sake of it, and she suspected that the buildings and the neat cobbled streets would have been just as familiar to her great-great-grandfather as they were to her.

Many of the families had lived there long enough that legends of the years before the elves were first exiled still echoed among the younger generations.

As they rode down a narrow side street, avoiding a massive puddle that had flooded the more direct path, she noticed an old woman wearing a kerchief peering through her front window at her. When she saw that Kessara had noticed her presence, her eyes went wide within her weathered face, and she ducked out of sight.

These people must never be forced to serve King Ursa. Their culture would be destroyed, dragged forward into a future that they never asked for and do not want. No. We will succeed here tonight, and soon, I will be queen. I will be able to protect those who have no one else to turn to.

Wes rode a few feet away from her on one of the donkeys that they'd been given, gazing up at the narrow facades with an expression of wonder on his face despite the rain that poured into his eyes. She smiled. Despite all of the traveling he had done as Envoy, and despite being raised in a stunning palace of his own, he always seemed to find new things in the world that fascinated him.

High One, You have done great things for Wes Cervos. Please help him to see it when he cannot.

She thought of the boy who she had promised to marry the first time, before the Septemvirate had hauled him off to prison for blasphemy and treason. She wasn't sure that she would recognize him if she met him now. Even after beginning to hear about the High One, he had still been so sad, so bitter about the life he had been given.

But he had grown. The sadness and bitterness might have crept up on him from time to time, but he managed to resist it, to fight it, to be good in spite of it.

Through him, through his faith, it was as though the most admirable parts of King and Queen Cervos had been resurrected.

Wes turned in his saddle, flashing her a quizzical expression, and she turned quickly in the other direction, trying to suppress a smile.

You will never be my Roven, and you don't need to be. But I am so proud of the man that you are.

She hoped that she would get a chance to tell him as much.

They had spoken little on their journey, in part because of the wind and rain, but also because she had too much in her mind that she did not know how to say.

Now that they had made their way down the staircase, the wind was much more bearable, and there were some overhangs from the buildings that gave respite from the endless rain. Still, they had been quiet, with only an occasional request from a guard or a bray from a donkey to break the silence.

They continued for several more minutes, until finally, up ahead down a long street, they spotted the North Sea.

"It's beautiful," she said, clearing her throat. It felt dry, as though dust had gathered upon her tongue.

"But a dangerous beauty," Wes said, not taking his eyes off of the crashing waves. Each one struck at the sand and rocks with a sound like thunder, but the donkeys paid it no attention.

"Good thing we left the stags," she said, gesturing behind her toward the plateau high above at the top of the stairs. "I'd have been thrown for sure if they heard that racket."

"Me too," Wes said, smiling at her.

"You would have been bucked off in two seconds! Remember the time at the archery tournament in Aridmoor?"

"Lord Henico's face is burned into my mind," Wes said, grinning. "Not to mention Lady Gwyn's expression when she set the tablecloth on fire while trying to shut him up."

"Trust Moorn to put out a fire with an entire bottle of spirits."

"King Radagar looked about ready to serve me at the feast after that stunt."

"At least Kylan wasn't King then," she said, laughing. "I'm pretty sure he would have actually had you executed."

A few minutes later, they were laughing uncontrollably,

happy tears mingling on their cheeks with the rain. Old stories passed between them, most of them involving Moorn or Roven or both getting into trouble, but he and Kessara were always there, too. Usually they were in the background, trying to keep the peace, but she had loved fooling around with their friends all the same.

"This is okay, you know?" she said once they had caught their breath, thinking of what it would be like to be just the two of them, going through life side by side as husband and wife.

"It is," Wes agreed. She knew that he knew exactly what she meant, and she found that fact comforting.

Friendship could become romance. She had to believe that. And even if it didn't, friendship was still a powerful kind of love, all by itself. Her love for Wes was just as real as her love for Alder, whether it became something more or not.

"Look," Wes said suddenly, leaning toward her in his saddle and lowering his voice to a whisper. "Captain Drohma, by those docks."

He only had a couple of his own men with him, but still, a ripple of apprehension passed through her. Kessara stood up straight in her saddle, hoping that every hint of merriment was gone from her face. She wouldn't let him sense any point of weakness. Not ever.

Out over the sea, she could see the three dragons flying, but Alder was not on any of their backs.

The two royal guards moved their own donkeys closer, but Kessara raised a hand and told them not to bother.

"The good Captain would never defy a decree of the King," she said, loud enough for him to hear. He smiled at her as they closed the gap between their parties.

"Our Princess is not only beautiful, but wise," he replied, giving her an exaggerated bow. She twisted her fingers in the sodden fabric of her cloak, remembering the piggish things he had said about her and her mother. She loathed flattery, especially when she knew the much less flattering thoughts passing through his vile mind, but she would not allow her emotions to show on her face.

"Thank you, Captain," she said, giving Wes a warning glance to keep quiet. Fortunately, unlike Alder, he was more familiar with the quiet skill of diplomacy, and gave the Captain only a nod.

"You're most welcome," he said, his words seeming to ooze out of him like tar. "In any case, there is little time for you to return a compliment. Look!"

There was a tremendous sound from the water, but this time, the wave had not yet hit the shore. A great tentacle stretched toward the sky before slamming down onto the surface, sending a plume of water nearly as high as the clouds.

"It looks like the Princess was right," he said, his false smile still plastered on his face despite the look of terror that shone in his eyes.

"I guess you had time for one more compliment of your own," she said, jumping down from her donkey's back and racing toward the docks.

For once, she wished very much that she had been wrong.

CELESYRIA

"Watch out for his arms!" Jaconial's voice sounded in Celesyria's mind as the creature struck upward, as though angry at the sky itself. Perhaps it was.

The sea boiled beneath her as she flew, moving as quickly as she could through the blinding rain. There was no lightning at the moment, but she knew that it could start at any time.

For the moment, though, she and her friends had other concerns. Jaconial and Nazzan rode just behind her, and the three of them made another high pass, trying to get an idea of what exactly they were dealing with.

The tentacles stretched much higher than she first thought, making it difficult to get a good look. Worse, the creature was blue, making it difficult to see amid the water and foam as it writhed in all directions.

"By the Dracodei, I never thought such a beast could still exist," Nazzan said in her mind as he dove lower, narrowly avoiding being lashed by a tentacle. *"Was it here beneath the surface all this time? Or did the elves keep it in the West Strait?"*

"It wouldn't fit! Look at the size of it," Jaconial said, pulling her wings taut as she caught a buoyant gust of wind and glided to the right. *"In any case, would you please be more careful?"*

"She's right, you're too close," Celesyria added, following Jaconial on the pocket of air.

On the shore, she could see Wes and Kessara, standing near Drohma and his men. She assumed Alder would have seen something by now and come running from the lighthouse, but she did not spot him. The heavy sheets of rain made visibility difficult. Of course, it was a perfect night to attack, at least from the perspective of the Gorok.

"You do realize that we will have to actually attack it at some point," Nazzan said, his voice teasing.

She glanced at Jaconial, who had fallen in beside her.

"Every species of man drives me crazy," Celesyria ventured, half-worried that she would be offended. To her relief, Jaconial only nodded and gave a quick smile, baring her sharp

teeth.

Before she could respond, the creature began to move, cutting through the current as though the choppy water was a still pond.

It seemed to use his tentacles almost to climb the waves, rising out of the water so that they could see more of its body. Nazzan pulled up at once, flying closer to Jaconial and Celesyria as the Gorok gave a roar from some unseen orifice.

"You were saying something about attacking it?" Celesyria said, gasping as they circled the monster, avoiding its flailing tentacles. It was many times their size, and she understood at once why the fishermen had all refused to sail. She eyed the fishing boats moored near the docks, sure that the creature could grab hold of one and tear it in two with ease.

"Ladies first," Nazzan quipped.

They watched in horror as the creature began to move again, using its tentacles to pull itself through the water. Waves crashed around what they assumed was its head, its full shape obscured by the water below and the curtain formed by the incessant rain.

"It's going for the shore!" Jaconial shouted.

It moved faster than she would have thought possible, twirling and writhing toward the docks. They flew as close behind it as they dared. Celesyria could see an eye the size of a barrel-lid peeking up from the surface. Its gaze was black and hollow, and she could not tell if it was intelligent or merely acting on pure instinct. Before she could examine it further, the eye sunk beneath the waves again, most of the body disappearing as the larger waves near the shore crashed over it.

Celesyria watched as Kessara and Wes retreated backward

off of the docks they had been standing on. Screams filled the air, rising in volume as more and more people awoke from their sleep. Fishermen and children, peasant women and well-dressed merchants, all joining together in a panicked mob. They raced across the cobbles, all moving toward the cliff.

Toward the staircase.

"Wes," Celesyria called to him in her mind as they circled back around.

"High One help us," he replied.

For a moment she could not speak. The Gorok moved ever faster, pressing toward the ships and the docks in great twirling strides. They had to fly higher as the creature paused for a moment, striking at the sky with its tentacles, though she did not think that its eyes were placed in such a way that it could see them from behind.

"Ask Kessara if her guards can get to the top of the staircase," she told Wes as she opened her wings, letting a draft of blistering wind draw her higher over the tethered fishing boats. *"Even some of Drohma's men, if he will listen. There's only one way out of Kingsvier Landing, and if someone was to attack the fleeing citizens from above..."*

She couldn't bring herself to say the words.

If the creature had indeed been drawn here by the elves, they couldn't ignore the possibility that more enemies might be hiding. If the crowd of people could not make it onto the plateau above, it would be a massacre. The Gorok would strike land soon, and if it wasn't stopped, it would tear through the city like the buildings were made of toothpicks, killing anyone who got in its way.

She wished very much that she could shout at King Manta. If he had listened sooner to his own people, the city might have already been evacuated. They might have had the men to truly fight back. As it was, she felt helpless, even with Jaconial and Nazzan beside her. As usual, the High One was their only hope.

22

Chapter Twenty-Two

WES

Wes watched as the Gorok drew closer, unable to make his feet obey him. He knew that he should run, to try and flee to the interior of the city, but he couldn't bring himself to move away from the docks.

Kessara stood nearby, her feet rooted in place as she stared.

The beast was like nothing he had ever seen, a great mass of slick tentacles attached to a body many times the size of a full-grown dragon. It cut through the gargantuan waves as though they were only air, its huge eyes staring up out of the water every few seconds.

Kessara choked out from beside him that the creature looked stupid, but he could not agree.

Somehow, even through the screaming wind and the driving rain, he could see something deeper within those black pools.

The darkness was there, a malevolent intelligence that could make even stupid creatures obey. He was sure of it.

For a moment, he forgot his headache, forgot the dampness

of his soaked clothing. He felt a chill rush through him at the thought of its tentacles touching his flesh, grabbing him, dragging him under the surface to the freezing depths below.

"We need to do something, Kessara," he shouted over the wind. She turned to face him, but she said nothing. He could see the worry in her eyes.

Alder had not yet arrived.

The two of them watched as Drohma shouted for several Red Army soldiers to make for the coast. Several ignored him, joining the press of civilians racing for the staircase, but some of the men drew their swords, rushing past Wes and Kessara onto the docks.

The Princess had sent her men toward the stairs as Celesyria suggested, but Wes wondered if they would be able to make it to the top in time to be of any help. He could only hope that the soldiers who had taken their stags when they had arrived would stay at their post. They might be the only protection the people would have if bandits or elves chose to try and cut off their escape route.

Wes felt a hard shove from behind as Captain Drohma raced past, nearly knocking him onto the worn gray boards.

"Coward," the man spat, following the others who were getting into a haphazard battle formation near the fishing boats. Ignoring him, Wes turned to Kessara, who looked about ready to throw the captain into the Gorok's waiting embrace.

"You need to get inside, Kessara," he said, watching as the creature struck out a tentacle and took hold of a dinghy that had come untied. With incredible strength, the Gorok hurled the small craft toward the rocks on the far side of the port, where it struck with a crash and shattered into a thousand splinters. "Go somewhere near the cliffs. It's getting closer."

"No," she said, shaking her head and stepping out of the way as some of the braver fishermen rushed onto the docks to join the soldiers. Even a few children had joined in the effort, attempting to pelt the monster with rocks from a safe distance while their mothers screamed at them to stay with the crowd making for the stairs. "My people are in need. Ask the dragons to land. We need to do something."

"What exactly do you think we should do?" he asked, exasperated, as he called out to Celesyria in his mind. Alder would no doubt appear at any moment and blame Wes for Kessara's stubbornness.

Not that he's any more likely than I am to be able to get her to listen.

The Princess gestured in the direction of the fishing boats, where a few dozen soldiers were racing toward the beast, swords drawn. A few more stood on top of buildings, firing arrows. The creature cried out, and Wes swore that he could feel the force of the sound deep within his bones.

A few seconds later, he saw the dragons landing on a flat patch of sand a little further to the west. It was near the water, but not as close to the beast. He and Kessara would be able to get to them.

"We must fight," Kessara said, nodding in the direction of Celesyria, Jaconial, and Nazzan. "In any way that we can."

Before they could move toward their friends, however, a huge wave spilled over onto the nearest dock with enough force to shatter the wooden support beams that rested beneath. Kessara screamed as the ground tilted under them, only just managing to avoid sliding toward the bubbling water.

"Get back!" Wes screamed as another wave crested behind the first one. It was even taller. To his relief, Kessara did not argue this time.

Taking her hand, he raced uphill, toward the residential part of town that lay just past the fishing district. He willed his feet not to trip on the old uneven cobblestones. There was no time.

They reached the end of an alleyway and turned around just as the sea poured water directly onto the spot where they'd been standing, shattering a large section of the dock and burying the area beneath filthy, mud-ridden water.

ALDER

Alder tripped against the thick sand, swearing as he slid to the ground. Within seconds he was on his feet again, the mud sucking at his boots, threatening to pull him back down.

"Are you alright?" Aelrie called as she passed him from behind, having no difficulty whatsoever navigating the terrain on her light elven feet.

"Fine," he grunted, but she was far enough ahead that he doubted she could hear him at all.

Good. Just find them. Keep them safe.

To his left, the waves were so high that he feared the entire beach would soon be covered with water, but he could not get out of the way. There were jagged black rocks to his right, slick with rain and impossible to climb.

They could only run.

He and Aelrie raced along the small strip of beach that remained, trying desperately to see what was happening out on the sea. Alder thought he saw a large tentacle a few times, but he could not be sure of exactly where it was, or if it was getting closer as he feared. Each crushing wave sent a cloud of white mist into the air, veiling the Gorok's movement even more.

He had to get back to the port. He ran harder, wishing he could shed his sodden clothes. *I thought we had more time. I would have never left to get a better view if–*

An enormous noise split the air. For a moment, he could not think even of Kessara.

The Gorok's call reminded him of the screech of a bird, only many times louder, and beneath the high pitched whine was a deep sound like shifting stone.

"High One help us!" he shouted at no one in particular, forcing his legs to move even faster. A second later, he tripped again over a jutting rock, sprawling to the sand. He could feel warm blood gushing from his knee, but he ignored it as the beast screamed a second time.

Finally, he reached the edge of the city proper, and raced onto the cobblestone. Aelrie had rushed ahead, and now he could no longer see her.

The entire place had erupted into a panic. Hundreds of citizens were rushing toward the cliffside staircase, shoving and trampling each other as they went. He watched as a young soldier shouted at them, trying to keep order, only to be shoved off of the road by a large woman in a blacksmith's apron.

Other soldiers from both factions were pouring down streets and stumbling out of houses, converging on the port. They were cutting lines and boarding the nimble fishing vessels, and several of the fishermen were attempting to stop them from commandeering their boats by means of their fists.

He saw Aelrie again, near the docks, standing atop a large stack of crates and firing at the creature with her bow. To his relief, none of the soldiers seemed to have noticed her presence, and if they had, they were leaving her alone. If anyone could get an arrow into the monster's eye, it would be the elf.

Hefting his sword into his hand, he stopped to breathe for a moment, noticing for the first time the filthy stench that the creature had dredged up from the deep.

He could see it now, out past the fishing boats, and there was no doubt now that it was coming closer. If there were any more men coming, they would have to hurry. The boats could be easily sunk by the beast on their own, but if enough of them could get close, he hoped that they'd be able to deal some damage.

Before he could join the soldiers, however, he saw the three dragons alighting on the patch of beach that sat near the docks. They were uncomfortably close to the water, but he knew that they had little choice. There were too many tight buildings on this side of the city for them to land elsewhere.

"Celesyria!" he shouted, running toward them, his knee aching beneath his wet trousers.

"We made a pass," she said as he arrived, giving him a quick nudge with her snout. "It's bigger and faster than it looks from here. If the soldiers don't stop it..."

Her voice trailed off.

They all knew.

The creature roared again, and Jaconial lifted her wings up in an attempt to cover her ears. "I didn't sign up for this," she said, shaking as the Gorok continued its demented noises.

"None of us did, including the men who are currently trying to kill it with arrows and swords," Nazzan reminded her, gesturing toward the docks. The soldiers had managed to get several more of the boats into the water, rushing up beside the beast before it could get any closer to shore. It had already turned over at least two of the vessels, but it seemed to be struggling to keep up with all of them as it was pelted with arrows from all directions.

High One help them.

"Where are Wes and Kessara?" he asked.

"They told us to land here," Jaconial said.

Celesyria cocked her head for a moment, probably speaking to Wes, but before she could tell them more, they heard a rush of water loud enough to drown out the screams of the Gorok.

They watched as Aelrie leapt from the top of the crates, racing out of the way just as the port was hit with a wave, tearing the docks straight from their pilings and eroding the sand beneath.

Alder stared at the destruction, waiting for the mist to clear, an unintelligible mix of words that might have been a prayer racing through his mind.

Before he could search for bodies in the water, he saw it.

A second wave, swelling to an impossible height as it moved toward the shore.

He saw Aelrie racing toward them, nearly falling as she scrambled past one of the broken boats that had been pushed onto the sand by the rushing water.

And then he saw a flash of blue on the street that led uphill.

Without a word, he jumped onto Celesyria's back and pointed toward the main street. The dragon leapt into the sky without comment, pumping her wings so quickly that she was flying faster than the wave, circling high above as it pummeled the docks.

Kessara and Wes stood safely out of harm's way, mere feet from the edge of the water.

"Can you get me down to them?" He called to her, glancing over his shoulder at Nazzan and Jaconial, who had followed close behind. Aelrie was already on Jaconial's saddle.

As they descended, he could see the look of annoyance on Wes' face below, and he was almost certain they were arguing. He was even more certain that Kessara's stubbornness was the cause.

He felt a smile tugging at his lips despite the chaos that threatened to consume them.

KESSARA

Kessara stood beside Wes, trying to steady her breathing. The wave had spared them, and from what she could see from where she stood, most of the soldiers were standing a bit farther toward the eastern end of the docks, which had not been badly damaged. She saw several fishing boats overturned in the water, but whether they had been capsized by the Gorok or by the water, she did not know.

She lowered her head in a brief prayer. Her country would grieve these men, whatever colors they wore, but not yet.

The creature was still attacking the other soldiers, guttural cries pouring out of it as it struck out with tentacles and moved fast enough to cause fresh waves to form.

She could see their archers spending arrows, but it did not seem to be doing much good. As she watched, four of the soldiers leaned over from their fishing boat and hacked at one of the tentacles with their swords, finally severing it. The pitch of the creature's scream was so high that she wished to cover her ears.

Maybe if we could remove more of the tentacles, we'd have a fighting chance.

An idea was forming in her mind, but before she could think about it further, she saw a flash of orange scales overhead.

CHAPTER TWENTY-TWO

"Celesyria!"

Alder was on her back.

Kessara's heart swelled with relief at the mere sight of him.

Celesyria landed, with Nazzan close behind her. Jaconial and Aelrie landed a second later. Alder climbed off of Celesyria's back, and without another word, Kessara raced toward him.

She fell against his chest, embracing him, hardly noticing the cold mud that now coated her dress and cloak. The Gorok screamed in the background, but she did not even turn. The rain pelted down with a new ferocity, but she did not wipe the water from her eyes.

For a moment, she could forget all of it. She longed for one more kiss, even though she knew it would hurt even worse than the last.

When it came to Alder, she was addicted even to the pain.

Before either of them could do anything stupid, Wes was there, and she stepped back to let Alder clap him on the back.

"Thank you, brother," Alder said, his eyes red with what Kessara suspected might have been tears. "Thank you for protecting her."

Kessara might have argued that she was protecting herself just fine, but for the moment, she could only be thankful to still be alive. The docks below were a mess of mangled wood and foaming water, and she could see even more of the soldiers' bodies bumping against the piles, lifeless. They had to act.

"I have a plan," she shouted over the rain. "Alder and I will go to the docks. The rest of you need to go back out over the water. Keep an eye on the beast as best you can. I may need you to help me direct the soldiers from the sky."

"We will try," Nazzan promised, looking at the others. Jaconial and Celesyria nodded.

"I haven't been to Kingsvier Landing in years, but I remember something from my most recent visit," she continued, her voice rising with her excitement. "There's a munitions factory here. A small one, but..."

"Calesca bombs?" Alder asked, his eyes gleaming. She could nearly see the wheels turning inside his head. Galeharbor was famous for producing the deadly munitions.

"Mostly, but they won't be of use here. Their blast radius is too large, and we can't risk blowing up the entire fishing district."

"If we don't kill the Gorok, the fishing district will be underwater anyway," Alder said.

"He's right, Princess," Wes agreed, shaking his head. "We should use the most powerful explosives we have. We can get the soldiers out of the way—"

"There's no time," she said firmly, standing as tall as she could manage. The three dragons tilted their heads in approval. "Even if I could get all of the soldiers to listen to me—and if Captain Drohma is still alive that is far from guaranteed—our people rely on this harbor for food. The majority of our fishing boats are kept here, and we've already lost several of them. We're hanging on by a thread as it is. We already rely so much on Aridmoor's grain. We cannot let the people lose fish as well."

Alder went to speak, but she continued, ignoring him.

I will not cower like my mother. There are times when a woman is right, and a man is wrong.

"I am the Princess of Galeharbor. This is my Kingdom, and considering that my father and mother are holed up in Windshear at the moment, I am in charge. We will not be using any calesca bombs. We will not risk destroying the remainder of the fleet."

For a moment, Alder and Wes both stared at her, but finally they nodded.

"There are other bombs we can use," she added. "Trust me. The rest of you, get to the sea. I may need Alder to help me talk to the soldiers, and it will be easier to speak to them if I'm not shouting from a dragon's back."

"You should stay here where it's safe, Kessara," Alder said, his objection lacking its usual force.

"We don't have time to argue about this," she said, watching as Wes climbed onto Celesyria's back. "You'll be right beside me. I'm not worried."

As she watched her friends flying toward the tumult below, she stood as straight as she could, trying to stop her hands from shaking. The munitions storehouse was close, and she remembered the way.

It was a long shot, but at least it was something.

Chapter Twenty-Three

CELESYRIA

A few minutes later, Celesyria circled over the harbor, comforted by the familiar weight of Wes riding on her back.

Below them, the Gorok continued to assault the ships in the dock, disappearing beneath the waves every few seconds to flee the hail of arrows before rising up again in another location. It was difficult for the archers to track him, and she feared that it wouldn't be long before their stock of arrows began to deplete. They needed more men, but she doubted that any would be forthcoming. Drohma would have sent for aid, of course, but even the fastest messenger would be too late if they could not at least injure the Gorok.

"Pull up!" Jaconial's voice sounded in her head. She obeyed the urgent command without question, narrowly avoiding being hit by the other dragon as she dodged one of the creature's tentacles.

"I'll vomit if that thing touches me," Jaconial added with a visible shudder as she flew back down closer to the surface,

Aelrie balanced expertly on her back.

An elf riding a dragon. These are indeed strange times.

"What's the plan?" Wes asked in her mind as they circled once again, making their way slowly toward the eastern side of the harbor. She still could see no sign of Kessara or Alder, but they could do little else but follow her orders.

"I have no idea. Let's take one more pass over the streets and hope Kessara knows what she's doing."

The lower part of the city had almost completely emptied out, but as they'd feared, the staircase was too narrow to handle the size of the crowd. Hundreds of people were gathered near the base of the cliff, jostling for space on the stairs. Over the shushing of the rain and the roars of the sea monster behind them, she could hear the screams of women punctuated by the occasional high-pitched cry of a child.

The Gorok was getting closer, and the people were panicking.

"Jaconial, Aelrie, you need to help them," Wes shouted. Celesyria agreed, nodding as she flapped her wings against a strong gust of cold air that had swept in out of nowhere. "If they tear each other apart, what good have we done?"

"They aren't going to listen to an elf," Jaconial snapped.

"They will listen to a Guardian," Celesyria said firmly. "And Aelrie's skills may be needed to bring calm. Please, you must try."

She caught a look of horror on Aelrie's face at her suggestion, but she could not dwell on it. She had to get back to the docks, even if all she could do was to try and fly close enough to tear at the creature with her claws. Wes would just have to wait with the men on land.

"Fine," Jaconial said, flying nearly low enough to hit the

tops of the buildings as she approached the crowd.

Celesyria turned back toward the North Sea and saw something that made her blood run warm.

"O, High One, no. Spare us. Have mercy," Wes was saying in her mind as she ceased flapping her wings, letting the air carry her toward the waves. She could not seem to gather her thoughts well enough to form a response. Breathing was suddenly difficult.

Along the horizon she could see four elven vessels, moving quickly toward the shores of Kingsvier Landing.

Managing to find the words to describe the terrible sight, she reached out to Alder in his mind, praying that wherever he was, he would be able to hear her.

AELRIE

Aelrie leaned against Jaconial's neck, trying to get a good look at the mob as they drew closer to the base of the stairs. She could see men with bleeding noses and bruised eyesockets, women crying, and children being ushered toward the stairs apart from their parents. There were a handful of soldiers, but they did not seem to be working together in any sort of organized fashion.

Several of the children pointed and shouted at the sky, smiles breaking on their sad faces as Jaconial approached.

"A dragon! Look!" she heard one of them cry, a young boy with blonde hair done in tight plaits against the top of his head. Several other children joined in, pointing and jumping up and down at the sight.

"There's an elf on her back, mama, look!" another one said, this time a tall girl. Her mother did not seem to have even heard her as she ushered her daughter toward the staircase.

To think that not so long ago, children would have often seen Guardians patrolling the skies, reminding them that they were safe.

Aelrie swallowed a lump in her throat, not quite able to bring herself to think about who exactly they had been kept safe from.

When they reached the stairs, every step crowded with people, Jaconial circled above. Aelrie searched the top of the plateau, her keen eyes alert for any sign of movement coming from the wrong direction, but there was none. All she could see was sparse, dry grass punctuated by dead trees, and a snaking line of people heading off toward other towns in search of safety. She looked toward the south. Somewhere behind the mist, Windshear stood. Many of the people would go there and rush to the palace walls, begging for aid from the King and Queen.

"Such foolishness," Jaconial said, her voice rumbling alongside the pounding of the rain. "This could have all been avoided"

"The King did what he thought was best," she said quietly, not sure if she wanted Jaconial to hear at all. The dragon said nothing, taking a final turn and sweeping along the edge of the cliff for a few moments before heading back toward the crowd waiting at the base.

Aelrie watched in disgust as a group of what she assumed were Lesser House nobles, all dressed in fine clothes, reached the top of the stairs. Behind them, taking up much of the available space, were several servants carrying their huge pieces of luggage.

"I have half a mind to throw their trunks to the Gorok," Jaconial said. Aelrie could feel the growl in the dragon's chest, even through the leather of her saddle.

"If you could get at them without harming the servants, I'd agree with you," she said, shaking her head. The selfishness was difficult to contemplate.

A moment later, they saw a group of five men in the middle of the huge waiting crowd, their fists and curses flying. One of the men took a punch to the side of the head and went down, nearly being trampled by the press of people trying to get past them.

"Look!" Aelrie said, hoping the dragon knew what she was referring to. It was difficult to pick out individuals among the chaos, but to her relief, Jaconial saw the fight and began to fly lower.

Before she could think of what they might do to bring calm, the dragon was approaching them, flying so low that a tall man could reach up and touch the scales of her belly.

Without another civilized word, Jaconial roared directly at the men, loud enough that they, and several of the others near them, fell to the ground in a clumsy heap.

She snarled at them. "Fight again, and I will kill you. Think of your hatchlings instead of yourselves."

Without waiting for a reply, she flapped her wings and headed back up higher into the air.

"I suppose we must do what works," Aelrie said, shaking her head in mock disapproval.

"Are you sure I can't do the same to the merchants?"

"Tempting," Aelrie admitted as she watched the expensive leather luggage being hoisted up the final steps and onto the plateau. Jaconial circled again, looking for more trouble, but the crowd seemed to be behaving for the time being.

The children began to point and stare with even more

excitement, several of their parents joining in. Not sure how else to convey that she was indeed a friend, she raised a hand in greeting, smiling down at them. Many of the children and some of the mothers did the same in return, but it brought her no relief.

She had not intentionally used magic to manipulate them, but still, she could never be sure of the reaction of any human. Elves were not like them. Her race poured darkness into their veins, tainting everything.

Is Wes truly my friend, or is he trapped in an elven snare that even I cannot see?

In better moments, she wanted to believe that there was indeed good within her, that Wes and the others saw something that made her life worth living. But more often than not, she doubted it.

She had come to Auranth seeking forgiveness, but how would she know if the High One would grant it when she was still too terrified to ask Him?

She could not dare. The High One was the God of light and truth. She knew only shadows and lies.

As if on cue, she felt a surge of darkness within her, the sensation pushing the breath from her lungs.

She gripped the leather straps of the saddle, only just able to stop herself from falling.

Her mouth felt dry, and everything was spinning, her vision dotted with stars. The force was stronger than anything she'd ever felt before, as if the entirety of the North Sea had crashed against her very bones.

Protect them. Protect him.

The words danced at the edge of her consciousness, beckoning for her to pay attention. She pushed aside the sudden longing to fall apart, trying to focus on what she knew that she had to do. She had to keep moving.

"Jaconial!" she screamed, not caring how insane she sounded. "Turn around! We have to get to the water! Now!"

Jaconial did not question her. The dragon banked hard to the right, her wing nearly touching the edge of a rooftop as she turned. She flew hard against the surging wind, covering the distance as quickly as she could, but Aelrie knew that she could run even faster.

"Go to that roof, get as close as you can!" she shouted as the Gorok screamed again, threatening to drown out her words entirely.

As soon as Jaconial was low enough, she leapt from the dragon's back and ran, leaping for the next rooftop and then racing down the stairs. She hoped Jaconial would find the others.

A single face filled her mind, consuming everything. She had to protect Wes, no matter what else happened. She didn't have much time.

They were coming.

WES

Wes clutched at his stomach with one hand as Celesyria raced toward the approaching elven ships. Flying always made him sick, but this was something much worse. Black light bathed the edges of his vision, and for a moment, he thought he would pass out and fall to his death.

Sucking in gasps of salty air, he forced himself to take careful hold of the saddle, looking over his shoulder at Jaconial's retreating figure. He thought of Aelrie on her back, riding with perfect grace, her braids flying out behind her, slick and ink-black in the rain. He hoped that the people would see that she was on their side, but even if they didn't, he trusted that Jaconial would find some way to keep them in line. There was no other option.

"We need to get closer," he said to Celesyria in his mind, eyeing the boats. *"We need to know how many there are."*

All he wanted to do was to run away, to let someone else deal with this evil, but he knew it was a child's wish. There would be no mysterious heroes coming to save the city. All of the heroes were already here, dressed in uniforms of red and blue, many of them floating face down in the water.

High One, help them to know that they are not alone. None of us are. You are with us.

They flew closer, and for a moment he could focus on nothing else but staying in place on the dragon's back. The wind was even fiercer this far from shore, and Celesyria had to use every ounce of her strength to keep their course.

The sails of the small boats below billowed gently, drawing the elves at a steady pace toward land. He could see men and women perched on wooden seats, wearing thick cloaks but otherwise unconcerned with the torrent of rain or the screaming of the wind.

"Looks like there's only five in each boat," Celesyria said, unmistakable relief filling her voice.

"That's a lot for so few of us," he replied, closing his eyes as the dragon took a sharp turn and made her way back toward land. There was no point in waiting around for an elven arrow to pierce the membrane of Celesyria's wing, but he did not wish to look down as she hurried.

"With the High One on our side, a thousand elf warriors would be nothing," Celesyria said firmly.

As they raced back toward land, they watched as the Gorok lifted one of the fishing boats with its tentacles, hefting it into the air with no effort at all. Wes swallowed bile at the sound of the screams that followed. He looked down into the maelstrom below, averting his eyes as several of the soldiers on board were hurled against the rocky edge of the shoreline, their cries going quiet in an instant.

"May the High One bring them to the Eternal Lands," Celesyria said, bowing her head as she flew. Wes said nothing, unable to bring himself to pray at all.

Celesyria could watch all of Kaveryth burn, still believing that they were doing the right thing and that the High One would restore everything in time. He envied her faith, and yet he did not know how to find it for himself.

How could he find the strength to keep going when everything was falling apart? How could he sleep at night knowing that the events he and his friends had set into motion had brought such evil to innocent people all across the continent?

He thought of the great spire, watching over everything, a constant feature of his life for all of his eighteen years.

Perhaps he should return to it.

Perhaps he should carry the treasures of the people to the sacred cave, taking up the role of Envoy that he had cast aside.

Perhaps the promise of protection from dying Guardians would come to pass once again.

He shook his head, smiling grimly to himself as Celesyria headed for the far side of the harbor.

Those promises were not enough, and nothing he could do would bring the old days back. He did not share Celesyria's unshakeable faith, but he had not yet lost all hope. He'd seen the High One move mountains before, and he trusted that He could do it again.

Perhaps trust was the only kind of faith that he had, for now.

It would have to be enough.

Chapter Twenty-Four

ALDER

The munitions warehouse stood on the eastern side of the harbor, a large gray building with no windows. To Alder's astonishment, it appeared to be deserted.

"Did none of the men think to use explosives?" he asked Kessara, staring at the imposing structure as they hurried along the docks. To their left, he could see the soldiers continuing to attack the Gorok, but their numbers had lessened. Many had run, he was sure, but he feared just how many had died.

They were running out of time. Kessara's plan had to work.

"Almost none are local," the Princess said, sounding out of breath as she hurried across the planks. "The fishermen may know of the explosives made here, but to remember that fact in the middle of a fight is another thing."

"And most of the fishermen have fled or been killed," he said, staring out at the floating remains of ships that the Gorok had destroyed. There were still many that remained untouched, but he saw no fishermen standing on their decks. Not that he blamed them.

"There he is," Kessara said suddenly, gesturing toward a group of Red Army men standing nearer to the creature.

Alder knew at once who she meant.

"Do not get involved. Please," she begged him, gesturing for him to pull the hood of his cloak over his head. He did so, hoping that his face would be obscured in shadow. She was right. However he felt about the man, this was no time for his ego and rage to take over.

"Captain!" Kessara called, quickening her pace as she took a few steps onto the narrow dock. "Come at once."

Captain Drohma turned, a look of surprise on his face. Alder suppressed a grin. The man was not used to being told what to do, except perhaps by King Ursa.

"My Princess," he said easily, striding toward her and kissing her hand. "How may I be of service?"

Alder watched them from beside a stack of storage crates, but his former Captain did not notice his presence.

"What is happening now?" she asked quickly, gesturing to the creature. "I require an update."

"Kingsvier Landing is being attacked by a presumed-legendary sea monster, and my men stand in the way. Along with the help of the good Princess and her band of traitors, of course."

Alder tightened his fists beneath his cloak, but Kessara only smiled, the backdrop of the pouring rain and screeching Gorok doing little to upset her regal expression.

"I must remind the Captain that were it not for King Ursa's threats, my father would not have sent our navy ships away to the West Strait. Nor would your men have been stationed here and put in charge of their departure."

"I would think you would be thankful to have my aid, however accidentally my men came to be here," he replied, taking a couple of steps closer, his face mere inches from hers.

"Alder," Celesyria said in his mind. *"I know you cannot respond, but I need you to listen."*

She paused.

"Of course I am thankful, Captain," Kessara said.

"There are elves here, on the North Sea, making for the Gorok. About twenty of them. Coming fast."

His head swam, and he pressed his palms into his temples, as though the pressure might help him to think of what to do.

"I've had to pull back most of my men," Captain Drohma was saying. "They did not sign up for a suicide mission, so I have sent them to help your people reach the plateau and get to safety. Some remain on the boats, fighting with bows and swords, but I suspect few will live."

Alder drew a breath, stepping out from the crates and flinging back his hood before Kessara could respond. She glared at him, and he could see the fire within her blue eyes, even through the pouring rain.

"There are elven vessels in the sea, my Princess," he said, ignoring Drohma's look of rage at being spied upon. "They will arrive within mere minutes."

"Alright," Kessara said after a moment. "That's concern-ing."

Drohma snorted, and Alder suppressed the urge to punch him in the face.

"I need your help, Captain," she said, her voice clipped. "I need you to recall your men for the time being and to order them to make for the munitions factory. They won't be able to use the calesca bombs, but there will be others. It will give us a fighting chance at taking this beast down." She pointed at the building.

Drohma did not respond, instead striding over to Alder and circling him like a hawk watching his prey.

"Cadogen," he said, spitting at his feet. Alder watched as the mucus was washed away by the rain. Still, he said nothing, not daring even to move. Drohma was a worm, and it was high time he stopped concerning himself with his opinion.

"Princess, I promised to obey the orders of King Manta. Considering that you act now in his stead, I will do as you ask. I will try and convince more of my men to commit suicide for the sake of your peasants."

"It is the duty of a soldier to fight battles, even ones they may lose," Kessara said, jutting out her chin. "I ask no more of them than what their vows to People, King, and House demand."

"And what is the duty of a princess, then?" Drohma asked, looking at her with hate filling his eyes. "To make demands, to exert a price from others that she herself will never pay?"

Alder forced air into his lungs, hoping very much that the Gorok might swallow the disrespectful lout whole.

"Go and do as I have asked, Captain," Kessara said, turning on her heel and continuing toward the open space east of the harbor.

Alder followed, watching as Celesyria and Wes came flying toward them across the sea, Jaconial and Nazzan approaching from the west. Aelrie was nowhere to be seen.

Within a moment everyone save the elf stood in a circle, reunited amidst the chaos, but there was little time for greetings.

"We need to help them," Kessara said, her gaze passing

over each of the dragons in turn. "You three can keep the beast distracted while Drohma's men ready their bombs. The rest of us will stay here with the soldiers and do what we can from the shore."

"I will assist the dragons," Alder said, his voice firm. Nazzan gave him a quick nod of agreement, followed by Jaconial. Celesyria stared out at the sea, waiting. "My sword will be more useful there than on the docks."

He waited for Kessara to protest, but she said nothing, only giving him a short nod. Instead, it was Wes who spoke.

"I will come with you as well. I will not abandon Celesyria to this monster by herself."

He strode forward, moving to climb onto her back, but Alder pressed ahead of him, standing near the dragon's shimmering orange flank.

"Nazzan and Jaconial will protect each other, and I will not leave Celesyria. Stay with the Princess, Wes. And ask Aelrie to come and help when she turns up."

"Thank you, Alder," the dragon said, her voice filled with sadness. He glanced down at the heavy manacles that still encircled her ankles.

You will survive this, and you will be rid of them, I promise you.

"I can fight," Wes protested, his brows knitting together over his dark eyes as rain flattened his curls against his skull. "I'm not as good of a swordsman as Alder, to be sure, but–"

"Your skill with a sword is irrelevant," Kessara snapped, cutting him off before he could say anything else. She strode forward until she was between the two men, staring between them. Alder could not tell if it was tears or raindrops that dripped from her perfect blue eyes.

"I will stand aside because the duty of a Princess is not to die as a soldier," she continued, pausing for a moment as the sound of an explosion filled the air, followed by a renewed battle cry. "As of now, my duty is to marry the Envoy of Silverfell, to become Queen, to rule our people, and eventually to produce heirs. Your duty is intertwined with my own. You must live."

Alder gripped the hilt of his sword so tightly that he was certain his palms would bleed, but he did not care.

Discipline.

"The Princess is right, Wes," he said, looking down at him from the height of Celesyria's back. "To fight the beast directly..."

He trailed off as he caught the glances of the other dragons, not wanting to say the words. They all knew it, and even they were afraid. As a mere human he was much more delicate than they were, and so was Wes.

"You should stay here and help where you can. But you must not let your pride get in the way if retreat is necessary," he continued.

Wes' eyes flashed with anger. "I'm not going to cower like a little boy."

"He's right," Celesyria chimed in, craning her neck so that she could look over at her friend. "The future of the Four Kingdoms rests upon you, Wes. You are too valuable to us all to die this night."

"Maybe I want to die," Wes spat. "Maybe I'm tired of bearing this burden. I never asked to be Envoy. I never asked for any of this to happen."

Alder recoiled, nausea rising in his throat.

After everything they had done to protect him, after all the sacrifices of so many people, he was going to stand there and wish for death?

The rage that had been simmering ever since Captain Drohma left threatened to boil over. He let go of the leather straps and slid from the saddle, landing hard on the stone and muck.

"Do you have any idea what is even being asked of the rest of us?" he demanded, tightening his fists as he stood, towering over the shorter man. Wes took a step back, stammering as he tried to form an answer, but Alder did not feel like hearing him speak.

"You are being asked to marry a wonderful woman, the woman that I love," he continued, jabbing a finger in Wes' face. The dragons and Kessara were saying something, but he couldn't hear them through the blood pulsing in his ears. "And I am being asked to fight to make sure that happens. I am willing to *die* to make sure that happens. So you will stop acting like a petulant child, you will stay here, and you will live."

Wes was apologizing, but he ignored him, climbing onto Celesyria's back without another word.

CELESYRIA

"He probably deserved that," Celesyria admitted, loud enough for the others to hear as she and Alder flew over the North Sea. Jaconial and Nazzan were flying as close to her side as their wingspans would allow.

They were keeping an eye out for Aelrie as they flew, but so far, she had not yet reappeared. Celesyria had hoped that she'd be able to put her sword to use alongside Alder, but it was too late to try and find her back on land now.

Below them in the harbor, the soldiers were igniting explosives and sending them toward the Gorok with catapults and other battle engines, but they struggled to hit their target. The beast moved quickly despite its size, and most of the precious bombs detonated beneath the surface, causing little if any damage. She could count only a few men who were continuing to try. She hoped that most of the others had fled rather than been killed, but a glance at the overturned fishing boats and broken dock piles did not inspire confidence.

"I tire of being right, Celesyria," Alder called over the wind. "But I understand his weariness. I just want this to be over."

The clouds were so thick that she could not even glimpse the sky. She was certain that night had passed into day by now, and yet the darkness remained. She glanced over at the boats that drew nearer and nearer with every passing minute.

Perhaps the elves bring their own night with them. Dawn will not come until we are free.

She closed her eyes for a moment as a vicious gust of wind blew from the west, stinging her face with tiny hail pellets. Nazzan and Jaconial pulled their wings in as close as they dared, and she followed suit, not wanting the delicate membranes allowing them to fly to be damaged.

"It seems our current predicament wasn't enough of a challenge," Nazzan called out, his deep voice rumbling in Celesyria's chest.

"Either we land, or we attack him now and finish this," Jaconial said, pointing a claw toward the Gorok as they circled above. "We cannot bear this hail for very long. If we go much higher where the ice is fresh, our wings may be punctured."

"*Alder, are you alright?*" Celesyria asked. She would not dare to try and turn to look at him in these conditions, but she could feel his weight settling heavily on her neck.

"This hail is big enough to bruise my pretty face," he choked out, his voice shaking. She watched as the surface of the sea began to boil more than ever, thousands of specks of ice pelting its surface at once.

Before he could say more, there was a screaming below, and Celesyria watched as one of the bombs landed squarely on the monster's back. It was a metal device with protruding spikes on all sides, and the bottom of it stuck into the Gorok's slick skin.

The fuse remained lit, the flame dancing along a greased string, a tiny star in the gloom.

The creature raged, tearing at its own back with its tentacles as it tried desperately to get the spikes out of its back.

"They got him!" she shouted at the others, nearly crashing into Nazzan as she tried to circle out of the way, toward the beach. There wasn't enough time.

"Get back behind that next wave!" she cried, unable to think of anything else as she pulled her wings as close to her body as she could and dove down. She could see the approaching elves, but even they had slowed, waiting. Nazzan and Jaconial were right behind her as the huge wave crested in front of them.

For a moment, she could not see the harbor. The water was a wall falling toward the shore, the surface rippling as the hail continued to strike every inch of it. She felt Alder flattening his body against her neck, bracing himself against her.

The hail and the wind continued to shatter and to wail, but there was nothing else.

A moment later, the wave was falling, the water churning up into white foam.

Behind it was the Gorok, tentacles writing as he grabbed for another ship, lifting it into the air and throwing it against the nearest dock, shattering the wood. Men screamed, and at least two that Celesyria could see fell into the water.

Below the surface was a rippling light, sinking down toward the seafloor, slow and gleaming, until she could see it no more.

Jaconial let out a roar, loud enough that Celesyria faltered in the sky. They were circling now, low enough that the hail only stung. Nazzan swore, using several words that she had not been aware of. She wished for the release of tears, but there was no time for pity.

The beast was winning, and the elves had picked up their pace once again, their boats sliding across the sea behind them, impervious to the hazards of the storm. The dragons would soon be within easy reach of their arrows.

"Celesyria, you need to take me to that demon," Alder called out. She felt him sitting up straight in the saddle, probably drawing his sword even as the ice burned in his eyes and stung at his cheeks. His voice was steady, the practiced delivery of a soldier giving orders. "Drop me on his head, and then get out of the way. I'm going to end this. Jaconial, Nazzan, get to land. You will be the only chance that the people have when the elves reach the city. Celesyria will be right behind you."

Jaconial and Nazzan obeyed at once, retreating to the beach. Most of the remaining soldiers had pulled back to the munitions building, but several had spread out, covering the main street where people were still making their way to the cliffs.

"I'm not leaving you," Celesyria said as she circled again, struggling to take deep breaths of the prickling air. She felt a panic taking hold of her chest, and try as she might, she could not quite get ahold of herself. It was easy to claim a love for the Eternal Lands when it wasn't your life on the line, but now that she was faced with death, every cell in her body wished to flee from it. "I will fly close enough for you to hit him."

"It does not make you a coward to live, Celesyria," Alder replied.

"I know. But I'm still not going to leave you."

To her relief, Alder did not say more to dissuade her. Ever since the day that they had met, while she was helpless in prison, he had been loyal to her. He had gone into Whitespire to save her mother, risking everything. If he was destined to die this night, she would die with him.

No matter how afraid she was.

"O High One, may your desires for our lives be fulfilled, even if they hurt," she said.

"So be it," Alder said.

It was a simple prayer, half hearted and cowardly and wavering even as she said it, but it was enough.

Peace rippled through her, and she turned sharply, heading straight for the creature from behind. She ignored the hail, and the wind ceased to bother her eyes. She could see him now, his eyes betraying no emotion, no feeling. There would be no guilt in slaughtering it. It was not a mere animal, not really, but something else. Something foul and filled with darkness.

"Now!" Alder shouted. More than ever before, they seemed to move as one. She reached the beast's flank, extending a claw and scouring its flesh as deeply as she could. It turned to face them immediately, its roar making her heart hammer in her chest as it raised several tentacles in their direction.

Alder leaned forward in the saddle, and she turned her head just enough to see the silver flash of his sword as it cut through hail, and then flesh. The Gorok screamed again, drawing back its tentacles before hurling them all down on the water, sending another huge wave toward the shore. But Celesyria could hardly see it.

All she saw was the wound that Alder had left, so deep that he had nearly severed the tentacle. It hung there like a hinge, the suckers undulating uselessly as blood like black ink poured from the gash.

It was working. They just had to stay alive long enough, and they would win.

Chapter Twenty-Five

KESSARA

The explosion never came.

Kessara and Wes stood to the side of the munitions building, holding their breaths as the fuse wavered in the mist, until suddenly it was gone. Neither spoke for several seconds, pulling their cloaks more tightly around their heads as the hail clattered against the roof, a fresh volley of stinging ice.

She wanted to swear, but she found she did not have the energy, nor did she wish to anger the High One. Perhaps they already had. Perhaps they were losing this battle because they had not done enough, or because they had done the wrong thing altogether. It seemed impossible to know.

She watched as more of the soldiers retreated, their faces red with the stinging of the hail, their hands chapped and raw from hauling explosives and rigging catapults. Some walked past her, heading for the cliffs, shaking their heads as if to apologize for their cowardice as they fled with the civilians.

For all of her talk of duty, she could not blame them. They did not fight for the High One, nor did they fight for the Dracodei, not really. They fought for bread and coin. They fought to go home to their comfortable wives and chubby little ones. She supposed that there was honor in that, too, even if it was a lesser kind.

Before she could decide what she and Wes could do next, she heard the sound of crashing water and splintering wood. Screams rang out, and water pounded against the front of the building. Wes was pressed against the wall, shoving his arm beneath a thick rope that was lashed to the sturdy stone. He reached out his hand to her, and she tried to get to him, but she stumbled, falling to the ground just a few feet away. She watched as he began to let go of the rope, trying to go to her.

"No!" she cried, but the water had already come, silencing her yell and lifting her up. Blinded, she couldn't think of anything but trying to breathe. The water was freezing, and she coughed as it poured into her mouth. Salt stung her eyes. She was pulled under, and she couldn't tell which direction was up. She felt weightless for a moment as she surfaced again, sucking in as much air as she could. She was unable to see the munitions building any more, and before she could figure out the location of the rocks that she could see, she was sucked under again.

Finally, she felt the water beginning to pull her in what felt like a backward direction. Righting herself, she grappled with her hands, desperately clutching at what seemed to be a metal railing. Her fingers were cold and clumsy, and she could not get a good grip.

"Come on!" she shouted, her throat burning as the words escaped in a growl. It had been a miracle that she hadn't been knocked into anything on the way up. If the wave pulled her back down, she doubted that she'd be as lucky.

Finally, she got one hand around the bar. With all of her strength, she took hold with the other hand, and pushed her foot in between the base of the rail and the stone edge beneath it. The water was receding now, sweeping down the hill, a great drain pulling everything toward the sea.

She closed her eyes as she saw several people floating by, trying to keep their heads above water. It was a small consolation that they seemed to be being pulled toward the beach rather than the treacherous wood buildings of the harbor, but there was nothing she could do to further aid them.

Finally, as the water level dropped, she could see where she was. She glanced at the railing, noticing the finely cast detail. It was a street she'd been to before, home to Lesser House nobles and rich merchants.

She got to her feet, coughing as she tried to settle the ache in her throat. Everything felt strangely silent, her ears ringing nearly loud enough to drown out the tumult that continued in the harbor below. She had to get back.

Let Wes be alright. Please, High One, this destruction cannot all be for nothing.

She raced toward the main street. If the Gorok was going to send another wave, she wanted to be standing nearer to the beach where she'd at least have a fighting chance.

She ran past civilians moving the other way, toward the stairs, struggling to catch her breath, trying to catch sight of Wes or any of the others.

Before she could cut back toward the harbor, however, she caught a flash of silvery gray out of the corner of her eye. For a moment, she thought it was Aelrie, and her chest swelled with hope. The elf would find Wes. She would protect him.

Barely a second later, the growing flicker of optimism was

snuffed out.

It was another elf, a male, with long hair done in black braids. The boats were not yet at the shore, but they were nearly there. Perhaps he had swum the remaining distance. She shook her head, ducking into the shadow of a nearby building. That didn't matter now. She could see the bow on his back, the wicked glint in his dark eyes as he made his way up a side street, heading for the cliffs.

She glanced around, hoping to see a soldier, or perhaps by some miracle, one of her own royal guards. She would have been thankful even to run into Captain Drohma. But she saw no one. Many of the men were in the middle of the vulnerable crowd already, and those who were not were at the beach, waiting for the other elves to land, or at the dock, continuing to attempt to bomb the monster.

She had to handle this herself.

She began to make her way up the street, keeping her steps as silent as she could. She felt the dagger at her waist, the same one she had used to free Wes from prison not so long ago.

There was no other option.

High One, care for Wes. Protect my future husband. Please.

She could not bring herself to pray for Alder, but she trusted that the High One knew. She had last seen him on Celesyria's back, circling the fighting with the other dragons. He was strong. She had to believe that he would come back alive, even if he would never be coming back to her.

WES

Wes held his breath so long that he was certain his lungs would burst. He felt the splintering rope against his hands as he tried to keep his legs secured, the surging water nearly pulling him off of the side of the building. When he was finally able to draw a breath, he watched for a moment, exhausted, as the dark currents raced up through the fishing quarter and into the rest of the city with astonishing force.

He looked around frantically, seeing only a few other soldiers standing nearby who had managed to get a strong hold on something.

"Kessara!" he cried out, his voice hushed by the pelting of the hail. The water level had lowered, but it was still too strong for him to risk letting go. Kessara had to be up in the city somewhere. He could only hope that she had not crashed into anything as she was carried there.

He closed his eyes for a moment, retreating into the crook of his arm, away from the biting hail. The water was receding now, drawing anyone and anything caught in it back down the hill. He heard cries, imagined children being ripped from the arms of their mothers and carried back toward the hungry sea. He could not bear to look toward the central area of Kingsvier Landing.

Instead, he turned to the other side, disentangling his legs from the rope as soon as the downward pull of the water let up.

I have to find her.

He turned back toward the Gorok and saw Celesyria with Alder on her back, swinging his sword at the beast, narrowly missing his left eye.

"Help!" came a scream from the docks. He let his gaze fall, and noticed a man, a lit torch in his hand as he tried to ignite a bomb resting in the bowl of a catapult. Standing next to him was an elf, his sword drawn, his white teeth gleaming as he grinned at his prey. "Somebody help me!"

Wes hesitated, watching as the elf drew closer. He risked a glance toward the beach, where the elven boats lay on dry sand, lifted there by the Gorok's huge wave. Men and women were pouring out of them, some heading toward the crowd of civilians on higher ground, others making their way to the harbor to finish off the remaining soldiers.

This one was on his own, and he could not see Wes from where he stood. Wes glanced at the bomb, the fuse waiting, stark against the dreary sky. The aim of the catapult looked to be true. Alder and Celesyria had forced the beast closer, into the shallower waters where it could not disappear into the depths and surface again somewhere else.

The rest of the soldiers did not seem to hear the man's cries.

He thought of the fury on Alder's face as they had parted, guilt and self-hatred hammering at him with each unsteady breath.

He knew that his own life had been difficult. As Envoy, he'd never had a real childhood as others did, and when he was not even yet a man, his entire family had been slaughtered. Now, many of his own people hated him, thinking him to be a blasphemer and a traitor.

He was tired.

Every part of his body ached.

The old familiar longing for oblivion tugged at him, pulling him down, telling him he was worthless. That everyone would be better off with him gone, especially Kessara and Alder.

And now, here he stood, mere feet from an elf who would relish his death. He could die, and better, he had a shot at saving someone else while doing so.

It is not a suicide. I will fight with all I have.

He drew his curved sword, admiring the sharp edge as it gleamed in a sudden flash of light. Thunder boomed overhead, loud enough to make his ears ring.

Alder is right about everything. This man is dead already, going to my death beside him will do little.

The elf was taking his time, taunting the man as he lunged for the bomb, trying to hold the torch steady against the fuse long enough to light it. He saw the elf's mouth curl into a cruel laugh as he knocked the wooden stick from the man's hand. Wes heard it hit the dock, the oil continuing to burn uselessly against the damp wood.

If I survive tonight, I will destroy Kessara's life. I will destroy Alder's life. I will spit upon Roven's memory.

I will keep falling for Aelrie, and I will break both of our hearts.

Thoughts of the High One swirled in his mind, but he ignored them, continuing to argue with himself. It felt almost as though someone else was there, taunting him, reminding him of all of the ways he had failed, and all of the pain that was to come for everyone he loved.

Every time he thought of a reason to walk away, to find Kessara, to live, he felt the dark tide within, dragging him down, calling to him from the black depths, promising bliss and silence.

"Help!" the man shouted again, weeping now. "High One, if you're real like they say, please, help me. I beg you! I know I've done many evil things, but please, have mercy!"

The elf had knocked him down, and was standing with his foot pressed into his chest, leaning over him. His knife was in his silvery hand, and Wes could not take his eyes off of the tip of the blade, sharp and vicious, longing to bite and tear at delicate flesh. Longing to bring forth blood.

The elf's braids bounced as he tilted his head back and laughed, a thin, barking sound that made Wes' head ache behind his eyes.

He leaned down, knife raised.

The helpless man closed his eyes, as though accepting defeat.

Wes couldn't breathe, couldn't move, both of his choices before him screaming that time was running out, that he had to act—

Light seared across the sky.

A bolt of energy slammed into the elf, knocking him onto his back, hair burned, skin singed.

Thunder crashed.

Wes stared open mouthed as the man who had been pinned got to his feet and ran, scrabbling up the hill toward the cliffs.

The elf didn't move.

Wes felt as though he had been struck himself. The High One was with the people of Kaveryth. How could he have ever doubted that, even for a moment?

Somewhere out there, beyond the mist and the gloom, the sun was waiting. Wes wanted to feel its warm light on his face again. The dark could not last forever, not even in such difficult times.

Even a single candle in the gloom was cause for hope.

"I want to live," he said aloud to no one in particular, rushing down the splintered wooden dock, where the lit torch still laid burning.

He took hold of it and carried it to the catapult, pressing the flame against the fuse as the hail and the rain assaulted him. Finally, after agonizing seconds, he watched as the fire licked its way along the fuse. He saw a wooden release at the base of the catapult. He had only seconds.

"Celesyria, pull back!" he cried out in his mind.

He watched as she obeyed immediately, nearly knocking Alder off of her back with the sudden movement. He held on, however, clutching at the leather straps with one hand and holding his sword with the other. The Gorok turned in the water, searching for the dragon.

Wes released the bomb.

He fell back onto the deck, chest heaving with anxiety as the explosive flew through the air, impossibly slow. Out of the corner of his eye, he could see elves and men fighting, but he couldn't move.

The bomb landed on a large floating crate a few feet from the Gorok. It tried to get away from the pointed metal object, but he could not move through the shallow water. All of a sudden, there was a bright light, as though the sun itself had landed in the harbor. There was smoke, a great wave of it, obscuring the creature. He could not even see Celesyria's orange wings any more.

For a second, he feared that the bomb had failed, malfunctioning somehow and giving off smoke rather than flame and heat. He got to his feet, taking a couple of steps forward, wondering if perhaps he could load the catapult again–

The wave of sound was so powerful that it knocked him to the ground.

He felt his head smacking into something on the way down, and the resulting headache made his usual ones seem tolerable by comparison. He lay there for a moment, staring up at the sky, the insides of his ears aching and ringing.

"You did it, Wes!" Celesyria called, her voice jubilant. *"Look at it, look at the tentacles... wait. No. It's impossible, it–"*

Alarmed, Wes got to his feet, ignoring the dizziness that threatened to knock him over once again.

The crate where the bomb had landed was gone, and several of the nearby docks were burning, their exposed pilings blackened and burning like torches.

The Gorok rested where he had been before, nearly half of his body missing. Burned tentacles floated nearby, giving off a smell so terrible that Wes only barely managed to stop himself from vomiting onto the deck.

The creature roared, throwing back what was left of its head, revealing a sharp beak filled with hundreds of pin-like teeth.

For a moment, Wes swore that the monster's remaining eye sought him on the shore, staring at him, the black circle filled with centuries of hate and malice. He couldn't turn away, couldn't stop himself from staring back, the darkness calling to him, telling him to walk closer...

The eye closed.

The beast was silent, staying so still that Wes nearly dared to hope it was dead.

"*High One, save us,*" Celesyria was whispering in his mind. He could see her now, circling near the surface, Alder gesturing to the beast with his sword.

And then Wes saw it.

The creature was changing, the surface of its flesh bubbling, rippling, churning itself up from the inside. The burnt, stinking stump where its largest tentacle had been began to heal, the blackened flesh once again becoming pale and slick. The suckers were undulating, and within moments, the beast was able to move the arm, striking toward the sky, narrowly missing the dragon.

"*What in the Wrathlands is happening?*" Jaconial asked in his mind.

Wes saw her near the beach, circling low with Nazzan, clawing at the elves that were clashing with the soldiers while trying to avoid being struck by archers. He could see several of them standing on rooftops, firing off arrows every few seconds.

"Just keep trying to help the soldiers," he replied. *"We can't let the elves make it into the city."*

He returned his focus to the beast.

It already looked whole again, scarcely scratched by the explosives or the swords. It began to raise its tentacles again, ready to slam them into the water and send another wave into the city.

All of this was for nothing. We all need to run.

For the first time in a long while, Wes felt very much like he was going to cry.

KESSARA

The elf moved slower than Kessara would have expected, slinking up the street like an alleycat in search of a mouse. He took his time, peering into windows every now and again, as though hoping to find some lonely soul he might be able to terrorize on his way.

The Princess followed, thankful that the sound of the storm and the city silenced her footsteps. Her palm was sweaty against the dagger, and she took it into her left hand for a moment, rubbing her right hand on her sodden dress before returning it.

She was not going to get a second chance at this. She couldn't waver, not even for a second. Any mistake would be her last.

They were nearing the outer edge of the crowd now. She could see people pressing and shoving, the stairs filled with so many people that she feared the wooden support beams might tear free of the cliff wall.

The elf ducked down a side street, and for a moment, she lost sight of him. Keeping to the darkest shadows she could find, she followed, her footfalls screaming in her ears as she moved away from the mob of voices. There was an overhang on the roof here, and without the sound of the hail, she feared that the elf would notice her approach.

He has superior senses as it is. All things considered, he should have found you already. He's proud. He's arrogant. It does not occur to him that a mere human would dare to sneak up on him in the first place.

She kept moving, and a few seconds later, she saw him again, standing on a small deck attached to a squat tavern. He was facing the crowd, cradling his bow in his arms like a child. After several long seconds, he pulled his quiver from his back, resting it against the wooden rail, and drawing one of the arrows.

No one in the crowd noticed as he nocked the arrow. Nor did anyone see him drawing it back, the string tensing beneath his strong silver fingers.

But Kessara saw the smile on his face, the longing he felt to kill, the sweet anticipation of death and ruin.

She saw the wooden stairs behind him, counting only six steps. They would creak, but it did not matter. By the time he turned...

She stepped from the shadow and crossed the narrow street, reaching the stairs. She dared to take a single breath. His bowstring was fully taut now, the arrow waiting to fly.

She held her dress up with her free hand, rushing up the steps, two at a time. She was there on the deck, the wood clattering beneath her feet, not caring.

She saw him tense his body, but before he could turn, she was upon him, eyeing the smooth gray of his neck.

Her palm was no longer sweating. She ignored the bite of steel against flesh, and then it was over. He crumpled to the ground, falling with what felt like a tremendous noise, his svelte body pure muscle.

She looked at the dagger in her hand. The rain was already washing the blood away, but she did not wish to look at it for a second longer.

She shoved it into its place on her belt, breathing hard, trying to push what had just happened from her mind and finding herself unable.

I killed someone.

Alder and Wes and Celesyria and the others needed her, but even thoughts of her friends could not calm the guilt that raged within her heart. There was a booming sound coming from somewhere behind her, loud enough that she could feel the rumble deep within her chest, but she did not turn to see what might have caused it.

She stumbled down the stairs of the deck, wandering aimlessly toward the mob of people. She had to warn them that the elves were already here.

She faded into the crowd, hood drawn over her hair and shadowing her face. No one took any notice of her as they pleaded with others to be allowed through, men trying to get their wives to safety, parents trying to get their children out even if they themselves were left behind.

She tried to spot a soldier who might be in charge, but the

only men in uniform she saw were part of the mass of people, shoving like the others. There was no order at all.

Suddenly, her ears filled with a familiar rushing sound, loud enough to drown out the cacophony that pressed on her from all sides.

Everyone in the crowd seemed to turn at once, eyes staring, mouths gaping.

Another wave was rushing up the main street toward them, knocking over benches and barrels and tearing signs from buildings.

Kessara rushed toward a side street and clambered onto a low balcony, narrowly avoiding being shoved to the ground as the people pressed as close to the cliffside as they could to avoid the water. She saw a young boy climbing a tall, sturdy-looking hedge nearby, beckoning another little girl to follow him. She tried to take hold of his hands, but she was too small to reach. The water was coming fast, nearly touching the edge of the crowd, where the slow and the old were struggling to keep up with the others.

She couldn't bear to leave them.

Climbing back to the ground, she rushed toward the little girl, offering her a hand up. Her palms stung as the girl's hard boot hit her fingers, shattering a nail as she shoved her toward her brother. The boy got hold of her and pulled her onto the hedge.

She did not wait. She saw a slight young woman with a cane nearby, and rushed over to her, half dragging her from the center of the street. As soon as she had helped the woman onto a patio, she went back, spotting a stumbling man who was missing a leg. Her shoulder muscles screamed beneath his weight, but she managed to support him, getting him to the relative safety of a side street.

The two of them stared as water rushed into the space where they had been standing seconds before. She saw others, those she had not had time to help. She looked away, swallowing tears as they were pulled under.

The seconds passed, impossibly slow, until finally the water began to descend down the hill, large hail stones floating on its surface.

"You saved my life," the man was saying, his eyes red with tears as he held out his arms to her. She accepted his embrace, hiding her own tears in the rough fabric of his wet jacket as she sobbed.

She pulled away, giving him a nod and heading back toward the crowd, resisting the urge to stare back at the North Sea.

Somewhere down there, her friends were fighting, perhaps dying. And yet here were her own people, citizens of Gale-harbor, so afraid of death that they would leave even disabled people and children to drown to save their own skins.

She threw back her hood and undid her cloak, throwing it onto the ground behind her. Even with her wet hair, torn dress, and bleeding hands, many of the people stopped short at the site of her.

"I am Princess Kessara Manta of Galeharbor," she called out, glad that her mother had insisted on teaching her to project her voice when necessary. "I am now in charge of this evacuation. You will let me pass."

People stepped out of her way, and she moved through the crowd, pushing toward the stairs. Every few moments, she was met with a new cluster of people who had not heard her, and she repeated her short speech. She had half expected them to ignore her, but instead, they turned to their companions,

298

urging them to make way for the Princess.

When faced with chaos, people wish to be led.

As she reached the base of the stairs, she felt a swell of pride in her father and her mother, despite the decisions that had led to this catastrophe. There was still hope in Galeharbor. The Manta family ruled with justice, and the people respected them for it. Even Kessara, even after all that she had done by publicly aiding the Envoy in his rebellion.

Those on the stairs scurried over to the rails, letting her through. When she was high enough that she could see the entire crowd, she turned to them, clearing her throat. Below, she could see the Gorok writhing about, Celesyria flying nearby, Alder on her back.

He's still alive.

The thought gave her strength. "Silence, please!" she shouted, surprised at how loud her voice was, even amid the storm. Lightning was crashing every so often now, thunder echoing against cobblestone, but still, the people were listening.

"Our remaining soldiers are fighting off a company of elves that has reached shore. Should those men fail, and they almost certainly will, the elves will reach us. I have already killed one that slipped past the others, armed with a bow."

The crowd began to cry out at that, people turning to one another with fear-stricken faces. She held up her hand.

"If we do not work together to evacuate, the elves are going to kill all of us."

She paused then, letting the screams and cries build. She needed them to be afraid.

"But if we can reach the plateau, we will have a chance. More Red Army men as well as Galeharbor soldiers will be coming to aid us soon, if they are not up there already. The elves are too few to be able to go after everyone."

Everyone was watching now, mothers clutching little ones to their chests, men staring up at her with grim faces.

She allowed all of her rage to fill her voice, her throat burning as she screamed at the crowd.

"There may be another wave even before the elves make it here. And you will not leave the sick, old, or helpless to die!"

Most of the crowd nodded, but others only stared, their eyes hard and defiant.

"I know I cannot enforce my command. There are no soldiers for me to command. I am only one person. But I can promise you that in the next life, the High One will know what you have chosen. Choose courage. Choose hope. Choose sacrifice."

Mouths fell open at the mention of His name, but she did not care. The people deserved to know the truth, to have it out in the open, whatever else happened. Death would come for all of them eventually, even if they escaped this city alive, and only the High One held the power to decide the fate of their souls.

"Now, if you will excuse me, the man that I love is down there. Let me pass, and remember what I have said."

Without another word, she headed down the steps. As soon as she reached the cobblestone below, she broke into a run, dashing down side streets and making for the harbor.

Finally, when she saw the munitions building up ahead, she paused for breath, turning to look back at the stairs.

The people were heading to the plains above, walking in orderly lines, with children nearest to the top. The rest of the crowd waited along the cliff wall, away from the threat of another wave, the old and infirm among them.

She looked up at the dark sky and smiled, tears filling her eyes once again.

That, Captain Drohma, is the duty of a princess.

26

Chapter Twenty-Six

AELRIE

Aelrie watched, wanting to be sure, wanting to see all sides of what lay before her before she made her decision. She had already seen everything that she would see, but somehow, that did not matter.

Certainty was not enough, not when such a price was demanded of her.

I need something else, High One.

Tear me apart, throw me from this roof, split the sky with lightning again.

I'm afraid.

I'm afraid of time, and I'm afraid of my eternity.

She pressed her slender body more closely against the chimney as two elves ran past her along a side street, no doubt heading toward the crowd of helpless civilians.

She closed her eyes, forcing herself to breathe until the longing to go after them passed. She could kill them, sparing some lives.

But if I am right about this beast, it will not matter anyway.

She knew the answer, but she could not make herself move. She knew that as soon as she left the roof there would be no going back.

The High One will forgive. I have to believe he will forgive.

She could see most of Kingsvier Landing from her perch, and her eyes roved from place to place, trying to see all of her friends at once.

Jaconial and Nazzan were near the beach where the elven ships had landed, guarding the main road as best they could.

Wes was standing at the edge of the beach, sword in hand, with three Red Army soldiers fighting beside him to block the elves from advancing along the streets leading from the harbor. For the moment, he was holding his own, but she found her eyes drawn to him every few seconds.

I can't walk away from this. Not even for you.

She wasn't sure if she believed her own words.

She could not see Kessara any more. A few moments earlier, before the bomb and the massive wave that followed it, she had watched in horror as the Princess followed one of the elves toward the cliffs. The chances that she had survived an encounter with him were small. She could only hope that she had not gotten too close.

Alder and Celesyria flew near the Gorok, Alder attempting to slash at the beast with his sword. It was useless, just as she knew it would be. Every time he was cut, he would heal himself, knitting the flesh back together from within.

If they did not flee, it was only a matter of time before the beast got lucky and struck him. If Alder fell from Celesyria's back, he would be dead just from hitting the water. And yet, the two of them continued to fight, coming around again and

303

again, occasionally stabbing the creature in the eye, making him roar and scream until he healed himself anew.

She shook her head, astonished by their stubbornness.

She turned to Wes. One of the soldiers had been cut down beside him, and he stepped over his body, his sword flashing and clanking as it connected with the elf's slender blade. Another soldier stepped in beside him, his own weapon joining the fray as they pushed the creature back.

Wes was not a very good swordsman, she knew, and she doubted even a trained soldier would be able to match the elf with his superior senses for long. The man was toying with them, playing like a cat chasing a beetle, prolonging the inevitable.

So am I, lurking in the shadows while my friends wait to die.

There was no flash of lightning, no gust of sudden wind, no ignition of flame.

The High One did not approve, that much she knew already, but He did not seem willing to strike her dead in order to stop her. That would have to be enough.

She drew a breath, trying to find courage amid the guilt.

She could stand beside Wes. They could go down fighting. They could save some lives. The dragons and Alder would help. If Kessara was alive, she was almost certainly near the stairs, getting her people to safety.

There was another path she could choose.

There was always a choice.

She closed her eyes for several seconds, until she was sure that the tears would not come.

I can't do it, High One.

I'm not strong enough.

Forgive me.

She rushed to the edge of the building and clambered down the water pipes to the ground, ignoring the snarls of the other elves as she rushed past them. They didn't matter. Nothing did now, nothing but what she was choosing to do.

If she was to be damned, she would damn the beast with her.

ALDER

"We have to go back!" Celesyria was shouting aloud as she circled low, narrowly avoiding the swipe of a tentacle. To Alder's horror, the creature had managed to get past them, away from the docks. It was still moving slowly, as though it enjoyed taunting them, but he was sure that soon enough it would reach deeper water. It would be able to hide.

"No," Alder shouted back, tightening the grip of his free hand on the saddle. "Nothing else is going to take it down. Maybe if I can strike at its brain..."

He let the sentence trail off as the creature roared, picking up a huge piece of wooden deck piling and throwing it toward shore like it weighed no more than a toothpick. The few soldiers that remained near the docks leaped out of the way, racing toward the others on the beach.

Celesyria pulled up and took a broader pass, and Alder squinted against the hail and rain, trying to see the clash of elves and soldiers. He was able to make Wes out, standing shoulder to shoulder with several of King Ursa's men, a single elf attempting to press through their line.

"They need us, Alder," Celesyria said, gesturing with a front claw. "Even Jaconial and Nazzan won't be able to hold the elves back much longer on their own. Their size is a disadvantage here. They need men with swords."

"There's only one of me," Alder argued, wincing as a fresh

gust of air hissed against his ears. "I'm not going to be able to do very much. Let me try to get the Gorok again. Please."

"One more time, and then we go to the beach," Celeysria said, her tone making it clear that the decision was final. Whether the dragon was in charge or not, Alder supposed that he had little choice but to listen to someone who could fly him over to the beach and drop him there.

"Bring me right over him. I need to get onto the top of his head, in that spot right between his eyes," he said, focusing his glance on the precise spot that he thought would offer them the best chance. "You need to drop me there and then circle around."

"Alder, you can't, what–"

"Do it, Celesyria."

She said nothing else. She knew as well as he did that it was the only possible way they might be able to defeat him.

The creature could regenerate, but even that ability had to come from somewhere, and the brain seemed the most obvious choice.

If it has a brain at all, and if said brain is actually in its head.

He gripped the hilt of his sword more tightly as Celesyria dove. Doubting was useless. He would take the chance, even if the hope of victory was only a small glimmer. Someone had to try, and with the exception of maybe Aelrie, who he had not seen in quite a while, he had the best shot. The dragons couldn't get close enough. They were too big, too easy for the creature to grab with its tentacles.

He had learned a long time ago that some battles could only be won by a hero with a sword.

CELESYRIA

CHAPTER TWENTY-SIX

Celesyria held her breath as Alder fell.

For a second, she thought that she had dropped him from too high up, certain that the creature was going to notice him and to get out of the way. To her relief, the beast was so huge that it did not even flinch as Alder landed feet-first on its head.

It turned to her instead, tentacles flying. She watched Alder stumble backward, slipping on ooze as the creature opened its mouth to roar at her, sharp teeth flashing. She turned back as they'd planned, flapping her wings hard against the wind, quickly moving high enough that it could no longer reach her. It still did not seem to notice Alder.

She looked down at him, his body small and seemingly useless against the bulk of the creature's body. It had moved farther out to sea now, and on all sides, Alder was surrounded by deep, churning water. If he fell...

He won't fall. He'll make it.

She circled above, straining to see through the rain, wanting to be ready if anything went wrong. The creature was turning to look at her, its screeches stinging her sensitive ears as it lashed out impotently with its tentacles.

Good. Keep looking at me, you demon. We're not letting you go home.

She took her gaze from Alder for a moment, doing a loop in the air, which had the intended effect. The creature snarled at her, moving in circles, trying to stay under her in case she flew back down within reach of its tentacles.

Alder held his sword at his side as he moved toward the creature's eyes from behind, stepping slowly, not wanting to alert it to his presence. Celesyria slowed, hoping that the creature would not roar or make any sudden movements with her friend so close to its mouth and eyes.

Alder looked up at her, giving a quick nod. She flapped her wings, trying to stay in place, mere inches from the ends of the Gorok's tentacles. The long Aridmoorian sword gleamed against the dullness of the clouds as Alder held it aloft, the tip pointed straight down. As far as Celesyria could tell, it was positioned precisely between both eyes. It was the best they were going to get.

"I'll be right there," she said softly in his mind, not wanting to distract him. She would have mere minutes to pluck him from the water if he succeeded, and only seconds for him to leap from the creature's back if he failed.

Everything happened at once.

Celesyria saw the sword move, piercing down. It sunk into the creature's flesh, straight to the hilt. She saw the beast's eyes go wide. For a moment, she could not breathe. Alder stood there, still gripping the hilt of the embedded sword.

"Alder, move!" she called out to him, but he did not seem to hear her.

The creature's head was undulating again, like it did before, but this time it was pulling the sword in deeper, dragging Alder with it.

She dove toward the beast, feeling a tentacle wrapping around her tail, ignoring its pull.

"Let go!" she screamed at him. Finally, as though awaking from a dream, Alder released the sword, stumbling backward. The creature's mouth was open now, its howls drowning out every other sound as it thrashed in the water.

Celesyria watched as the sword disappeared into the beast's head, smooth flesh covering over it like it had never been there at all.

She got her legs over the beast, and Alder took hold of one of her manacles, using it to climb up her leg and into the saddle. She tried to fly away, but the creature had the end of her tail in its grasp, and she could only flail back and forth helplessly like a chained dog.

Briefly she considered getting Alder to crawl to the end of her tail and hack the tentacle off, but then she remembered that his sword was on the bottom of the North Sea. Worse, she could not feel him moving on her saddle.

"Alder? Are you alright?" she asked in his mind.

She could just hear his grunted response over the wind. He was alive, but it was clear he was hurt. The last of his strength had been spent.

She flapped her wings harder than she ever had before, sure that the delicate membranes would tear. They remained intact, but it was pointless. They were still trapped.

The creature drew closer, its other tentacles wriggling through the sky. Within seconds, it would take hold of her legs and drag them down.

Out of the corner of her eye, she could see a fishing boat on the water, but no one seemed to be on it, certainly not enough navy soldiers to aid them now.

She desperately wanted to call to Jaconial or Nazzan. Perhaps one of them could get Alder from her back before she went down.

She glanced over at the beach, a numb feeling in her tail beginning to race up her back. If she did not get away, the Gorok wouldn't even need to grab her with his limbs. She'd fall out of the sky herself if she couldn't feel her wings.

The two dragons were there as she'd left them, each trying to hold back five elves from passing into the city. Far away in the distance she could see the staircase leading up the cliffs.

It was still filled with people.

Grief seemed to crush her chest from within. Alder wouldn't want them to save him anyway, not if it meant so many civilians would die. He had taken the vow of a soldier at fourteen, and even now that he offered no fealty to an earthly king, she knew his loyalty to the High One was something much greater.

Her voice shaking, she began to pray aloud. It felt right, somehow.

The creature had taken hold of one of her back legs now, taking its time, knowing that the victory had already been won.

"High One, let my dear Alder pass into the Eternal Lands. He has fought bravely in Your service. Please, protect the others. Do not let the elves or the Gorok kill the citizens," she began, her voice shaking.

She could not seem to stop the shivers that poured through her body, despite the numbness. She wondered if this was what it was like to feel cold. Despite the chill of her reptilian blood, she was certain that the tentacles of the creature were doing something to her. The suckers probably deposited some kind of poison, but there was little point in worrying about it. She did not fear the pain. It was the fate of her soul that concerned her now.

"Let Wes and Kessara live. Help them to love each other as husband and wife, for the good of their Kingdoms and of all Kaveryth. I beg this of You."

Her throat ached, and she could not bring herself to say any more.

Praying for herself was unnecessary.

A sad memory rose, a verse from the Codex Veritatis that

she could never manage to forget.

The fire-breathers have come to us out of the Farplace, and to the Farplace again they must return. The worst among them and the best alike have no place in this world the High One has made. A soul is necessary for all who belong here, and a soul that race will never possess.

27

Chapter Twenty-Seven

AELRIE

The sails of the fishing boat billowed out, pulling the vessel through the water at a blistering speed. Aelrie sat against the deck's railing, perched behind a stack of barrels, not wanting the creature to notice her. Perhaps he would think the boat was empty, floating from the docks on its own.

In any case, if the Gorok wanted to take hold of the boat and throw it into the sea, it would have to let go of Celesyria anyway.

The elf glanced behind her at the beach, where her countrymen pressed forward, trying to get through the two dragons, Wes, and the remaining soldiers. The Envoy was still fighting, and she chided herself for doubting him. When it came to protecting the innocent, Wes was stronger than anyone would expect, least of all himself.

It's because the High One is with him. Any other explanation is only foolishness.

She pushed the thought aside.

He and the others would not be responsible before the High One for the decisions that she made.

She watched Celesyria struggling against the beast. Her tail had been ensnared easily, and now it had both of her back legs in its grip. The strength of her wings was keeping them in the air, but soon the toxin would reach them, too, and the dragon would be paralyzed.

Alder half-sat, half-laid in the saddle, holding onto the straps, eyes closed. His sword was gone, he was hurt, and she could imagine the pain he felt thinking that it was the end.

Aelrie closed her eyes for a moment, drawing a breath, feeling the power of the sea beneath her. She could feel every droplet of water that plummeted from the thick clouds over her head. She could sense every current of wind that passed over the waves.

I am not innocent, Wes.

I was born into darkness.

She stood, feeling the blood rushing through her legs, down her arms, into her fingertips. She felt as though she was buzzing with energy, like lightning had struck her and continued to course through her body, making her strong.

She dared to glance at the beach for a moment. The elves had not noticed her.

She strode forward, onto the center of the boat's deck, feeling every knot and bit of grain from the wood beneath her feet. She imagined great trees, entire forests, green leaves and roots that stretched into the depths of the world.

All of it gave her strength, but there was one more thing that she needed to find victory.

She raised her hands, watching as Celesyria and Alder continued to struggle against the Gorok's grip. She could feel everything, sensing every piece of hail, every little fleck of ice. She called to them, speaking a language that had no words.

An ancient language, far older than the Gorok.

A language of darkness.

She opened her eyes. The ice was there, cascading toward the Gorok from all directions, tiny flecks of hail converging into a churning white mass, rollicking over the sea.

She held her hands aloft, controlling it, forging it into a huge, living, frozen spear.

It punctured the side of the Gorok before the beast could attempt to flee. The creature screamed, its tentacles retracting. Celesyria broke free, flying upward as fast as she could flap her wings.

Aelrie pulled back the ice and then sent it into the beast again, and again. The screams continued as great splashes of ink-black blood poured from the creature. Its eyes were cast upon her, the hatred of a thousand wicked elves staring out from the black depths.

The ice encased the creature, squeezing it, tearing it apart. The screeches went silent. Somewhere on the beach, she could still hear shouting, but she did not dare to turn, could not risk breaking her focus before the deed was done.

She gathered more and more hail, sending the creature down into the water as she did so. Soon, it was held still, broken and silent, beneath a glassy surface of ice.

The North Sea moved around the new island where the Gorok rested, the waves unchanged, the storm continuing to howl.

KESSARA

Kessara sat against a building along Kingsvier Landing's main street, sobs wracking her chest, struggling to breathe.

314

She had seen Alder in the distance, on top of the creature, his sword raised, Celesyria circling overhead. She had watched him fall, heard the creature roaring, saw its horrific teeth bared at the sky.

For a split second, she knew that the man she loved was dead. The terrible truth had coursed through her, igniting her veins, shattering every bit of strength that she had left.

Alder had been willing to sacrifice his life for her people, but he had failed.

And then she had seen ice rising out of the sea from nowhere, rushing at the creature, stabbing it like the North Sea itself had come to life.

The Gorok had crashed down into the depths, sending water and crystal rushing onto the shore.

Behind her, there were cheers. All the way at the staircase, the people saw the defeat of the beast.

She wanted to cheer along with them, to thank the High One, but she could not bring herself to do anything but cry.

She watched Alder on Celesyria's back, rushing for the safety of the harbor, with no Gorok to chase them, far from where the elves still battled the others.

He was alive, she could see it, but it was not enough to mend her heart.

Even living through one second where she was in the world and he was not had been too much for her to bear.

28

Chapter Twenty-Eight

WES

Wes felt his feet digging into the muck as he stumbled backward. The elf who was attacking him was coming fast, towering over him, all silver skin and hard muscle. He felt a jolt shudder through his arm as he blocked the elf's blade with his own.

He tried to call out to the soldier who had been standing near him a moment before, but the cry caught in his throat.

He was on the ground, dark blood seeping over his Red Army uniform from a wound in his chest.

He lunged at the elf in front of him with a ferocity he did not know he had, slashing at him, his blade flying through the air. The elf's eyes went wide for a moment as he regained his stance, but not even a second later, Wes could see a teasing smile rising to his lips. He was not afraid.

For Wes, it had been the most difficult fight of his life. For the elves, it was a child's game, a training exercise, no more.

He dodged to the left, narrowly avoiding the tip of the elf's sword as the man pounced. He gripped his own blade as tightly as he could, stumbling back against the wet sand.

Without the aid of the soldiers, he would not last much longer, and he doubted that the elves would kill him quickly. Torture awaited him.

He made his way across the beach, trying not to trip on the detritus that the waves had brought out of the sea. Old pieces of driftwood and bits of metal were everywhere, wrapped in thick seaweed that threatened to catch on his boots and trip him. The elf followed, stepping easily through the mess.

Nazzan stood closest, several arrows sticking out of his green chest, blood dripping in dark rivulets onto the sand below. Jaconial stood a little behind him, shielded from most of the arrows.

Wes felt guilt at the idea of taking refuge behind him as well, but he pressed on. A new flame had been lit within his heart, warming him, giving him strength. He would do all that he could to live. Not because he thought that he deserved it, but because the High One had given him a calling, and he could not dare to reject it any longer.

An arrow shot past his face, disappearing into the city beyond. A moment later, there was another, and another.

"Get behind me!" Nazzan was shouting. He fell to the ground, tripping over a broken anchor just as another volley passed just over his head.

He got to his feet again, ignoring the pounding in his head, ignoring the ache of his turned ankle. He was running, his chest heaving, the muck sucking at his boots, slowing him.

He could hear laughter at his back. He could almost see the bows being drawn, arrows nocked, white teeth grinning.

And then he saw it.

The sea and sky both seemed to be moving. For a second, even the elves went quiet, staring out at the water.

Ice was being drawn from below, pulled from the sky, converging on the Gorok. He blinked, unable to move, unable to comprehend the impossibility of what he was seeing.

Celesyria and Alder flew away from the creature, high into the clouds. The beast screamed as the ice hit him, again and again.

Aelrie.

He knew it before he saw her, standing there on the deck of one of the fishing boats, out in the middle of the harbor. Her arms were raised, and her lips were moving. The creature was being dragged now, pulled beneath the surface as ice bloomed over his head, imprisoning him.

Somewhere in the city he could hear people cheering. The elves would recover soon and resume their assault, but he still couldn't make himself run to safety. He was transfixed, watching her, so beautiful and terrible, her face gleaming from within despite the dullness of the sky.

She turned to face him.

Her eyes were all wrong.

The pounding in his head became a deluge of pain. He dropped his sword into the sand, clutching at his temples, closing his eyes against the burning light, but it did not help.

He could feel sand against his cheek, but he did not remember falling.

Celesyria was screaming in his mind but he couldn't find the energy to make out the words, or to say anything back.

The pain was all there was, loud and close and pulsing, drowning out everything else. He felt his stomach clench, and then he was sick on the sand. It brought no relief.

Tears dripped from the corners of his eyes. He couldn't pray. He couldn't think.

"Get him on my back. Now!"

Wes couldn't be sure who was speaking. Hands took hold of his body, and then he was on his feet, unable to bear his own weight. He watched three pairs of boots crossing the sand, unable to open his eyes all the way, the pain in his head so intense that he thought blood would pour from his ears.

He saw a wall of green scales, and then he was being lifted again. His fingers fumbled for the familiar leather straps of the saddle, and he managed to get on, pressing his body low against Nazzan's neck as he took off into the sky.

He did not pass out. He forced himself to breathe slowly, letting the air fill his lungs.

He knew.

I'm going to live.

CELESYRIA

Celesyria watched in astonishment as the elves below fled to their boats, pushing off into the sea, their strange sails pulling them toward the horizon.

They're retreating. They're giving up.

She flapped her wings and flexed her claws, trying to assess the damage. The numbness had passed quickly, and for that fact she was thankful.

The beast was dead, encased in his prison of ice and dark water.

It was over, but she felt no relief. Too many questions still plagued her, along with an uneasy twinge in her gut that she could not shake.

She could see Aelrie on the deck of the ship, laying still

against the wood. She could not tell if she was still alive, but Alder was, and he was badly hurt. She had to care for him first.

She flew toward the harbor, watching as the soldiers from the beach made their way up toward the crowd at the base of the cliff. She could see smiling faces as the news spread. Some of the people abandoned the stairs, heading back toward their damaged homes, ready to begin the long process of rebuilding their city. Most of the others continued toward the plateau, not ready to trust that their nightmare could really be over.

She did not see Wes anywhere, nor Kessara.

I have to get Alder to safety, and then I will find them.

Her own limbs ached, and she was sure her tail was badly broken, but she had to keep going. The immediate threat had been vanquished, but she would not rest until she knew that all of her friends were alright.

She saw the munitions building and flew over it, landing in the large patch of open space that lay at the back. She moved to lie down, wondering how she was going to get Alder off of her back without help, when Captain Drohma stepped out of a nearby door.

"Oh good, a visit from my former soldier," he said flatly, walking over to Celesyria and clapping a hand onto Alder's back. She could not feel him move.

"Help me get him down," she said, suppressing a growl as the man smacked him again, harder this time. "Please."

Drohma placed Alder's arm over his shoulder without another word, dragging him down from her back until they both landed clumsily on the ground. The Captain turned him onto his back, pressing his ear to Alder's chest.

Celesyria held her breath.

"He's breathing fine. I suspect he will come around soon

enough."

"Thank you," the dragon said, finding that she meant it. Despite their animosity, Drohma's Red Army men had fought bravely, and she doubted that Jaconial, Nazzan, and Wes would have been able to protect the city from the elven assault without them.

Without another word, Drohma drew his sword, pressing it against the pit of her throat in one swift movement.

"The Princess is not here to offer you protection," he said, his voice sounding far away as blood surged in her ears. "I see no soldiers of Galeharbor, either. I respect King Manta, of course, but he will never know what I have done. The Gorok nearly killed you already. People would assume that the injuries you sustained were too severe for you to survive."

"Leave Alder alone," she choked out, struggling to speak, the blade pressing into the sensitive skins surrounding her vocal cords.

"Alder Cadogen is a deserter and a traitor. He's also unimportant," Drohma said, waving a hand. "I know that now, though I didn't always realize it. Kaveryth swarms with men like him, men with more muscle than strength, selling their loyalty to the highest bidder."

"Alder fights for the High One."

"And this supposed god of yours promises freedom, joy, and repose in the Eternal Lands. I see no difference from any other employer of mercenaries," he said firmly. "In any case, I am still considering killing him. Though I never expected it to be so easy."

He paused, glancing over at Alder's silent form. Celesyria took a step closer, pressing herself more firmly between the men. She could feel blood seeping from a shallow wound at her throat, but she did not care.

"You will have to get through me."

Drohma laughed, his mouth a grimace.

"You know as well as I do that I hold you in a vulnerable position. It is unfortunate for you that I paid attention to my governess when she taught me dragon biology."

He was right. Dragon scales were incredibly strong, but where they were absent, dragon skin was thin. Still, even with blood gushing from her throat and mere seconds left to live, she would kill the man if he dared touch her friend.

"Why do you hate me so deeply?" she asked instead, stalling for time. Her friends had to be nearby, had to have seen her and Alder come this way.

"I told King Ursa about your silly little playhouse in Auranth, and about your army. I expected him to allow me to raze it and to kill the usurping Envoy, but he refused. He feared splitting his forces. Feared it would hinder his acquisition of power to kill Wes, at least for now."

Celesyria felt a glimmer of hope at his admission. King Ursa was capable of cruelty, to be sure, but it seemed his thirst for power still drove him most of all. They could work with that, if necessary.

"Anyway, he refuses to see that you and the Envoy are the worst kind of threat," he continued, still holding the heavy sword to her neck, his arm not so much as flinching. "You do not only seek military power, but power over the minds of the people. Your Codex Veritatis, your talk of this high god, he does not treat this threat with proper care. But I do. Ever since you brought your foolish ponderings to the Envoy, the secure traditions of the Four Kingdoms have been upended. And for that, I believe, it is necessary to kill you."

Behind him, she saw a flash of shimmering scales.

"As you say, Alder is a nobody. He poses no threat to you, certainly not at this moment. I care little for my own life, if you will only spare his. Call to your men, find him a healer, and I will not resist you."

It was not a lie, even as she watched Jaconial land behind the Captain.

Drohma was right. What the High One promised to those who loved Him was worth the pain of this life. And even if those promises did not apply to her, she had had a hand in bringing them to others, and that was a precious gift that even the grave could never take from her.

He was powerless already.

Jaconial roared behind him, making such a loud and sudden sound that he dropped his sword in surprise. Celesyria caught the handle of the hilt with a claw, flinging it off into the distance.

Before he could say anything else, the two female dragons were standing over the Captain, fangs bared.

"You will die," Jaconial said, lowering her face until she was inches from his head. He fumbled in his belt for a dagger, but she only laughed. "You are a pathetic coward."

She raised a claw as though to tear at him, but Celesyria leaned in front of her, raising a wing to form a shield.

"Run, Drohma. The next time you seek to harm us, your life will not be spared," she said, ignoring Jaconial's incredulous expression.

The Captain raced toward the main city, and Celesyria noticed that the hail and the rain had stopped. Everything had gone still and quiet, and she could see the first hint of sunlight peeking between the clouds.

"He is still a threat to us," Jaconial said finally, moving to examine Alder as best she could.

"I will pray for him to find the truth before it is too late. Those who live by the sword will die by the sword, one way or another."

To her surprise, Jaconial did not argue.

"Thank you," she added quickly, bowing her head. "I never thought you'd be the one saving my life."

"I assure you, Celesyria, that I never planned to," she said, a hint of a smile on her face.

She will find you, High One. Give her time.

WES

Wes opened his eyes. Jaconial and Celesyria stood below, near the damaged harbor, and Alder was laying on the ground nearby.

He took the leather straps of the saddle more tightly in his hands as Nazzan took a sharp left, preparing to land. His head was still aching, the headache worse than any he'd ever had before, but with each minute that passed, the pain's hold on him was loosening. Thoughts returned, and then prayer.

Thank you, High One. Thank you for letting me live, and for giving me the desire to live in service of You.

As Nazzan touched down, he found himself able to get out of the saddle. On shaky legs he strode over to Celesyria, pressing a hand against her flank as she touched the top of his head with her snout. They did not need to speak.

Alder was on the ground, and two Red Army men rushed over with medical kits and knelt over him. They treated him with evident care, and Wes felt a rush of gratitude that nearly made him forget his pain.

When the external threat was great enough, even adversaries could stand as brothers. Perhaps there was more hope for a truly unified Four Kingdoms than he had once thought.

Satisfied that Alder would be alright, he turned back to Celesyria.

"Where is Aelrie?"

The dragon opened her mouth to answer before closing it again.

"Is she alive?" he demanded, staring at Nazzan and Jaconial, panic seizing his chest. She had killed the Gorok and scared the other elves away, so he was confident that she was on their side, but her eyes...

"She fell," Celesyria said, bowing her head. "On the deck of the ship. I'm not sure if she lived."

"Nazzan, we need to go to her."

"I will go," Celesyria said, stretching out her wings.

"You're bleeding!" Wes protested, looking at a gash in her neck.

"He's right," Jaconial added. "You need a healer."

"I'm not sure the Red Army soldiers are going to know much about dragon medicine," she retorted.

"It's alright," Nazzan said, striding over to Wes in a few steps. "I'll go. I will not let Wes come to harm."

KESSARA

Kessara watched as Nazzan jumped into the air, Wes on his back, heading for the sea. She had to speak to him, but there would be time later. At least he was alive. She raced through the narrow streets of the fishing district, trying to remember the way through the winding alleys and tight passages.

She lifted her skirts, her lungs burning as she ran. She

had seen Celesyria and the other dragons heading for the munitions building. Alder had to be with them, and he had to be alright. She could fathom no other possibility.

She saw him lying on the ground, two soldiers in red uniforms standing over him.

"Let me see him!" she demanded, collapsing onto the ground near his chest, tears pouring from her eyes. She saw Celesyria giving the men a nod out of the corner of her eye, and they retreated, probably heading back into the city to give medical assistance to the many others who had been wounded.

She had done everything she could to care for her subjects. Wes and the others were alive. All she wanted now was him, to be near him, to feel his hand in hers once more.

"We should help," Jaconial was saying. Kessara heard the sound of dragon's wings flapping overhead, and then there was silence.

There was sunlight on Alder's handsome face. The storm had finally broken, and it was morning. Even the treacherous North Sea looked almost pleasant. She drew in slow breaths, feeling her heartbeat returning to normal, savoring the familiar taste of salty air.

She reached for Alder's hand, stroking at the back of it, brushing aside dried blood and dirt that had stuck on his knuckles.

"You're alive," she said, tears flowing freely. She could not stop the fresh sobs that wracked her body, relief and joy and pain mingling into one feeling.

"Yes. And you're getting my shirt wet," he said.

She leaned back, staring into his perfect green eyes, not caring that her nose was running and her own eyes were bright red with tears.

"I'm okay, I promise. I'm bruised and I need to sleep, but I'm okay."

She threw herself onto his chest, and he held her, his fingertips brushing against her filthy hair.

Too soon, she rose to her feet, noticing two fishermen who had returned to the harbor.

"Gentlemen, I need help," she called out to them. For a moment, they stared at her, until recognition dawned and they collapsed to their knees, bowing low.

"Please, I need to get this man to a bed," she said as they rushed over, bowing once again and helping Alder to his feet.

Within a few minutes, he was in bed in one of the fisher-man's own houses, and they were alone.

It was a small but decent house, with tidy rugs and a thick quilt for him to sleep under, and she was thankful for their decency. Kingsvier Landing had been severely damaged, and many had been killed, but at least they were free once more to fish the North Sea. They would be able to rebuild.

"Can you stay a little while?" Alder asked from the bed, not opening his eyes. She sat at a stool beside him, her hand clasped firmly in his.

"Of course," she whispered, watching as his chest rose and fell.

Within minutes, he was asleep, his face peaceful. There would be time for food and drink and a bath when he awoke, but for now, she was thankful that he was comfortable.

She felt a sob rising again, and she clapped her free hand over her mouth, not wanting to wake him. She could not stop the tears that trailed down her cheeks.

The room was impossibly silent and still. In another life, she would have found it peaceful. But now the solitude filled her with dread.

"It will always be this way, if we let it," she whispered to his sleeping form, tears rolling over her lips. "We will be together, we will be friends, but there will be a wall between us that we cannot climb. I will look at you, but I will not be able to see. I'll cry for you, but you won't be able to wipe my tears."

He stirred, and she brushed a lock of red hair from his eyes, waiting for the tension in his forehead to smooth.

"Alder," she continued, the words catching on her tongue. "Alder."

She could not take them back once uttered, even though he could not hear. The High One could hear. And she would know. But she could not walk away, not now, not anymore.

Not for her people, not for the whole world.

"You are much stronger than me, Alder. You are willing to watch me marry for the good of our people, but I am not. I can't do it. I won't. I lived for one second today when I thought you were dead, and I knew. Without you, life is devoid of color."

She pressed her lips to his forehead, savoring the touch, terrified that she would never kiss him properly, terrified that their stars were already set in motion, unchangeable as the setting of the sun.

"No," she whispered to the shadows, getting up from her chair. "There's another way for us. There has to be."

29

Chapter Twenty-Nine

WES

Within a few moments, Wes and Nazzan were over the harbor.

He felt the familiar twinge of nausea whenever the dragon made a tight turn, but on the whole, he found himself relieved that the worst of the pain was gone. He still did not know what had caused it, but it did not seem to have had any lasting effects.

He looked over at the horizon, where the last elven boats were passing into the north. He feared it would not be the last they saw of them, but for the moment, the people of Kingsvier Landing had been spared.

The hail had let up, or perhaps it had all been pulled from the sky. The air that hit his face was cool and fresh, smelling of the sea. The stench of the beast was gone, buried with it beneath the ice. The sun was beginning to show through the clouds, and Wes wished that he could lay on the beach somewhere, feeling its warmth on his face.

But first he had to know that she was alright. And even then, he feared that it would be a long time before they could truly relax. Their larger enemies had not been destroyed, only thwarted. New alliances seemed more possible than before, but possible was not the same as easy. The autumn feast was drawing near as well, sure to bring its own tumult.

He leaned forward, gripping the saddle straps as Nazzan banked right, his green scales along the edge of his wing sparkling in a ray of sunlight.

The boat waited, bobbing gently on the subdued waves.

At the very edge, near the bow, he saw Aelrie.

She was not resting on her back as he'd assumed, but rather bent to the side, her legs askance.

Her eyes were closed, but she did not look peaceful.

"I need to get to her," he told Nazzan in his mind, swallowing the sob that threatened to rise from his throat. *"Go closer, please."*

She couldn't be dead. She had to be alright.

"Are you sure?" the dragon asked, making a tight circle over the top of the mast.

"There's an open space near the stern. Fly as straight and low as you can, please."

Wes sat up straight in the saddle, lifting his legs until they were both on one side. The sun had slipped behind the clouds once again, and the sea below no longer looked welcoming. Though the storm had mostly passed, the waves were still substantial, and the dark water was still deep.

A second later, the deck was below him.

Before he could change his mind, he pushed himself off, sliding down the dragon's flank toward the solid wood. The fall felt like it took a very long time, his eyes stinging from sprays of seawater as his body rushed toward the boat.

Somewhere deep within him, without him being quite aware of it, memory of Alder's swordplay training kicked in. As his feet touched the deck, he tucked his body into a tight roll. He felt a twinge of pain in his shoulder as he came to a stop, but his ankles seemed to be intact.

"Aelrie!" he cried out, getting to his feet again and racing across the slippery surface, dodging lobster traps and piles of rope that moved with each strike of a wave.

She said nothing back.

He rushed forward, glancing up at Nazzan, who was keeping watch overhead. The sun had come back out, and beneath his feet, puddles of pooled water glimmered in its light.

She was close now, behind a pile of old crates. He clambered over them, and once again his head began to ache. As he took the few final steps toward her, the pain intensified. Tears sprung to his eyes, but he wiped them away with the back of his hand.

He tripped over a mop that was leaned against the railing, dizziness rushing over him. He fell forward, his nose almost touching the deck before he caught himself. The scent of old fish that permeated the worn gray wood was so foul that he felt his stomach lurch, but all he wanted to do was to lay down and to rest.

The sun was no longer welcome. The bright rays made the back of his eyes ache. He longed for a soft bed, a dark room, and a huge mug of cool water.

No. Not yet.

He forced himself to his feet, clutching at his head. Nazzan was saying something in his mind, but he ignored it. The dragon would tell him to leave her, to get someone else to check on her, but he would not walk away, not now.

As he reached her side, stumbling across the tilting deck, relief rushed through him. He could see the steady rise and fall of her chest. She was alive.

She looked just as beautiful as ever, her dark hair pooling out behind her on the deck, her silvery cheeks gleaming, her lips soft and pink with life.

For a second, an image flashed in his mind of the way she'd looked before, standing there commanding the ice and the rain.

He knelt down beside her, blinking away thoughts of black eyes and power and despair. She had killed the Gorok. She had saved their lives.

"Aelrie," he said again, his voice a whisper. It hurt even to speak. The pounding in his head was pushing everything else away, dragging Wes under into a place where only pain mattered.

It hurt to look at her, but somehow he knew it would hurt even more to look away.

He reached out a hand, fingertips shaking, and placed it upon her cheek.

He paused, barely touching her, a feeling of dread pouring over him, but it was too late to draw back.

His skin was lit on fire.

The pain raced through his fingertips, traveling in an instant along every nerve, red and burning. He cried out, falling backward, his feet scrabbling against the deck as he tried to get away from her.

His head slammed hard against the floor, but he barely felt it.

The other pain, the impossible pain, was coming, racing through his body. He thought he screamed, but he couldn't manage to open his mouth.

The pressure inside of his head was like nothing he had ever felt. He could not compare it to anything, but somehow, he found himself for a split second, long enough to give the torture a name.

Darkness.

He heard Nazzan shouting, and saw a flash of green beside the deck's railing, but he could not move any closer to the dragon. His muscles were spasming now, great wracking shakes that spread from his feet into his neck.

He felt spit bubbling up into his mouth, choking him. With great effort, he turned his head, his jaw pressing his teeth together until they too ached.

He saw her there, just as she was before, eyes closed, lungs taking in a steady stream of air.

High One, save her. He let his eyes close.

Darkness was all he could see.

TO BE CONTINUED

Read *Maker*, the fourth installment in the Storm & Spire series, coming spring 2023.

Dear Reader

Thank you so much for reading *Maelstrom*, the third book in the Storm & Spire series.

If you enjoyed this book, I humbly ask you to consider leaving an honest review. It can be just a sentence or two if you like. Thank you from the bottom of my heart for your support & encouragement. It's hard for me to believe that this series is nearly over!

If you want to stay up to date with my writing (including the release of Storm & Spire book four) please consider signing up for my newsletter. My newsletter family also named the Gorok monster featured in this very book!

I can't imagine him being called anything else.

You can sign up at https://authorstefanielozinski.com/newsletter

In Christ,

Stefanie Lozinski

Behind the Scenes

Maelstrom was an absolute blast to write, even though I definitely had certain points in the process where I was certain that I was actually the worst writer on earth.

Fortunately, as my husband often reminds me, I *always* feel like that during my projects, and I always survive in the end. And I've learned a lot along the way. =)

The Stats

I took a little longer with *Maelstrom* than with *Majesty* as far as plotting goes. That part of the process ending up taking right around **30 hours.** I suppose it's not surprising, considering that it's a later book in a series that has grown more complex than when I was first writing *Magnify*!

Drafting was faster, ending up taking me right around **77 hours.**

As for editing, this book went really well. I think I only spent about **16 hours** on my end.

Of course none of these numbers include all of the hours that go into talking with my cover designer, formatting, uploading, creating ads, writing newsletters, social media, etc. Writing a book is a time consuming task, but I'm so thankful I get to do it.

Being an author has been my dream since I was a little girl, and it's a blessing to get to do it.

Oh, Kessara, I feel you.

A lot of the struggles that the Princess of Galeharbor goes through in this book were surprisingly emotional for me. No, I have never had to marry someone in order to become a queen! Like most of us, though, there have been seasons in my life where my heart was crying for one thing and God was leading me another way.

This is a bit personal, so if you're not into that, thanks for reading and feel free to skip this part. :)

To be very open and vulnerable with you guys, I am very much in that sort of season right now. I have two children, and my husband and I have been actively trying to have a third for over a year now. My other two were easy.

This time, it's different.

I never expected the tidal wave of emotions I'd experience every month with yet another negative pregnancy test. It has truly tested my ability to trust in God, and that test is ongoing!

We had so many plans in our minds, assuming we'd have more babies right away. I think that expectations can really steal your joy. Not to say we shouldn't make plans, but everything is ultimately up to God's will in the end. I've really been trying to be grateful for the many blessings we have, while still trying to remain hopeful for the future.

Kessara is in a much tougher situation in a lot of ways. She loves a man she cannot have, and because of it, she's lost the support of her family. The scene where she tells her father she's not marrying Wes was an emotionally painful one to write, but it really made me relate to Kessara and feel for her and what she was going through.

Our culture tells us we always need to "follow our hearts". And hey, sometimes that's good advice. Our intuition and our deep desires can be helpful in making decisions, taking risks, and chasing dreams. I don't deny that at all.

However, our minds must rule over our hearts.

The Bible tells us in Jeremiah 17:9 that "The heart is perverse above all things, and unsearchable, who can know it?".

I can empathize with Kessara's decision to turn from marrying Wes. I think a lot of readers will think she did the right thing, and I can empathize with that opinion as well. However, when it comes to the big picture, I think Kessara (and I!) have a lot of growing to do in learning to trust God's will for our lives, even when it seems impossible for us to follow it.

Maybe God will bless my husband and I with a few more babies. But maybe He won't.

Maybe the High One will give Kessara a way out of this impossible situation. But maybe He won't. (Yes, this is a not-so-subtle argument: buy *Maker*, the fourth book in the Storm & Spire series!)

I need to trust that whatever He has laid out for my life is going to be the best thing for my soul. And when I reach the end of this pilgrimage here on earth, my soul will be what truly counts.

In any case, I humbly ask your prayers that we will be able to conceive another little Lozinsksi.

May God's will be done.

Acknowledgments

To everyone I thanked in book one, thank you again. You're all still wonderful, especially my dear husband Jordan, my fearless beta reader Jacinta, my wonderful kiddos, and each and every one of my readers.

Jillian - Thank you for coming up with the perfect name for Meraxes, and for being such a wonderful supporter of the Storm & Spire series. <3

Lady Gwyn and Lord Henico - you know who you are. Sorry one of you had to be a boy to make the anecdote make sense. ;) Thank you for everything.

Antonio - no way am I naming a dragon in a completely made up fantasy world "Cleopatra the Alchemist" (???), nor am I ever writing a romantic suspense that centers around a prion disease outbreak, deadly mosquitos, or a nuclear attack. I do, however, hope to keep receiving your very "dudes rock" ideas.

About the Author

Stefanie Lozinski lives in Ontario, Canada, with her husband, two young children, two cats, and a whole lot of books. When she isn't homeschooling her little ones, you'll find her on a long walk, drinking coffee, praying a Rosary, or working on her next novel.

You can connect with me on:

🌐 https://www.authorstefanielozinski.com

📘 https://www.facebook.com/authorstefanielozinski

Subscribe to my newsletter:

✉ https://authorstefanielozinski.com/newsletter

www.ingramcontent.com/pod-product-compliance
Lightning Source LLC
Chambersburg PA
CBHW051320190726
48290CB00001B/240